LINCOLN

VH NICOLSON

Emma,

"You complete me."

V. H. Nicolson
x

B
Boldwood

First published in 2022. This edition first published in Great Britain in 2025 by Boldwood Books Ltd.

Copyright © VH Nicolson, 2022

Cover Design by Lori Jackson

Cover Images: Depositphotos and Shutterstock

Every effort has been made to obtain the necessary permissions with reference to copyright material, both illustrative and quoted. We apologise for any omissions in this respect and will be pleased to make the appropriate acknowledgements in any future edition.

A CIP catalogue record for this book is available from the British Library.

Paperback ISBN 978-1-83678-606-1

Large Print ISBN 978-1-83678-607-8

Hardback ISBN 978-1-83678-605-4

Ebook ISBN 978-1-83678-608-5

Kindle ISBN 978-1-83678-609-2

Audio CD ISBN 978-1-83678-600-9

MP3 CD ISBN 978-1-83678-601-6

Digital audio download ISBN 978-1-83678-602-3

This book is printed on certified sustainable paper. Boldwood Books is dedicated to putting sustainability at the heart of our business. For more information please visit https://www.boldwoodbooks.com/about-us/sustainability/

Boldwood Books Ltd, 23 Bowerdean Street, London, SW6 3TN

www.boldwoodbooks.com

For my mum.
The funniest, feistiest, and strongest woman I know.

AUTHOR'S NOTES

Please note this book comes with a content warning.

My books all come with the guarantee of a happily ever after, but sometimes the journey to get there can be a hard-fought one. The main focus of my books is love, romance, and happiness.

However, just in case you aren't sure, and if you are a sensitive reader, then please proceed with caution. Here's a content warning list:

Triggers: Absent parent, abandonment, loss of a parent.

1

LINCOLN

I fly out of the changing rooms and get the fright of my life when I step straight into the path of someone I wasn't expecting to be here.

"Holy shit, you scared me. I didn't realize you were starting tonight." I extend my hand to welcome the new cleaner and flash the stunning dark-haired woman a smile.

Rio, the gym manager, said he needed a deep clean before a big announcement meeting with senior management tomorrow. I'm positive he said the cleaner was coming in on the morning of the meeting to do that, though.

Maybe I heard him wrong.

She props the mop she's holding against the wall before shaking my hand, then pushes her long hair over her shoulder nervously as she stares back at me with her deep-brown hypnotic eyes that look like they're sprinkled with gold. As she clears her throat, I instantly release her hand, step backward, and take her in.

Gorgeous from head to toe, she's got the most perfect hourglass body.

She's possibly a wannabe actor or model, which would be about right for Los Angeles. She's certainly got that whole X-factor vibe about her.

"You don't need to sign the visitors' book. It's just us two in this evening." I look around the drab gym. It's a ghost town as usual and nothing like the five-star gym my father and I created at our hotel resort back in Scotland.

I turn my attention back to our newest member of staff. "You know you don't have to wear gym gear just because we are a gym, right?"

She stares back at me. "Yes."

I turn my baseball cap around and flash her a smile. "I'm Lincoln, by the way. My work visa runs out in six weeks, and I'm only helping for the next five weeks. Then I'm taking a week off before I return home to Scotland."

I can't wait.

Six weeks left.

Los Angeles has been great but I'm excited to see my family again.

"So." I clap my hands together. "We have the new buyer coming in tomorrow. She's apparently a proper ball-breaker and we need this place cleaner than clean." I gesture to the enormous space. "I'm actually surprised we didn't have to paint the grass green outside for her." I should have kept that to myself. "Your name is Lucy, isn't it?"

She nods at me with a smirk.

"Great."

Maybe she's nervous as it's her first shift, but she's not much of a talker.

"Come this way. I'll show you where everything is."

Following my brief tour of the gym, where Lucy barely said

two words to me, I leave her to get on with her cleaning duties and head back into the reception area.

Through the large window that separates the gym from reception, I find myself unable to concentrate on the laptop screen and stare at the quiet girl as she moves about the gym.

She shouldn't be cleaning. She should be sprawled across my bed, begging me to take care of her.

Stop it, Lincoln. No-women rule.

And she's probably got a boyfriend anyway. No one can be that beautiful and not have a boyfriend.

She turns suddenly. Our eyes lock before she looks away again.

I want her.

But that's not going to happen as I have inflicted a sex sabbatical on myself while I've been traveling around America.

Four and a half months and no pussy and now is not the time for my cock to decide it's time to want to have some fun again.

Before I left Scotland, I realized that I wasn't exactly picky with my choice in women, and my home had become a conveyor belt for one-night stands and so I decided my playboy status needed to be reset, and traveling was the perfect opportunity to do that.

I've been a good boy... so far.

I inhale deeply. *Right, Lincoln, spreadsheet, then have a quick look at the agenda for tomorrow's entire team meeting with the new owner.*

Has Lucy been invited?

Making any excuse to speak to her again, I return to the main gym area. "Lucy, did Rio invite you to the team meeting tomorrow?"

"Yes." She turns to face me, holding a roll of blue paper towels and a spray bottle of sanitizer.

"Great. Nine thirty sharp. We don't want to annoy the new boss, do we? Especially if she is as badass as they say she is."

"Noted." She flashes me a cheeky white-toothed smile.

"You're really pretty. Did you know that?" I blurt without a second thought.

Sucking her plump lips into her mouth, she looks back at me wide-eyed.

"Fuck, sorry I said that. Crap, I'm sorry for swearing, too. My mouth has a tendency to say what my brain is thinking around beautiful women. Shit, I shouldn't have said that either because we have a no relationships with staff and sexual harassment clause in our contracts. Fuck. Forget I said anything. I'm sorry I swore again. I wasn't coming on to you. Well, maybe I was, but I didn't say I wanted to fuck you right here on the weight bench or anything." I hold both of my hands up in a stop gesture. "And I said 'fuck' again. Sorry." I flap the neck of my tee shirt back and forth nervously as my body fires up like a furnace. "What I was trying to say, well, that I think, you're really—"

"Pretty." She finishes my sentence.

I'm never getting to return home to Scotland. I'll be in court next week for sexual harassment.

Biting my tongue to stop me from making a bigger fool of myself, I hike my thumb over my shoulder. "I'd better get back to work. Forget what I said. As soon as you're finished, I think we will close up because no one has been in after ten at night for months." I look around the unwelcoming space. "The remodeling I would do to this gym."

"Oh, yeah, what would you do?" she asks.

I love her sweet harmonic American accent that pulls at my dick.

"For a start, install security cameras inside and out. Security men on the doors at night. A woman-only section over there." I point to the area that could easily be sectioned off. "Better lighting outside. The place needs painting and modern fixtures. The showers need upgrading, and then there's the dance studio. It could do with a sprung floor. Then I reckon the local cheer teams would hire the facilities. Interactive touchscreen fitness mirrors so people can work out with a virtual instructor. I'd also have a no-mirror section too. For those conscious about their physique." That would entice more members. "That's for starters. I know this place could be outstanding."

"Wow, you've really given it some thought. What do you do in Scotland?" she asks.

"Hospitality." If I tell her I co-own a five-star spa and hotel resort, it makes me sound like an entitled dick. Which, maybe I am, but my father made me work in every section of the hotel to learn the running of the place. My share in the hotel wasn't given to me; I had to earn it, and I did. I'm itching to get back.

Time stretches between us like an elastic band when she doesn't ask me anything else. "Okay. I'll leave you to it." I walk backward. "I'm sorry about my motormouth."

"I've forgotten what you said already." Her mouth hitches sideways in a smirk.

"Great." I turn and walk straight into a machine, battering my shin against the rigid cold metal.

"Fuck," I hiss. That's going to leave a mark, and I bruise like a goddamn peach.

Smooth, Lincoln. Real smooth.

I hear a soft giggle. "Are you okay?"

Casually flapping my hand in the air, I give her a thumbs-up and hobble back to the office. Over the next hour, I keep my head down and work on the membership attendance spreadsheet Rio asked me to compile. Eventually, I close my laptop and psych myself up to speak to Lucy again, but I discover she has left.

Without saying goodbye.

2

LINCOLN

"Morning," I cheerfully greet everyone in the staff office.

Lackluster *hello*s and *hey*s mumble back.

If this were my team, I would motivate them to do their best at work. But it's not my place. It's a temporary work placement after all.

"Morning." Lucy sits down beside me and I'm instantly surrounded by a warm blend of vanilla and pear. She smells divine.

Today she's wearing a figure-hugging purple dress paired with candy-pink killer heels, which is such an unexpected contrast to last night.

"Morning," she says again.

I say a shocked "Hi" in response. I think I've forgotten how to breathe. I may have also forgotten how to form words and blink too. She's beautiful, even more than she was last night.

Granting me a giant smile, she asks, "You all set for the big meeting with the bitch boss from hell, Lincoln?"

I shuffle uneasily in my seat. She seems more confident

around me today. Maybe it's because we aren't alone like last night.

"Well, now, I never said that." I trip over my clipped words.

"You might as well have." She winks at me.

Winks.

She *is* different from last night.

"Are you going to an audition? Are you an actor?" My eyes flit up and down her outfit.

"Something like that." She grins at me cheekily.

A loud clap startles me from our staring contest as Rio addresses the room. "Great, everyone is here. Thank you all for arriving on time. Before we start, I want to say a few words. Be prepared for significant change, but remember, it's all for the greater good. Without further ado, I would like to pass you over to Violet West, our new investor. Please give Violet a warm welcome." He claps and everyone joins in.

Beside me, Lucy runs her dainty fingers down the fabric across her thighs, then rises to her feet. Holding her hand out for me to shake, she stuns me and says, "Hi, Lincoln. Pleased to meet you. I'm the ball-breaker."

3

VIOLET

I would pay a lot of money to see that look on Lincoln's face again.

Letting go of his muscular hand, I turn on my thin-as-a-pin heels and take quick steps to the front. I know for a fact he's staring at my ass, so I give it an extra wiggle.

He can kiss it.

What a dick Lincoln was for assuming I was the cleaner last night. I thought it was easier to go along with his assumption. Especially after he called me a ball-breaker.

I guess I can't really be upset, especially since he mistook me for Lucy, the new cleaner. Honestly, I didn't correct him either, considering I was trying to sneak in unnoticed last night. Unfortunately, my plan didn't go quite as smoothly as I'd hoped.

To be honest, my mouth went drier than the Sahara when I laid eyes on him.

He's so handsome. Too handsome for his own good.

Sexy, deep Scottish accent, muscles, dreamy eyes, he's perfection. He's clearly been soaking up the sun while he's here; even his tan is perfect, too. And he's deliciously dark. Everywhere.

Eyes, hair, skin. He's Italian or Greek, maybe Spanish. Whatever he is, he's admittedly gorgeous but way too cocky for my liking.

So not my type, and I am so *not* his type. I bet tiny blondes are more his thing.

Casting my gaze around the room of people, I address the room. "Hello. It's wonderful to meet you all. I am Violet West, and I am one of the operations managers at West Oracle Corporations. I'm not actually the investor, but my father, Anthony West, is." I continue, "My job is to ensure a smooth and seamless merger and, more importantly, make sure you are all looked after." I love my job, but I have given this same speech at least ten times already this month alone. "I'm here today to show you exactly what we have planned for S&M Gym. For starters, the S&M Gym brand is no longer. Yes, we inflict pain here at the gym, but not of a sexual nature or that would be a different type of presentation I would deliver to you today."

Lincoln laughs louder than anyone else. "Sorry." He shakes his head and pulls his lips into his mouth.

His velvety laugh kindles a flame of heat between my thighs.

Focus, Violet.

I turn the presentation board on the easel next to me over. "Ladies and gentlemen, may I present to you Urban Soul Studios."

A gentle thrum of gasps sounds through the small team as I reveal the logo. "Here at Urban Soul Studios, we will offer services for the mind, body, and soul. It's a full rebrand, new timetable, and refurbishment. It's out with everything old and dated in this place and in with modern fitness and health equipment, new fitness classes, security, and new dance studios to accommodate events."

I deliver an empowering proposal for the next twenty minutes and the room buzzes with excitement.

An enthusiastic blonde-haired girl throws her hand in the air as I take questions.

"I would like to know if our jobs are safe?"

"Great question. I guarantee all of your jobs are safe as long as you have the motivation, qualifications, and drive to be part of a thriving and successful business." The qualifications statement is the loophole I need to replace two of the current members of the staff.

She beams back at me. "I'm a certified dance teacher. I would love to run dance classes."

"Already on it. I have identified your qualifications and within the proposal, you are to run dance classes for all ages."

"Yes." She clutches her hands in front of her.

She's going to be a star instructor; I can feel it already. "If you are worried the space we have isn't big enough for these proposals"—I point to the presentation board again—"you'll see this part here is an extension. That's the building to the right of us. We have purchased that too. Urban Soul Studios will be the most sought-after gym on this side of town."

I grab my water bottle out of my bag and take a sip of the cool liquid. "Tomorrow we will all be attending a team-building day. It's a fabulous way for us to get to know one another, plus you will also meet my father. You have the weekend off, then, on Monday, you will start five weeks of training at our head office on the east side of town. If you have any problems with travel arrangements, please come and see me." I take another sip of water. "I am overseeing the remodeling and will be here when the contractors are, so if you ever need to speak to me, you will find me here or via email. Does anyone have any further questions?"

Lincoln waves his shovel-sized hand in the air, which looks like the right size for spanking. Not that I would know what that is like as no one has touched me in a *very* long time, but the thought of Lincoln spanking me sends a wave of arousal deep in my core.

Not now, Violet.

"What about me? I'm only here on a temporary contract. Am I still required?" He tilts his head to the side, probably longing for me to say no, but because I'm a sucker for punishment, and as payback for calling me a ball-breaker, I say, "You will be my right-hand man while Rio is completing his management training. That work for you? Happy to break a sweat for me, Lincoln?"

"Sure." His Adam's apple bobs up and down, which has me all hot and bothered; he's so masculine in every way.

I clear my throat and try to focus. "Great. Alright then. Today I need you all to pack up any belongings, as the moving company will be here tomorrow. I cannot wait to work with you all. As soon as you're all set, you can leave. You have the rest of the day off. And Lincoln, can I have a word?" I call out to him across the room as I eye him scooping up his black backpack. Lincoln carries his enormous frame toward me, and I can't help but notice his tanned, sculpted thighs.

I love a man with thick thighs.

He's ticking boxes I didn't know needed ticking.

And he's tall, maybe six foot four. Nice.

Another tick.

As everyone leaves, Lincoln apologizes, "I am really sorry about last night." He nibbles on his bottom lip as if he's nervous.

And *wow*, I do love that Scottish accent of his.

"It's fine." I ignore the way my nipples harden against the lace of my bra when he rolls his Scottish tongue around the letter *R* and get back to my job. "I would like you to be here to take deliveries, flag problems, and point out any areas you think we need to improve on. Rio tells me that you know the building like the back of your hand, and you pay attention. He has nothing but good things to say about you. He trusts you. And you can grab me coffee too from time to time."

His eyes fill with amusement. "So, I'll be your assistant?"

"Yes, sort of," I say playfully.

"Dry cleaning to pick up too?"

"Perhaps." I'm testing him to see what his limits are. Apparently, nothing fazes Lincoln.

I pull my planner out of my purse.

"Is that yours?" Lincoln snorts.

I jump on the defense at my multicolored unicorn design planner. "Planners are life." I pop a hip.

"I didn't take you as a rainbow unicorn kind of girl." Lincoln struggles to hold in a laugh. "Is a simple black planner not enough?"

I bug my eyes out and wave my planner in front of his face. "No one will steal this hideous thing." That's a bald-faced lie. I love anything brightly colored or sparkly on a planner. On weekends, you'll find me perusing every aisle of every stationery shop within a fifty-mile radius of my house. It's my weakness and I have at least another ten more of these bad boys in my cupboard, ready to plan the shit out of my life, all with sticky notepads, inserts, and extra customizable pages I can add in myself. What can I say? I'm a sucker for stationery.

I continue my lie to hide my obsession. "This thing sticks out like a piranha in a punch bowl. It's not going anywhere." I flick it open, and a photo of my beloved white teacup Pomeranian, Pom-pom, falls to the floor.

Instinctively, I crouch down to pick it up as Lincoln does the same. Our bodies tilt and our heads collide, creating a *thump* sound as they clash together.

I throw my hand to my now-throbbing head. "Holy Mother of God. Argh."

"I'm so sorry," he mumbles. "Are you okay?"

"I think I'll live." I wince.

"You sure? Let me have a look."

I don't know why, but I tip my head forward and let him part my hair to inspect my newly formed bump. "Ooooh, it's the size of an egg already. Are you sure you're okay?"

"I'm fine. I'm used to it. I'm super accident-prone," I whisper.

He smooths my hair back in place, much tenderer than I imagined.

Our eyes lock and some kind of weird static energy passes between us.

Tucking a strand of my long locks behind my ear, a hot shiver runs down my spine. I can't stop looking at him. "You need arnica on that. My father swears by it," he advises.

I become aware of his thumb brushing back and forth across the skin of my cheek. *When did he cup my face?*

He takes a deep breath, removes his hand, and promptly stands to his full height and I instantly miss the warmth of his touch.

I give my head a swift shake to wake me up from my Lincoln fog and go to stand up, but I end up leaning back too quickly, wobbling on my towering heels, and lose my balance completely.

It happens quicker than the flicker of a firefly.

My feet go out from beneath me and I end up flat on my back with my feet in the air. I let out a high-pitched screech as my planner flies out of my hand and the pages scatter everywhere.

Oh shit. I don't have any panties on.

I stayed at the hotel around the corner to avoid the manic

rush hour. It was the only way to ensure I would be on time for the meeting, and goddammit, I forgot to pack clean underwear.

Laying my legs flat against the floor swiftly to hide my indecency, I silently die of embarrassment. There is no way Lincoln didn't see my freshly waxed pussy.

Closing my eyes, I throw my hands over my face to cover the hot color I feel myself turning. "Oh, my God. Please tell me you didn't see anything." I part my fingers slightly to peek through them to find Lincoln staring at the ceiling, his face as red as a tomato.

He saw.

"Not a thing." He continues staring at the ceiling. "Did you hurt yourself?"

"What did you see?" I coax.

"Nothing." He clenches his eyes shut and bites his bottom lip.

"You're lying."

"I'm not."

"So, why aren't you looking at me?"

"It was in case your dress had slid up," he splutters.

"Are you sure you saw nothing?" My body heat turns up a notch.

"Promise." He holds out his hand. "Am I okay to look now? Can I please help you up?"

I let out a defeated sigh. I do need help. There is no way I can get up off the floor without looking like a complete fool. I push both of my arms out for him and he grabs my hands, pulling me to my feet like I'm a featherweight; I smack into his rock-hard chest and he loops an arm around my waist, which feels nice. Good.

"Hi," he says softly.

"Thank you," I say under my breath.

"Does anything hurt?"

"Just my ego."

Lincoln gives me a gigantic smile. "And your egg-sized bump on your head."

"I'd forgotten all about it." I don't want to let go of his hands.

"I'm a qualified first-aider. I should check you over."

"You should." But neither of us moves.

"I've never had a California girl fall at my feet before."

"That implies lots of girls have."

"In the past, perhaps, but not since I arrived in America. I'm on a self-inflicted sabbatical."

My eyebrows fly up. "So, no women? Or men?" I add.

His chest rumbles as a warm and rich chuckle sounds across the quiet room. "I'm into women."

"Right." My voice is low and breathy. "Good to know. No women at the moment or men ever. Got it." Why do I care?

"Do I have the day off too?" he asks, still clutching my hand in his between us.

"Yes. I was just going to give you the work schedule. It's in my planner and outlines the workflow for the next few weeks, but I can email it to you instead if you prefer. You'll be my right-hand man for five weeks. An extra set of hands would be beneficial to the project."

"You've said that already. *Beneficial* for the project?" he asks as if not believing me.

"Yeah." I blink. My eyes zone in on his lips. He's got a beautifully defined top lip that most women would die for. "*Beneficial* for the project."

Lincoln leans in closer and just as I think he's about to kiss me, he rests his cheek against mine. "It's going to be a dream come true working with you now. Do you know why?"

"Why?" I feel hot all over.

He moves his lips to the shell of my ear and whispers, "Because of all the places I've visited on my travels, Hollywood is by far my most favorite place. I'd like to take another visit, though, maybe have a privately guided tour. I've already seen it once. But I'd like to get a better look. Up close."

Shit, he means my Hollywood wax.

"You said you didn't see." I gasp and try to pull away, but Lincoln firmly holds me in place.

"I wasn't lying. I saw nothing." He releases my hands and takes a step back, then looks at me innocently. "Team building tomorrow, then?"

I simply nod because I can't seem to make my body work.

Frozen to the spot, I watch the athletic and tanned Scottish man, who does things to my heart rate, pick up all the sections of my planner that have scattered all over the floor. He carefully places them in a neat pile on the desk to the side of us. "I'll let you sort that out. I'm guessing you have a particular way it all goes back together." He points at my discombobulated planner I'm secretly going to enjoy reorganizing again.

"Thank you." I smooth my dress across my hips.

Lincoln grabs his black backpack off the floor that fell off his shoulder when we collided, and shouts back over his shoulder, "See you tomorrow, Violet."

4

LINCOLN

I'm lost.

I pull my black Camaro over to the curb and look around. Every street looks the goddamn same.

Opening my emails to double-check the zip code, I realize I've typed a digit wrong. I'm only five blocks away from my destination. I was so close.

Driving in the correct direction this time, I put the windows down and enjoy the sudden gust of warm air that enters the cockpit of my air-conditioned car, and I run my hair through my overgrown floppy locks.

Having let my hair grow over the past few months, I need a good barber. A good shave is also required. I've never had a long beard before; scruff and goatee are my usual look and I always like to have my beard shaped, short and sharp, but it's a lifetime away from that now.

One minute away from the venue and my mind wanders.

The last twenty-four hours have certainly been interesting, and my trip has become more exciting.

After I left the gym yesterday, I may have spent way too

much time Googling Violet West, and I discovered a few things about her.

One, she's thirty-two and a savvy businesswoman. Two, she supports a local children's charity for fostered children. Three, she has thousands of friends and followers on social media. Four, in every photo of her, she's smiling, laughing, and having fun.

I also concluded she doesn't appear to have a man in her life.

I don't know why I feel some sort of satisfaction with that piece of information.

Having read her many online interviews, she appears to be *too busy* to have any kind of relationship and implied she was married to her job.

I couldn't help but laugh at that statement. We are a lot alike. I'm also happily married to my job, but I would love nothing more than to have someone to share my life with.

In fact, I've never been in love.

Loveless Lincoln.

I round the corner of the street I should have been in fifteen minutes ago, quickly park my car and I'm grateful the helpful receptionist within the chic, white, glass-walled building escorts me directly to the meeting room where my fellow teammates are seated, announcing me as we walk through the door.

Everyone turns to greet me with a joyful wave and a quiet hello. I mouth a *Sorry* and roll my eyes at Rio as I take one of the seats that are laid out in a semicircle shape.

"Sorry. I'm still trying to find my bearings."

"Ah, that accent is not local." A tall, thin-as-a-drainpipe, gray-haired gentleman standing in the middle of the semicircle gives me a welcoming grin.

"Scottish," I confirm.

"Beautiful part of the world. I've been once. It stole a little piece of my heart. I would love to go back." He claps his hands together, then rubs them. "You haven't missed anything, sorry, what's your name..."

"It's Lincoln. Most people call me Linc."

"Great, well, Linc, we were discussing the day ahead, but I have already partnered everyone up, which leaves you with Violet." He smiles across at Violet. "Violet usually works the room to get to know each of you, but we have an odd number of people today. You might enjoy partner work today, Letty."

Letty?

"Uncle Hank, don't call me Letty." Violet rolls her eyes with a smirk.

Hank cheekily smiles back at her. "As long as you don't call me 'uncle' again." He waggles his finger in the air at her, and the mood in the room lifts at the easy exchange.

"Deal."

She looks stunning again today. Hair pulled up into a high, tight ponytail, she's fresh-faced and freckled. In simple black wide-legged pants, a tight white tee shirt, and pure white chunky-soled trainers.

How the hell am I gonna focus today?

5

LINCOLN

"Okay, everyone." Hank, our team coordinator, addresses the room. "This morning was a tremendous success. I am sure you have all had a lot of fun. I especially like the moment Jasper faked his own shark-infested custard death. You deserve an Oscar, my friend." Hank winks at him teasingly before he continues, "Work is supposed to be fun. It's where you spend most of your days and there is no point in spending the rest of your life with regrets. This morning was about finding new ways to work together as a team, but it's time to go deeper. To get to know each other even better. This afternoon's exercises are based on building trust, being honest, and showing how courageous you can be." Hank rubs his hands together again. "I want you to find the partner I buddied you up with this morning. Are you ready? I need a hell, yeah." He punches the air, and we all laugh and parrot his *hell, yeah* back to him.

After a few minutes of moving our seats around, Hank instructs us to sit facing our partners.

I sit down opposite Violet. "Hi." I feel her nerves. "How's your head today?"

"It's better. Thank you."

Hank dishes out the rules of the next activity. "This exercise is called three lies, two truths. You are to tell your partner three lies about yourself and then two truths, and they have to figure out your facts from your fiction. The rules. They can ask you as many questions as they want to discover your truths. There is a fifteen-minute time limit and make your lies believable. No one will believe you if you say you can speak fifty-seven languages. This exercise is to demonstrate how trust*ing* and how trust*worthy* you are. Are you willing to share your innermost secrets with someone you work with without fear of being judged?" He pauses. "It's time to be courageous and show your vulnerability. Do you fully trust your partner to share? If you are brave enough to do so, it shows the true meaning of trust. Whatever is said between you two remains a secret." Hank eyes the wall clock. "You have thirty minutes, fifteen minutes each, and I will tell you when your time is up. Go." Hank sets us off.

"I'll go first." Violet wiggles side to side in her seat. "I love buying stationery and have a special cabinet full of it in my house. I collect dog ornaments. I've never been in love before. My sister and I are best friends, and I've had over ten assistants since I started my job at West Oracle."

I eye her suspiciously. She has a great poker face, but I am looking for her tell. I start by asking her questions about the dog ornaments and eventually I work out that's a lie.

"What was the name of your last assistant?"

She hesitates before answering. "Alfred."

"Alfred?" I can't hide my amusement. "What, as in Batman's butler?"

"Yes, he happens to have the same name." She tries to be cool, but the tone of her voice went up by at least two octaves.

"And the one before that?"

"Geoffrey."

I scoff, "*The Fresh Prince of Bel Air*'s butler, Geoffrey?" She's not a good liar.

Sucking her lips into her mouth, she snorts. "I'm not very good at this. Sorry, that wasn't very ladylike." Her rosy cheeks deepen in color.

"So that's a lie. How many assistants have you had then? A couple?"

She shakes her head. "None. I've never had an assistant. I have a kind of secretary instead. She's based at head office and only sorts my emails and organizes my calendar. No grabbing coffee or dry cleaning." She grants me a blistering smile that makes her eyes crinkle at the sides, illuminating her entire face.

This weird flip-flop sensation in the depths of my stomach begins and I try to think of paint drying to calm my half-mast erection and focus on our task. "Okay, so three things left: stationery, sister, and never been in love." I list them out loud. "You're thirty-two years old this year; I know that already."

She gasps. "How did you know that? You looked me up?"

Shit. "I did."

"Stalker."

"Research. You're my new employer."

"It's temporary work."

"And I want to know who I am working for. You could be trafficking women and have fifteen sex clubs for all I know."

"West Oracle is not *that* type of corporation." She leans toward me, her eyes narrowed.

"Good to know. Just checking." I wink. "Thirty-two?"

"Yes."

"You have to have been in love, surely. I reckon that's the lie. Which means your two truths are you love stationery and you're best friends with your sister." I fold my arms confidently.

Violet makes a buzzer noise. "Wrong."

Dammit. I thought I had it.

"Are you telling me you've never been in love and you're best friends with your sister?"

"Nope." She shakes her head again.

"You've never been in love and you love stationery?"

"Got there in the end."

"Are your sister and you not close, then?"

"I barely speak to my sister, Francesca."

"Why not?" My brows pull together.

"I work. I mean, what is the world coming to? Women *working*, making a living for themselves. Pft." She rolls her eyes, making me laugh. "And then, of course, there is how I look. Look at me." She makes a sweeping motion with her hands down her body.

"I can't stop looking at you."

Her eyes bug out. "You're a great liar, but I've got you pegged already. I bet busty blondes are your type, right? Your turn."

"Not yet." I flash the palm of my hand to stop us from moving forward. "You don't believe me?"

"For Christ's sake, why are we doing this?"

"Hank said complete honesty. I'll be dead straight with you."

"Okay."

"Yes, I like blondes. But until yesterday, they *were* my type."

"What changed yesterday?" She audibly gulps.

"A beautiful busty brunette with the peachiest of asses fell at my feet and made me question my entire existence. Tell me about the relationship with your sister."

She's still looking at me like she doesn't believe what I just said. "Okay, well, Francesca likes to keep reminding me I work too much. I talk too much. I need to settle down. I'll never get a man if I keep working all the time and don't look after myself."

"You are the most beautiful woman I have ever set my eyes on. I can tell you look after yourself."

"You're only saying that because I'm your new boss and you want to stay on my good side." Absentmindedly, she chews her lip.

"Throughout my entire twenty-nine years on this planet, I have never set eyes on anyone as gorgeous as you. I mean that. No BS." I slice my hand through the air.

"It's not always about appearance."

"I'm fully aware of that, and it's what makes you even more attractive. You're smart, talented, driven, caring. I could go on."

She scratches her neck with her perfectly French-manicured nails. I've made her nervous, and she's obviously not great at receiving compliments. "Did you find all of that out last night, too? When you were on your little research trail?"

"I did, yeah."

"What else did you discover?"

I lean in and she moves closer. "I know the camera loves you, Violet. I spent way too much time on your social media accounts last night looking at you. You are dazzling and I can feel your energy through the screen. You have beautiful eyes that I would like to lose myself in. I love their color. I learned you are one of life's gems and have a heart of gold. You invest your time and money in a kids' fostering charity that was almost closed down a couple of years ago, but you kept it afloat, and you've helped to rehome several hundred children since. You only have two close friends, Hannah and Ruby, whom you trust with your life, and you go out with them on the first Friday night of every month to a nightclub called Xenon. Harvard University gave you a first-class degree with honors." Her nostrils are flaring, and I can't work out if she's mad at me because I know so much or if she's mad at herself as her social profiles are set to public. "One last thing. Your sister sounds like a narcissist, but I think if you dug a little deeper, you will find that she's jealous of you because you're an incredible woman. She's intimidated by you. Hell, *I'm* intimidated by you, but it doesn't deter me from wanting to ask you out on a date. I would like to do that." It's not a question; I'm stating facts.

The whole time I've been talking, Violet's face has softened. Her golden eyes dance back and forth between mine as we stare at each other. "What about your no-women rule?"

"I'm in charge of the rules and I just ripped them up. But only for you."

She's looking at me like she can't actually believe what I am saying.

Violet flinches as Hank bellows, "Time to switch. It's your partner's turn now. Fifteen minutes, everyone."

I sit back. "You okay?"

Violet blinks several times and then leans back in her chair too. "Thank you for all those kind things you just said." Her voice is quiet, and I struggle to hear her over the faint hum of chatter in the meeting room.

"You're welcome." I take a deep breath in. "Okay, here goes, three lies, two truths. I can speak four languages." That's my first lie. I can only speak two. "My mother left my father when I was only a few months old and he brought me up by himself, and therefore I have never met my mother. I have never been in love. I'm a twin. I am completely color-blind."

She instantly pounces on my lie. "You said you loved the color of my eyes, so you're not color-blind."

"Well done."

"You can't be a twin or you would have said your father brought *us* up, not *me*."

"Well done, Detective West."

Narrowing her eyes, as if thinking hard, she finally says, "I don't think your mother left your father, so I think your two truths are you speak four languages and you've never been in love."

"Nope."

She inhales a sharp breath, as if in shock. "Did your mom leave you?"

"Don't look at me like that." When people find that out, I can't abide the look of pity in their eyes. The head tilt and the strike of pain across people's faces. It seems to hurt them more than me. My father is an incredible man. He gave me everything I ever needed and more. I never felt like I missed out on anything, and no one should feel bad for me.

Although that's a partial lie. I've always wondered what a comforting cuddle would feel like from my mom.

"What am I looking at you like?" she asks.

"Pity. Your sad eyes, the head tilt. I'm good. My father, my *yaya*, and my grandfather brought me up and I think I turned out okay."

She sits bolt upright, correcting her sympathetic body language, her brows knit together. "Your *yaya*?"

"Grandmother—she's Greek. My grandfather is Scottish."

"You only speak a couple of languages? Greek and English?"

"Well done."

Violet remains quiet as she looks at me. She's trying to figure out if I'm damaged and I can see her doing mental gymnastics.

"I'm not broken, Violet. There is nothing wrong with me. Or my father. My mom..." I shrug my shoulders. "She decided after she had me, she didn't want to be tied down. I was a *whoopsie*, and she was only seventeen at the time. I wasn't part of her life plan, so she left us." Although, as I say that casually, it stings a little.

"She left *you*?" I can tell Violet is struggling with that information.

"Yeah."

"Your dad?"

"Is an amazing man."

"You've never met your mom?"

"Never. Please don't feel sorry for me. I had a brilliant childhood, and my dad is an exceptional and selfless man. He's the reason I'm here. Traveling."

"Explain?"

"Not much to tell. My father and I work together."

"In hospitality?"

"Yes. He wanted me to find myself. Make sure working together was still what I wanted to do. So he sent me packing. Literally. He wanted me to experience my own life adventure. But I love my home, my family, and I can't wait to go back to Scotland."

Violet looks me dead in the eyes and frowns. "Why are you working? Why are you even here? I can't figure you out."

"I'm bored. I'll become a pro-surfer at this rate and sunbathing really isn't my thing. I enjoy working." I smile. "A bit like you."

"Cut from the same cloth." She changes direction. "You've never been in love?"

"Married to my job."

"Me too."

"I know."

"You don't really know me."

"I want to get to know you. All parts of you. Are we still playing the game?" I ask.

"Yeah."

"Can I tell you three other truths?"

"Yeah." She tucks an invisible hair strand behind her ear.

I take a deep breath. "One, I want to take you out on a date. Two, I'm flipped out by how attracted I am to you. Three, when you fell over yesterday, I didn't see anything because you are completely bare." I lower my voice further. "Bonus truth. It's the prettiest I've ever seen."

She gasps.

I tap my temple. "Embossed in my brain forever."

"You should try to forget."

"I can't," I whisper.

Time stands still for a beat too long as we survey one another. "You have nice lips," she says, staring at my lips as if hypnotized.

"All the better for kissing."

"And perfect white teeth."

"All the better for biting." I lick my lips.

"Tongue."

I lean in toward her ear. "All the better for licking and tasting illicit things."

She makes a faint whimpering sound that makes my cock bounce in my boxers.

"Time's up," Hank shouts, and the two of us spring backward in our seats.

Violet smooths her hands down the thighs of her black trousers, fixes her perfect ponytail, and then fans her face with her hand, muttering words I can't hear under her breath. It's then I notice her hard nipples piercing the thin fabric of her tee shirt.

She likes me.

6

VIOLET

These team-building days are to analyze the team, but today I could not concentrate on what our new employee, Judith, was saying during our afternoon snack break because all I could think about was Lincoln.

My stomach felt like an Olympian gymnast was doing a back handspring and roundoff when he spilled his heartfelt words and he told me he is attracted to me.

He was sincere, too. I could feel it. He doesn't mince his words and I really like that about him.

I want to take you out on a date.

Dating. That is something I haven't done in a very long time. Too long, come to think of it.

The last guy I dated, Chad, was a nice guy, but I never saw myself with him long term. We were never on the same page and I'm not sure why I stuck it out as long as I did. And the sex, eesh. It was, well, it was just sex. Two years of just *sex. What was I thinking?*

Following our midafternoon break, Uncle Hank marches us outside for the last activity: the leap of faith.

I'm not a fan of heights. My heart ricochets around my chest at the thought of having to climb the thirty-foot ladder to the top of the foot-wide totem pole.

That's not the part that scares me the most. It's jumping off, harnessed in some kinky-looking bondage harness, and then trusting it will hold the weight of my body while I'm suspended in midair.

And I have to jump off at the same time my partner does.

It's petrifying.

Beads of perspiration appear along my top lip and my hands feel sticky to the touch. I've had nightmares of splatting to the ground from thirty feet up. It's a step too far for me and a demon I'm yet to face.

Everyone gets harnessed up while I stand over in the shade, watching from the sidelines.

Observing each paired-up team, I watch as they climb the pole, work together, communicate, encourage each other, take their leap of faith, and come back down again.

I think this is one of the best teams we have gained for Urban Soul Studios so far. They are motivated, they communicate well, and they are willing and ready to learn. I'm too busy daydreaming, looking out across the open football fields to the left of me, when a Scottish voice startles me.

"Are you not joining in?" Lincoln in a harness is doing nothing to hide his enormous package. Man meat galore. *Someone send help.*

"Violet?" Lincoln calls my name to get my attention.

Thank God my lowered gaze is disguised behind my sunglasses. "I'm not a fan of heights."

"Am I doing this one myself, then?"

"Yes. You'll never catch me doing that." I arch my neck back to get a better view of the enormously long pole that looks like it

disappears into the sky from this position. "It's so high." I
wrinkle my nose.

"Do you trust me?" he asks.

"Um."

"Not even after our truth and lies game?"

"I do. It's... I..."

"I would never let anything happen to you. I've done this
before." Lincoln holds out his hand. "Trust me. Do this
with me."

Oh, no, no, no, no. "I can't. I'm too scared. What if I splat all
over the grass and then those poor people will see my ass go
through my face? And that's only the tip of the nightmares that
will live in their brains forever. Those poor people will need
therapy. For life. And it's so high and what happens if I get to the
top and I can't jump, and, and, and..."

Before I know what's happened, Lincoln's cupping my face.
"Breathe, Violet, breathe."

He slides my sunglasses on top of my head, then gently dusts
my cheek with his thumb. "In and out. Deep breaths." He pulls
me back from the brink of my mini meltdown.

I copy him, breathing in and out slowly.

"That's it, Violet. You okay?"

My heart slows down in my heavy chest.

"Yeah." I stare up at him. "I like your eye color, too," I admit,
bringing my thoughts to life.

"Oh, do you now?" He smirks.

I take a step back.

"I'm sorry. I shouldn't have said that." We're at a staff event. I
must have had a lobotomy I wasn't aware of.

Lincoln chuckles and points to the sky. "Come with me up
there. Face your fear. Don't do it for me; do this for yourself.
Trust me, please."

I shift on my feet from left to right, considering his invitation.

He adds, "It will be the best thing you ever do and you'll be telling everyone about it for years to come. I promise." He holds out his pinky for me to take.

He wants to make a pinky promise with me; that's cute.

I chew my lip. "You'll watch out for me?"

"Hundred percent."

"And you won't let me fall?"

"Never." He shakes his head, making his dark locks flop onto his forehead.

I grab his pinky with mine before I change my mind. Squeezing our fingers together, he pulls me closer.

"Good girl."

Those two words send a rush of arousal to my pussy; my panties will be soaked by the end of the day.

"Let's do this, Violet."

"My thighs will never go through the harness loops. Will it take my weight?" I blurt.

"Shut up, woman, you have amazing thighs. You are damn fine, girl. Where are you getting this shit-talk about yourself from?" he scolds.

My water during the break was clearly spiked with bravery pills because, before I know what is happening, I am harnessed up and standing at the bottom of the pole with Lincoln by my side.

Uncle Hank chatted to me the whole time I was getting equipped, but I can't repeat a single thing he said because there's a high-pitched squeal piercing my ears. It hasn't stopped since I stepped foot into the stupid harness.

"Violet." A muffled low tone comes from my right. I think that's the Grim Reaper calling me.

"Violet." Lincoln's voice makes me jump. "Look at me."

I do.

"You are going to go first, and I will be right behind you. Once we're up there, we will count to three, then jump. We are jumping into a void, but see these?" He pulls on my harness, and I nod. "If you miss the swing, these straps will support you. You won't fall. Okay?"

I hope my father knows I would like white lilies at my funeral, a black gloss casket, and I've always loved that slow Hawaiian version of "Over the Rainbow." I would like them to play that at my funeral.

"Violet, did you get all of that?"

"I think so," I lie; I have no idea what he just said.

Lincoln chuckles. "C'mon. Let's do this. You first. I'll be right behind you."

"What if I fall down the pole? I'll squash you. My ass will be in your face."

"What a way to go. Sounds like heaven."

I swat his arm as he lightens the mood.

"Now, stop stalling and climb the pole, Violet."

"You're so bossy."

"Just get up this pole and make it your bitch. Face your nemesis. You can do this, and I am behind you every step of the way."

"Watching my ass."

"It's a nice ass."

I take my first step onto the pole, muttering about his behavior since we met and move higher so we are out of earshot from the rest of team. "First, you tell me you saw nothing." I take another step. "Then you tell me you saw *everything* and that you'd like to visit Hollywood. I mean, really? That's a cheesy line if ever there was one. I thought I had you all figured out, but then I didn't and now I am back to thinking you just want to check out my ass." Another three steps up and I tell him how his smooth talking won't work on me. I grip the peg above and move up again. "You are just like all the other men, aren't you? Only after one thing." I ascend step by painful step. "Wow, it's hot up here." I keep focus on my hands, determined not to look down.

A chuckle from behind me alerts me to just how close Lincoln is and his laugh makes my pulse race.

"Are you mad at me?"

"Yes."

"I never would have known," he deadpans. "You've reached the top."

"What?" It's windier up here, making it difficult to hear. "Oh my God, Lincoln." I suddenly feel dizzy and sick all at the same time.

"Focus on your hands."

"This is where I die, isn't it? Can you tell them I want lilies at my funeral, please? And if my sister cries at my funeral, it will be crocodile tears. That girl will be glad I am gone. And please find someone to look after my dog, Pom-pom. He's my baby." I think I might start crying.

"You are not dying. Now listen to me, Violet," Lincoln coos softly from below. "You are going to pull yourself up onto the pole. But there is only a foot width to stand on, which means, when I pull myself up, I need you to stand still. You hear me?"

"I can't do this," I wail.

"You can. You're a force to be reckoned with. I know you can do this."

I pull myself up. God, that is hard with only a tiny space to maneuver on. I keep my head tilted back, only looking at where to put my feet through one open eye.

Lincoln suddenly appears by my side and wraps his powerful arms around my waist, and we wobble slightly.

"You made it." He pulls me closer.

"Everyone will be watching. You're cuddling me." My heart picks up a faster tempo.

"We have to. There's no space."

"We made it," I say unbelievingly.

"*You* made it, Violet. *You* did it."

"Only because of you," I whisper, holding on to him for dear life.

"Nope, because of you. You did this yourself."

"I made it." I feel such a sense of achievement.

"You did. Now, are you ready to take a leap of faith with me?" He looks me dead in the eyes as the warm wind swirls around us.

"No." My shout gets lost in the wind because he grips me tighter and jumps us both sideways off the tiny pole like he's freaking Batman. I scream at his moment of insanity, and a sudden jolt makes me wince. I look up and find Lincoln gripping the trapeze bar above with one hand, the other still wrapped around my waist.

"I've got you, Violet."

I pant heavily in and out.

"You're so goddamn beautiful. I really want to kiss you." Lincoln stares at my lips.

"I want you to kiss me too," I whisper. I've never wanted to kiss someone so badly.

"Say yes."

"To what?" I frown.

"Going out on a date with me."

I don't hesitate. "Okay."

7

LINCOLN

Almost time for my date with Violet, I scurry about my hotel room. After the long day of team building, I'm exhausted, but adrenaline is running through my veins like a wildfire tearing through a dry forest, setting my senses ablaze. I'm buzzing to see her again.

"I can't talk too long. I'm going out."

"Who with? Are you wearing a shirt? Is that new?" My father's voice sounds across the room from our video call on my laptop. "Are you going out on a date? When did you last wear a shirt?" His voice is laced with humor. "And you've had a haircut, and the long straggly beard has gone. Definitely a date."

I fasten the last button on my black shirt, then plonk myself down on the edge of the bed to face the screen.

"In answer to all your questions, yes, I am." I reach for my aftershave and splash some on my neck. Fuck, that stings. I haven't shaved in months. My goatee and beard are back to exactly how I like them: short and sharp, as I wanted to look smart tonight for Violet.

"What about your no-woman rule?"

"Things change. But it's just a date."

My father raises a black eyebrow in amusement. "But you only have a few weeks to go. Could you not last?" My dad flashes me a smile and tilts his head. It's uncanny how much I look like him.

"Should you not be in bed?" I brush him off.

"It is time for bed. I'm exhausted because we were at the zoo today. It was carnage." He yawns.

My stepmom, Eva's, voice whisper-shouts from somewhere behind him. "Knox, who are you talking to at this ungodly hour?"

"Shh, you'll wake the kids. I'm talking to Linc," he says in a hushed tone.

Her face suddenly appears on the screen. "You look very dashing, Lincoln. Who's the lucky lady?"

"Violet."

"That's a pretty name." She smiles.

"She is really pretty. Beautiful." I can feel my entire face lighting up.

"Oh, crap." Eva gasps.

"Yup, I know that look," my dad says.

"What look?" I'm confused.

"The 'she's the one' look." Eva gives me a cheeky wink.

"Okay, Mom. Whatever."

"Don't call me Mom. It's weird when you call me that." She scrunches her nose up.

She's right; it is still weird that Eva is only three years older than me and is married to my dad, but they couldn't be more perfect for one another.

"Sorry, Eva. She can't be 'the one'." I frown. "I'm only here for six more weeks."

"What's she like?" Eva asks.

I run my hands down the thighs of my newly purchased black jeans. "She's brunette."

"Wow, not blonde?" My father calls me out.

I ignore him and carry on. "Golden-brown eyes. Beautiful. Smart. She has no idea how funny she is. I really like her."

"Oh boy. Definitely smitten," Eva teases, then yawns. "I need my bed."

"Oh, goodie. I can't wait." My father smiles into the camera.

I stick my fingers in my mouth and fake gag. "I don't need to hear this. Go, you two. I'll call you tomorrow."

My dad grabs Eva's hand and kisses her wedding ring. "Night, Linc. Enjoy your date." My dad waves me off.

Eva gives me a little wave, too. "We can't wait to have you home. Your dad is really missing you."

"I am. I love you, son," he says.

"Love you too, Dad. Speak tomorrow."

"I want all the details," Eva says and they both wave goodbye as they hang up.

A text message alert appears on my laptop screen.

UNKNOWN

Hey. It's Violet. *smiley face*

I save her contact information.

ME

Good evening, Ms. West. I'm about to leave. What's your address?

She sends me it. Of course, her house would be on the most elite beach road in town.

ME

I'm coming to get you.

VIOLET

Looking forward to it. I'll meet you outside;
otherwise, Pom-pom will bark his head off at
you. *winking face*

I feel nervous, which is something I never feel when I go out on dates usually, but I tonight I'm flustered, and so far out of my comfort zone that I'm not even in the safety lane.

Checking my outfit in the mirror, I run my fingers through my freshly barbered hair and grab my car keys off the dresser.

Wallet, check.

Credit card, check.

Condom.

I take it out of my wallet and lay it on top of my chest of drawers. It's been in there since before I traveled to America. Second-guessing whether I should pick it back up again, I hover my hand over it.

Fuck it. It stays in my hotel suite.

I am determined to show Violet I'm more than just a one-night-stand kind of guy.

I'm a new man.

8

LINCOLN

She opens the glass door of her white, three-story beach house and slams it shut behind her. My mouth falls open as I take her in. Underneath her sheer lilac shirt, a dark-purple lace bra peeks out the top of an unbuttoned collar, showing off her glorious and bountiful cleavage. The devil has already reserved my space in hell because those beautiful breasts are going to be the only thing I see when I jerk off in the shower from now on.

Her shirt is tucked into tight black leather pants and she's wearing shiny black heels.

I groan, and she obviously hears.

"You like?" she asks, strutting toward me; confidence bounces off her.

"You look incredible." She looks fuckable.

"Hi," she says softly. "You look different."

"Okay different, or not so okay different?"

"Okay different." Eyes locked on mine, she stares at me.

Shit, I should have left my beard and long hair.

Now she can see my face. I'm not sure she likes it.

9

VIOLET

Hell's bells.

He's more gorgeous without a long beard. His now razor-sharp scruff makes his chiseled jaw look even more defined. He's had a haircut too. His hair is now shaved up each side of his head into the perfect skin fade, but he's left a little length on top to style. His black locks are swept back with not a hair out of place.

He's striking.

Lincoln leans casually against his black Camaro and he looks every bit the expensive bad boy. Black designer jeans, black suede boots, black shirt, sun-kissed skin, and a wristwatch that probably cost as much as his car. My nipples harden against the soft lace fabric of my bra. No one has ever had this effect on me, and I feel an odd warmth ignite between my legs. Lincoln pushes himself off his car and holds his hand out for me to take.

My petite hand gets swallowed up in his warm, spade-sized palm. It's the perfect spanking size. Oops, where did that thought come from again?

I hold on to my bravery from earlier. "I can't decide if I love the fact you are even more drop-dead gorgeous without a beard or if I should hate you because every woman in town is going to wish they were out on a date with you tonight."

He throws his head back, laughing. "Thanks, you're doing everything to boost my ego. I thought you didn't like my face for a minute there." He runs his other hand through his hair. "Now where are we going, m'lady?" Lincoln opens the passenger door, and I muster all the elegance I can to slide myself into the seat of his car.

"Indigo Zen." I place my purse on the floor as he pushes my door shut.

Lincoln jogs around the front and I can't take my eyes off his athletic body. I've hit the jackpot tonight.

He pulls open the driver's door and jumps into his side of the car, sending a gust of his addictive zesty scent my way, pushing my senses into overdrive.

He smells good enough to eat.

"Your house is very cool." He looks out his window at my beachside home.

"It's my father's. He bought it for family weekends together, but when he and my mom split, he left it sitting empty for a few years. I live in it now and look after it for him."

"What a shitty job that must be. Sounds painful."

"Sunrise and sunset are the worst." I sigh.

"I can imagine."

We both burst out laughing.

Lincoln pushes the start button on his car, and it roars to life.

"Your car sounds like an angry bear."

"V8 engine. She's an epic-sounding beast. I'm shipping her back with me." He pats the dashboard. "I've always wanted an American muscle car. She's beautiful."

"Did you buy this new?"

He turns his head to look at me. "Are you trying to figure out where I got the money from, Violet?"

"No, I, it's just…"

"How can the beach bum who works at a gym afford this?"

Dammit. "You got me. I'm curious."

"I have money." He gives nothing else away.

"Because you work in hospitality in Scotland?"

"I do." His face lights up as he puts two and two together. "Ah, you looked me up?"

I scrunch my face up.

"And you found nothing out?" He confirms my findings. Or lack of.

I throw my arms into the air. "You have one private social media account and nothing else. You could be a serial killer."

"I don't like social media."

"That's weird," I huff.

"But smart. You are very public. If I was clever enough, I could probably pinpoint when you ovulate next. And if there is a serial killer on the loose, he'll come for you before me, especially if you keep 'checking in' to places."

"And you only have a private Instagram account; you follow three people, and no one follows you."

"I don't use it to post, just to find out when the latest sneakers I want are going on release." He winks teasingly. "But we have a family group chat. Would you like to see?" He reaches for his phone.

"I don't need to see that." I wave my hand through the air. "Is that how you share your photos of your adventures? Hidden away within a private group chat?"

"Yes. Who the hell is interested in seeing my photos? I don't see the point of taking photos of your food or the sunset. Just enjoy the fucking moment. Hell, you know what I just realized?" he says with a serious face.

"What's that?"

"I've turned into my father. It's official. I'm a grumpy bastard."

I burst into a fit of giggles.

"If there is any more laughing at me, I will have to put you over my knee and spank you." He reaches up and cups my face, running his thumb back and forth across my bottom lip. I'm tempted to open my mouth and suck his finger, but I resist.

He groans, pulling his hand away to rearrange his thick length that's now visible through his jeans. "But I'm trying to be good for you."

"I don't need you to be good for me." I'm almost panting.

"Well, I need to be good for myself."

Disappointment hits me like a tsunami.

"For now, Violet. I'll be good for you for now."

10

VIOLET

Lincoln and I haven't stopped chatting since we sat down at our ocean-view table.

He's the first man to take an interest in my life and work.

After dessert, I plucked up the courage to ask what he does back home.

I'm currently sitting with my mouth wide open. "Your father and you own a five-star hotel? In Scotland?"

"Yes."

"With your grandfather?"

"Yes."

"And you're a director?"

"Yes. All three of us own it. We have the only privately owned, family-run, five-star hotel in Scotland. We're currently working toward becoming six-star rated. We'll be the only one in Scotland." He looks excited about that. "You should have dug a little deeper trying to find the information you were looking for about me. Google would find the good stuff. Not social media."

I have to force my jaw not to drop to the ground. I can't work him out. "Why the hell are you working for the gym?"

"Boredom. I told you; I like to work." He shrugs as if his explanation makes any sense. For the record, it doesn't.

"You're a weirdo."

"A workaholic weirdo." He picks up his phone, taps it a few times, then turns it around to show me whatever he was searching for.

Right enough, there he is. Lincoln Black, Director, The Sanctuary Hotel and Spa.

"That's you," I squeal.

"It is."

"In a suit."

"In a suit," he confirms.

I scroll through the pictures of the hotel. It's out of this world. I look up from his phone. Elbow bent, he's resting his cheek on his hand, and I feel his mood plummet.

I place his phone back on the table. "You think this changes how much I like you, Lincoln?"

He pops a shoulder.

I slide my hand along the table and turn my hand over, palm up, inviting him to take it. He surprises me by accepting.

"I like everything about you. I want to know more. Trust me, I know exactly what it's like. Superficial friends and men who want to date me or be my friends all the time. I get it, I do. They think being seen with me will lift their profile, increase their popularity. With money comes fake friendships and it can bring out the worst in people."

He rubs his thumb back and forth across my knuckles.

"I like you for being you, Lincoln. Funny, caring, boyishly handsome, and the fact that you went traveling just to make your dad happy tells me what type of man you are."

His eyebrows spring up.

"You're different and I want to have more date days and

nights with you while you are here in California." I give his hand a firm squeeze.

"Well, if that's the case, can you dance?" he asks out of the blue.

"I love to dance."

"No, I mean, *really* dance?"

"Like ballroom dancing?"

"Kinda. Do you trust me?"

"After today? Always."

He summons the waiter, pays our bill, and we promptly leave the restaurant, excited at the prospect of dancing.

As we make our way out of the restaurant, Lincoln's warm hand presses against the base of my spine. He ushers me out of the glass door, and we are hit by a wall of warm evening air.

"Are you not hot wearing those leather trousers?"

"Nope. I'm a born and bred Cali girl. It hasn't been that hot today."

"It was seventy-eight degrees Fahrenheit today." He moves his hand to the side of my waist and gives it a squeeze. I cringe, knowing he's probably felt my flabby bits.

"Meh, that's cooler than most days," I tease him, trying to push down my insecurities.

When we're almost at the car, someone calls my name. I turn and spot Chad confidently striding toward us. I'm sure he follows me everywhere I go.

"Who is that?" Lincoln asks through the side of his mouth.

"Ex-boyfriend."

I swear Lincoln grows a few inches taller and broader. "Doesn't look your type."

"He's not."

"Preppy."

"Male chauvinist."

"Missionary position?"

"Every time. Like clockwork, once a week."

"Once a week? Fuck, once a day is too little. How boring."

More than once a day? Holy shit, bring Momma some of that, spank you very much.

"Orgasms were just a rumor," I whisper as Chad gets closer.

Lincoln snorts and I burst out laughing.

"Hey, Violet." Chad goes to lean in for a kiss but thinks better of it when Lincoln pulls me closer. "It's good to see you," he says, eyeing Lincoln.

I wish I could say the same. "Oh, I know. I haven't seen you in at least, oh, a week. Going for something to eat?" I don't actually care what he's doing. I'm being polite.

"Yes, meeting Jezza and Ryan."

"A throuple? Nice." Lincoln's voice is laced with sarcasm, but his face remains stoic.

I tuck my lips into my mouth to stop myself from laughing.

Chad frowns. "No, nothing like that."

"Forgive my manners." I lay my hand on Lincoln's chest. *Oh wow, that is firm.* He flexes, looks down at me and licks his lips. The tension between us is becoming unbearable.

"Lincoln, meet Chad; Chad, meet Lincoln."

Lincoln squeezes his hand in an overly firm grip, making Chad wince, but he says nothing.

"Was lovely to meet you, *Chad*, and I would love to stand and chew the fat with you. But I have somewhere to take my girl."

My girl.

"Chew the fat?" Chad frowns. "Sounds disgusting."

"Oh, it's British for small talk. We don't have time." Lincoln promptly guides me to the car.

"Where are you off to?" Chad shouts from behind me.

"Private club," Lincoln answers.

Are we? How exciting.

11

VIOLET

"Where are we?" I look up at the distressed wooden sign above an even tattier-looking red wooden door.

"Come."

"It doesn't look safe." I look up and down the empty street for evidence of life. It's darker now. No one is around and I can't even hear any music. "It's not safe on this side of town," I whisper.

He whispers back, "Why are we whispering? There's no one around. Be brave. C'mon, Petal." *Petal?*

Lincoln pulls his phone out, taps open an app, and then holds it up to the corner of the door. "Concealed camera. Members only."

I jump as the junkyard door swings open and a fusion of sensual, slow-tempo music bellows into the empty street.

"Soundproof door." He tugs my hand.

"Is this a sex club?" I pull my hand out of Lincoln's and take a step back.

He gives a brief laugh. "Nope."

"You sure?"

"Yes. I have never been to a sex club in my life."

"Liar."

"I'm not lying. Strip club with my friends twice, yes. Sex club, no. I don't need to pay for sex, Violet."

"Because most women simply fall at your feet?" I don't know why I'm suddenly annoyed. I fold my arms across my chest.

"Are you jealous, Ms. West?"

"No." I pout. *I am*. It's a feeling I'm not familiar with.

Lincoln holds his two fingers up to the camera and mouths, *Two minutes*.

And the door closes again.

He moves toward me and gently cups my face. "Back home, I may have slept with a few girls in the past. But I have changed. I wanted to change. I haven't slept with anyone in months. I also have never paid for sex. Ever. That sounds nasty." He shakes his head. "I like you and only you. Violet West, God made you fucking perfect because you are the most knockout woman I have ever laid eyes on. I would love nothing more than to take you back to my place, peel off these sexy clothes, and learn every single glorious detail of your beautiful body because I have been hard for you since the moment you set foot inside the gym the other night." He moves his lips closer to my mouth. "Now, unfold those arms because all it does is push your tits up even further, and it makes me want to slip my dick between your delicious cleavage and ride it so fucking hard." His breath airbrushes against my skin.

Holy shit.

"But tonight, I am taking you out on a date. A proper date to remember. So chill, sweet flower."

"Okay," I submissively agree.

His hooded eyes drop to my lips. "Can I kiss you?"

"If you don't, I might die."

He grins and my arms fall to my sides. Finally, his soft, full lips press gently against mine and he lets out a low moan. As he opens his mouth slightly, mine responds, allowing him to slip his tongue between my lips.

It's a kiss unlike anything I've ever experienced. Something changes between us and desire runs through my veins.

Lincoln threads his large hand into my hair, pulling me hard against his mouth, deepening our kiss. I wrap my arms around his neck, holding him close, his hard length against my hip. Grabbing a handful of my ass, he pushes my pelvis into him and a gasp of enjoyment leaves my lungs. "Lincoln," I sigh. "I want you."

"Mmm, I want you so bad," he mumbles between kisses. "I'm so hard for you."

I rock my pelvis against his to relieve the tension building between my thighs.

"I'll come if you keep doing that," he pants as he digs his fingers into my hips to stop me moving. "Shit, I promised myself I wouldn't do this tonight."

"I promised myself I *would* do this tonight," I counter.

He dips his head and nibbles my jaw. "You're a devil woman."

"I am."

"A wicked woman with a delicious body I want to fucking devour." He moves back to my lips and kisses me.

"I could kiss you all night," I mumble against his lips.

"You just made dancing with you even more impossible. I can't dance with a hard-on."

"Let's go back to my place, then." I don't care how forward I am being. I'm a woman who knows what she wants... him.

"Don't tempt me." He presses his forehead against mine.

"I was trying to." I smile coyly.

"Trust me, I know." He presses his soft lips against mine in a last kiss. "Let's go dance. It's time to show me what you can do with this insane body of yours." He runs his thumb along my now-swollen bottom lip before he steps backward and eyes my body.

He shakes his head. "You are so fucking hot," he mumbles, as if talking to himself.

The door magically opens again, and we descend the dark stairs. At this point, I don't care where they lead.

Because after that hot as hell kiss, I'll die a lucky woman.

12

VIOLET

Lincoln clasps my hand as we make our way through the sea of dancers, dragging me through the crowd of hot bodies. With each step I can't believe what I am seeing.

Dancing. Erotic dancing. Well, it's not, but it looks like everyone is having sex on the dance floor as they all writhe against one another. Is it salsa? Holy hell, is this what Lincoln wants me to do?

For someone who has only lived here a few months, he knows his way around better than me and I've lived here all my life.

I didn't know this place existed.

I slow down to get a better look at the sexy couples. A brief tug of my hand is a reminder to keep walking.

The music is so loud, making the liquid in the bottles behind the bar jump around. The swirl of the exotic music, the maracas, the high-pitched guitar, the easy tempo of the beat, it's an energetic cocktail of sounds, and I can feel my hips automatically wanting to join in.

The entire club is clad in raw wood, pieced together with

rusty nails. Exposed silver-foiled air-conditioning pipes, copper piping, and lighting cables run along the ceiling. Every makeshift light is covered in a thin film of red or orange, making the cozy club look warmer and deeply sensual. Unique brightly colored abstract paintings hang in every recess on the wall, and along one side of the club, deep-red leather semicircle seating is filled to capacity with cheerful people all shouting at each other above the soulful music.

A "Wow" leaves my mouth.

"You like?" Lincoln moves his lips to my ear.

"I love. Do I have to dance like that?" I point to the sexy, gyrating couple in front of us. *I should have worn a skirt.*

"Do you want to dance like that?" Lincoln yells.

"Can you dance like them?" I feel stupid asking. He's a member here; he must be able to.

"Yes."

"Right."

"I can teach you."

"I'm a little clumsy."

"I got you. Would you like a drink? I was thinking of leaving my car. I can get it tomorrow."

"Tequila." *I need bravery juice.*

Lincoln laughs, then turns to face the bar, while I watch these beautiful people dance.

Glistening bodies shine under the low lighting, hands on hips, arms, backs, behinds as they all move in time to the music, lost in their own bubbles.

My eyes lock on a couple to the left. She arches her body backward, inviting her partner to touch her. He accepts by running his hand between her cleavage, skimming it across her stomach before he pulls her closer.

I'm so turned on.

Lincoln taps me on the shoulder as the bartender lays our shots on the bar and I immediately grab the salt, cover my hand, then Lincoln's, lay it back down on the bar and lift the shot glass. "I want to dance." I confess.

Lincoln *chinks* our glasses together. "After three, Violet. Ready? One... two... three."

In harmony, we lick the salt off our hands, throw our heads back and down our shots, then shove the lime slices into our mouths and suck.

I let out a whoop then say, "Another."

Lincoln holds two fingers. "Two more, please." He points at our shot glasses to give the bartender our order, and the bartender overfills our shot glasses clumsily.

"Slower this time." Lincoln winks as he picks up the salt-shaker off the bar. He leans forward and, ever so gently, pulls back the collar of my thin shirt. "Tilt your head to the side."

Before I have time to ask him what he's doing, he lowers his head and flattens his tongue across my collarbone. I shudder at the unexpectedness before he drizzles a little salt onto my skin and a few unstuck grains escape, cascading down into my lace bra.

Picking up the refilled shot glass, he slowly drags his tongue from my collarbone up my neck and when he gets to my jaw, he takes his tequila shot, then quickly covers his mouth with mine, driving his tongue deep.

He tastes of citrus and sin, all rolled into one. Raw and wild passion bounces between our pressed bodies.

When he stops kissing me, he's almost panting. "Your turn."

Taking his hand in mine, I position it palm up and pour a thin line along his pointer finger. I pick up my shot glass as Lincoln watches intently, waiting patiently to see what my next move is.

Licking the salt off his finger, I down my shot, then draw his finger into my mouth and suck hard.

He pulls me toward him, and I think he's going to kiss me; instead, he grabs my hand and pulls it between us. "You feel that, Violet?" He rubs my hand over his hard, thick length. "That's what you do to me."

I gasp and would love nothing more than to rip off his clothes but can't.

"Let's dance, not that it will calm *that* down." He points to his crotch and readjusts himself then slips his hand around my waist and guides me onto the packed dance floor.

I look around, internally freaking out that I might not be able to dance like everyone else.

"Violet, look at me." He's so serious when he stops in the middle of the dance floor and eases his thigh between my legs, bending lower to accommodate my height. I'm now fully aware both of his hands are on my ass.

"Kizomba—the dance everyone is doing—is slow, steady. I'm going to show you the basic moves, then you'll know what they are, but I will lead and all you have to do is follow. Okay?"

Over the next three songs, he teaches me the moves. Hips bump, hands skim, and cheek to cheek touches make me want him all the more and to drag Lincoln into a bathroom and fuck him senseless.

"You're one of those people who can turn her hand to anything, aren't you?" Lincoln rubs the base of my spine with exploring hands.

"I never got the hang of playing the piano." The song changes and everyone whoops, making hordes of people hit the floor. It's a tight squeeze, but it urges Lincoln to hold me closer, as if he's my protector.

The lights dim even lower, almost plummeting us into darkness.

I relax in his arms, feeling his hard body against my soft one. Temple to temple, we dance and it's the most romantic, sexy thing I have ever done with a man.

Holding me firmly in his brawny arms, he places the palm of his hand in the exposed gap of my unbuttoned shirt, gesturing for me to bend backward against the top of his broad thigh.

Taking my full weight, he arches me further back.

Gliding his hand further down my exposed skin, he splays his fingers as he reaches my cleavage and rolls my body back up. Once upright, he dips his head and lays a path of kisses from the top of my cleavage, up my chest, and across my neck.

Despite the air-conditioning, my body is molten hot with pleasure.

He grinds into me as we sway again, and I feel how hard he is for me.

"Will you come back to my place?" The tequila is doing the talking for me now.

"I'm not sure that's such a good idea." Lincoln pinches his brows.

My heart stalls. I'm instantly snapped out of this lust-filled haze by his rejection, making my face redden with embarrassment. "Okay. I think I would like to go home now."

"You sure?" he asks, confused.

"Yeah, I need to get back and let Pom-pom out. I'll go to the bathroom first. Can you order a cab, please?"

He nods, his face full of concern as the air grows icy around us.

I weave my way through the crowds with a heavy heart, and escape to the bathroom.

Lincoln is already standing on the sidewalk with the cab door open, waiting for me when I get outside. "Are you okay?"

"Yeah." I lengthen my spine and pull a fake smile to summon some positive energy back into my body.

The cab journey is a complete contrast to the whole evening, and you could cut the atmosphere with a knife. Lincoln doesn't utter a word, and his knee has bounced the entire way.

As we pull up outside my house, I lean in and peck his cheek. "Stay in the cab. I'll see myself in. See you Monday."

He doesn't move as he says a soft good night.

By the time I let myself in, let Pom-pom out for a quick pee, remove my makeup, and have a quick shower, my mind is more awake than ever as my head hits the pillow.

The ringer on my phone makes me jump. *Lincoln.*

I sigh and accept the call. "Hello."

"I'm sorry."

"For?"

"For tonight. It's just..."

"I know. You are taking a break from women." I rub my forehead.

"It's not like that," he says softly.

"What's it like, then?"

"You're different."

"Different how?"

"I can't put it into words. But you make me feel things I haven't felt before and you make me want to be better. For you."

I roll my eyes. "Okay." That sounds like a load of bull. "Well, thanks for calling to tell me that."

"I can't stop thinking about you."

Silence fills the void between us.

He continues, "I've screwed up in the past. Had a lot of one-night stands and I've never had a relationship that's lasted more than a couple of weeks. No one has ever felt right. Until you, I was beginning to think something was wrong with me. I often feel like there is a tiny part of me missing. You know, with the whole mom abandonment thing?" He doesn't let me answer, but adds, "I don't appear to be very good with matters of the heart. I've never been able to settle with anyone before. But then you came along and blindsided me. You're everything I could ever want in a woman. You're *more* than everything and my heart feels so fucking happy when I'm around you. But I leave in six weeks." He pauses. "Why did you have to come along when you did? The cosmos is fucking with me." I think he's talking more to himself now. "I meet a goddess of a woman, a fucking queen, who is funny, switched on, successful, and smart, with an utterly banging hourglass, painfully perfect body, and she can't be mine." His voice gets louder with every passing word. He's mad at our situation.

The sweet things he says about me set off a kaleidoscope of butterflies in my belly.

I hold my breath to listen. It's only then I detect the faint whoosh of the ocean waves crashing in the distance.

Is he outside?

Throwing my comforter back, I leap out of the bed and peek through the gap in my drapes. Sure enough, he's pacing back and forth outside my house. "I'm only here for six weeks, Violet. Why do you not live in Scotland or why was I not born here in your hometown, or why did I have to cross paths with you to begin with?" He lets out a *humph* noise as I watch him pick up a stone off the sidewalk and throw it angrily over the road. It disappears into the darkness on the beach. "Why did your father buy that fucking gym?" He pulls his hair. "We live over five thousand miles apart. I know because I looked it up. I'm mad at myself for asking you out on a date tonight. All it's done is made me want you more. I don't know what's wrong with me. I've never been like this with anyone before."

I stay quiet.

"Life is so unfair. I really liked you and for the first time... I felt things for you." He clasps his chest.

Liked?

I give a soft *ahem*. "I'm mad too."

"Yeah?"

"Yeah. I met this perfect guy, who is simply gorgeous inside and out. But you forgot something."

"What did I forget?"

I bounce down the stairs and cross the white-sparkle-tiled floor. Unlocking my front door, I swing it open and hit the switch to unlock the electric gates, granting him access, making him spin to face me.

"That this isn't a one-sided decision, Lincoln. You didn't let me decide or have my say. You made a decision that involved two people, and I disagree with you."

He walks slowly up my drive, his phone still glued to his ear. "What don't you agree with?"

"Not giving us a shot. You didn't ask me if I wanted to see what would happen between us. Or at least consider being exclusive. You wouldn't be breaking your stupid self-inflicted ban either. You'd be embracing a new adventure with someone who might just end up being your forever." I test him. "And what if it is only six weeks of fun? Does it matter? Where did your sense of adventure go? We only get one chance in life, and if we make mistakes, then we'll make them together. But you will never know if you don't try."

"I think I would need more than six weeks with you." On my doorstep now, he stares down at me in my purple pajama booty shorts and lilac tank top. I'm suddenly conscious that I have very bare legs, no bra on, and the girls are facing south.

He pulls his phone away from his ear. Now only two feet apart, I say, "I want more than six weeks with you too, but you might turn out to be a complete asshole. You were an eighth of an asshole tonight."

He gives a genuine chortle, finally ends the call, and pushes his phone into the pocket of his jeans, and I lower my phone.

"Just an eighth?" he asks, amused.

I lift a shoulder to my ear. "Meh, the rest of the night was okay."

"So, seven-eighths of the night was just *okay*?"

"Yeah, I suppose," I tease, then I put us back on course. "Also, it's been a very long time since I had sex too. Six weeks of it together could be fun. You mentioned something earlier about more than once a day. Where do I sign?"

He shakes his head. "You, Violet West, have thirty-foot poles that are your nemesis, but you are my undoing."

"Your leap of faith?"

"Yeah."

I hold out my hand. "Are you taking it? Or are we going to play a game of verbal gymnastics all night?"

13

VIOLET

He doesn't take it.

Instead, he steps toward me, moving inside my house, coaxing me to take a step backward, then with one foot, flamingo style, he slams the door behind him and the automatic catch locks us in.

He launches himself at me, crashing his lips against mine, while simultaneously lifting me into his arms. My phone slips out of my hand, falling to the floor. I don't even care if it breaks.

"I'm too heavy." My automatic default saying flies out of my mouth as I stop kissing him.

Cupping my ass with his hands, he narrows his eyes. "Lock your legs around me."

I follow his instruction.

"Let's make a new rule. No more negative self-talk," he mumbles.

"Okay." I'd agree to anything right now.

He slams me against the wall and all the air leaves my lungs. "You, Ms. West, are not heavy." His deep voice sounds dangerous and drips with desire as he runs his nose along my jaw. Inhaling deeply, he breathes me in. "You are the perfect weight for me to do my bicep curls with. I'm going to work out as I lift you up and down my cock."

"Two-for-one experience."

"Exactly." He thrusts against me, then assaults my mouth, touching, tasting, licking. This kiss is different from all the others tonight. It doesn't end with dancing or tequila; it's full of promises of what's to come and a *this is it* attitude. It's happening.

Lincoln keeps grinding himself against my perfectly aligned center, causing a small whimper to escape my lips.

His large, warm hand moves underneath the fabric of my shorts, his fingers exploring my bare backside before he takes a handful of my ass and squeezes hard.

Throughout the open expanse of the house, all I can hear is the smacking noise of our lips locking together and heavy breathing.

His fingers find my pussy and I throw my head back, gasping as he cups my now-swollen lower lips.

I let out a low, long groan as he plunges a finger into my pussy. "Fucking soaking, Petal," he mumbles against my collarbone.

"Only for you." I ride his finger, pushing myself up and down the wall, my entire body humming in response.

"Shit. I don't have any condoms. Do you?"

"I don't."

His forehead rests against mine. "I wasn't doing this with you tonight."

"I can be very persuasive."

"Fully aware," he grumbles.

We lock eyes. "I'm clean. I haven't had sex for over a year and I'm on the contraceptive shot. Like clockwork," I inform him.

"I'm clean. Have been for months. I got tested before I started traveling and I haven't been with anyone. Are you sure you want to go bare with me?" His brows pinch together.

I nod slowly with a smirk; his megawatt smile dazzles back at me. "We're doing this."

"Fuck, I need to lay you down and get a proper look at your pretty pussy. Where are we going?" He nips at my skin with his wicked mouth.

"Elevator."

He pulls back suddenly. "You have an elevator? You're so fancy."

"Shut up and start walking."

He moves his towering body into my hall and stops dead in his tracks, suddenly distracted by something I can't see behind me. He removes his finger from my wet center and I whimper at how empty I suddenly feel.

"There is a four-legged fluffy tampon standing in your hall. It's staring at us," he says through the side of his mouth. "And it's wearing a black bow tie."

"The bow tie makes him look very smart. He's not a tampon."

"Cotton candy?"

"Shut up and walk."

"A cloud?"

"Oh my God, if you don't start moving toward the elevator, I will have sex with you here in the hall while my dog watches."

His eyes bug out.

"Thought as much. That way." I hike a thumb over my shoulder. As we pass Pom-pom, Lincoln gives him a wide berth. "He won't bite."

"He might not like me touching his owner," he whispers.

"He won't care. But I care. So, for the love of all things holy, get in the damn elevator." I lean back out of our hold slightly, bang the call button on the wall with the palm of my hand, and the doors open. "Pom-pom, go back to bed," I command. "And you." I place both my hands on either side of his handsome face. "Get in there and kiss me."

He steps into the elevator, and I hit the number three on the panel, instructing it to take us to my bedroom on the top floor.

"So bossy." He traces soft kisses down my neck.

"You ain't seen nothing yet." I tilt my head to give him better access.

"My dick just grew even harder for you. I'm going to let you do whatever the fuck you want to me."

"I can't wait." As soon as the doors ping open, it only takes him four long strides to reach my bed.

"On the edge of the mattress," I order.

He turns around and lowers us and I let out an unexpected jumble of words when his thick clothed length brushes against my clit.

"Sorry, what was that?" He grins against my mouth.

"Felt so good," I whisper.

Running his hands up my sides, he slowly peels my lilac top up over my head.

"These nipples are begging to be licked, Petal. Fucking gorgeous." He tilts his head forward, sucking my nipple into his mouth. He flicks it with his tongue, bites it with the perfect amount of pressure, then lashes at it, teasing it.

I gasp, threading my fingers into his hair.

"I can't get enough of these." He squeezes my heavy breasts gently. "You have amazing tits. Do you remember the name of the club tonight?"

"Was it Agastopia?" What a time to ask a silly question.

"Do you know what that means?" He gives my nipple

another flick with the tip of his tongue, sending shock waves of pleasure across my skin.

I shake my head. My mind has gone completely blank.

"It means admiration of a particular part of someone's body. I'm obsessed with yours. Every single part of it."

Oh God, who sent this man my way?

I push him away from me, urging him to lie back.

"What are you doing?" He reaches for me.

"Just lie back and enjoy." I move down his body, and he watches in wonder when I begin to peel his clothing from his mouthwatering body.

His black shirt is the first to go. I unbutton it and he pulls it off his arms to help me.

My eyes can't take themselves off his sun-kissed washboard abs. "Sweet Jesus." My breath catches in my throat.

A deep groan leaves his chest as I kiss each divot, causing him to shiver at my touch and I move lower.

Slowly undoing the top two buttons of his jeans, my mouth salivates at the thought of what's beneath.

I unpop the other buttons, sliding the thick designer fabric down his hips and dropping them to the floor.

His dark, heated gaze looks down at me, scorching my skin. "Commando," I mumble, mesmerized by his huge, thick length. Will it fit? It's the biggest cock I've ever seen in the flesh.

An amused smile dances across his lips. "I've been commando all night."

"You wax?" I raise my brows in amusement at his smooth skin.

"Back, sack, and crack. It's the only way." He winks, making him look devilishly handsome.

I move to kneel between his legs and I watch with fascination as he fists himself like he's too impatient to wait.

"Your turn." He juts his chin. "I'm going to enjoy watching you while you take off those wet shorties."

With one arm behind his head, Lincoln continues to pump himself slowly. His eyes darken and his breathing becomes heavier with every long stroke, pre-cum glistening across his thick crown. "Show me that pretty pussy."

I stand on the mattress, being careful not to fall, and wiggle my shorts down my hips.

"Fuck," he hisses, looking up at me as he jerks himself harder.

"Ready for your private tour of Hollywood, Lincoln?" I skim both my hands over my heated skin, to my lower lips, then I ease them apart.

"So pretty," he mutters breathlessly.

My pussy pulses with anticipation. I touch my clit and a burst of energy surges through my body.

"Holy fucking shit. I'm not going to last. It's been months for me, and you are so sexy. I need you, Violet." He reaches for me.

And I kneel between his legs again. "Not yet. Patience, Lincoln."

He groans in frustration and goes back to pumping his cock.

I kiss his lean, sculpted body. First his stomach, then I lick his abs. He removes his hand from around his cock and weaves his fingers into my hair.

Skimming my hand lower, I wrap my hand around his cock and finally lick him from root to tip in one sweeping motion, then pull him into my mouth, making him jerk.

"Oh, dear fuck," he cries, grabbing my face with both hands.

He thrusts, but I know he's holding back. "So good, baby, so, so good."

Massaging his balls, gently at first, I then give them a squeeze before moving my hand toward his taint and massage it in circles, licking and sucking his cock much harder now.

"Oh shit," he gasps.

His saltiness floods my tongue.

His thumb caresses my cheek repeatedly, feeling like such a tender sentiment during our untamed moment.

Running my tongue around his crown, I use the opportunity to suck one of my fingers into my mouth to make it wet, then suck his hard length back into my mouth.

Edging my finger back across his taint, I move further back, this time to find his puckered ring and I circle it.

He shoots upright, pulling his cock out of my mouth. "Wh-what are you doing?" His eyes grow wide.

I don't move my finger.

"Do you trust me?"

He looks at me suspiciously and takes at least ten seconds to answer. "Fuck it." He lets go of my face and I push him back in my mouth before he can change his mind, inserting my wet finger into his tightness. "What the fuuuucccck?" He clenches the bedsheets.

I push my finger in another inch, curving it toward his stomach to I find what I'm after and give it a press, making him groan. I press again, and he finally starts to relax.

"I've never had anyone do this to me before. Jesus Christ, what are you doing to me? Why does that feel so good?"

Between his P-spot massage, me sucking, and him gently thrusting himself into my mouth, his moans grow louder.

I stop sucking his cock and kiss his glistening crown. "You're holding back, Lincoln. Let go and come for me," I urge him in a low, gentle tone.

"I don't want to hurt you."

"I can take it. Now fuck my mouth," I demand then seal my lips around his cock and I swallow him down.

He gasps. "The word *fuck* from your pretty lips is so hot."

Curling my finger again, I rub his sweet spot with my fingertip. He lets out a long, guttural groan and really begins to thrust himself into my mouth, making my eyes water.

I gag slightly as he hits the back of my throat, picking up the pace, letting him fuck my mouth much faster now. I gaze up just as he's throwing his head back and he loses all control, aggressively digging his fingertips into the sides of my face to get himself off.

"Aw, shit. I'm coming." He thrusts himself deep into my throat, then roars as he comes. Thick cords of cum fill my mouth and I swallow him down.

Covered in a thin sheen of perspiration, his stuttered pants and hip jerks are such a turn-on and have me dry humping the bed with need, my juices wetting my thighs. Every nerve ending throbbing with deep longing for him to be inside of me. I need to come.

I let him lie there, allowing him to catch his breath and ease my finger out of his tight hole, then kiss the end of his cock, making him flinch. He moans before running his hands down his face. "What the fuck just happened?" He looks at me through his spaced fingers, seeming almost embarrassed. "Did I hurt you? I'm sorry if I went too deep. I didn't mean to be that aggressive."

I drop a gentle kiss on his stomach. "I wouldn't have told you to fuck my mouth if I didn't want you to." I move off the bed. "Two seconds while I clean up."

I catch him digging the palms of his hands into his eyes, as he mumbles, "Fucking hell."

Entering the bedroom again, I see that Lincoln hasn't moved.

I crawl up over his gorgeous body.

"You like?"

I don't expect him to grab my waist and flip me over in his muscular arms.

"You, Ms. West, are in a heap of trouble." He nibbles the skin on my neck. "I have to teach you a lesson for surprising me the way you just did."

"Oh, yeah?" I slide my hands up his strong back; he's as wide as a football field.

"You, sweet Petal, are not so sweet, but a whole heap of spicy, and I just might fucking like it."

"Thought you might," I counter.

His gaze meets mine. "I've never done that before."

"You don't say." I thumb his cheek.

"What are you doing to me?"

"The same thing you're doing to me. I think."

"I need to taste you. I'm gonna lick you up so fucking good, Petal."

He moves down my body, placing a path of kisses as he heads south, nipping, licking, and biting as he moves. Where he is hard, I am soft, and where he's all bronzed, I am much less sun-kissed than him.

Close to my pussy, he makes himself comfortable between my legs. "Spread your lips for me," he instructs, which I do.

Closing in, he gives me one last look and says, "You have the prettiest pussy I have ever seen."

Oh, dear Lord.

"You are beautiful everywhere. Inside." He pushes his rigid tongue into my soaking core, making the whole room spin.

"And out." I watch intently when he circles my clit, causing my hips to buck off the bed. Steadying me with his hands, he flicks it then sucks it into his mouth and I almost come there and then. "Spread them wider for me."

I spread myself further, and I lose myself in his touch.

Before I know what is happening, his entire mouth devours me. His plump lips and tongue brush against my fingers, increasing the intensity.

I gasp when he inserts his finger, then another.

"Let me take it from here. Remove your fingers." Placing his other hand over the top of my hips and stomach to stop me bucking, his fingers never stop moving in and out of my body as he fills me deliciously with his expert digits.

This is exactly how I imagine sex should be. It's taken all these years to finally find someone who knows what he's doing.

"Oh, Linc, I'm going to come." It's embarrassing how quickly.

"Fuck my fingers and come on my tongue," he commands.

I arch into him to find my sweet release and he pushes them deep inside of me and I come.

Harder than I ever have before.

It's the ultimate joy as my body shatters into a million pieces and happiness dances across my skin. "Lincoln," I cry, my toes curling into the sheets.

Completely uninhibited, I let go of everything I've been holding on to because he's unclipped my wings today and I'm flying.

Grabbing on to his hair, my frantic hands pull him tighter onto my pussy, making his deep baritone moans join my high soprano ones. He continues to work my clit and wet center as wave upon wave of divine pleasure rolls through my body.

Behind my clenched eyes, white and gold paparazzi flash-lights dazzle my senses.

I'm breathless as I begin my descent. Lincoln gently kisses my still-sensitive clit, making me squirm, and I clamp his head between my thighs, which makes him laugh and his hot breath floods my swollen pussy.

I move my hips against his mouth. I'm so turned on, I need to come again.

Taking it as his invitation, it all happens so fast. He moves up the bed, sucks my nipple into his mouth, cups my ass cheek in his hand, locks my leg around his waist, and pushes his cock into me. Deep. Making my eyes roll into the back of my head as I cry out at his welcome invasion.

"Aw fuck, yeah," he groans.

Holding himself for a moment, he allows me to adjust to his size.

And hallelujah, he's got stamina.

"I've never been skin on skin with anyone before. You feel amazing. You are soaked, and so fucking tight." The veins in his neck are thick with tension, as if he's struggling with the plea-sure overtaking his body.

We both let out a giant moan as sparks fly between us.

"You're hard again? How is that possible?" I ask, with a mix of astonishment and excitement.

"Been hard for you since you flashed me..." He pulls his cock out slowly, then punctuates his last three words with deep thrusts, making my jaw hang open. "In... the... office..."

The fire between us licks flames across our self-control and I claw onto him. "Fuck me harder," I beg. "Fill me up."

He fucks me so hard that it makes my heavy breasts bounce with every pump of his hips, driving me up the bed and I have to grab on to the white wrought-iron frame to push myself back onto him.

Needing more, my hips rise, giving him as much as he gives me.

"Fuck, Violet. You're unbelievable."

He pulls himself out of me unexpectedly, leaving me feeling empty, my walls twitching as I'm teetering on the edge of my orgasm.

"Turn around. On your knees." His gruff voice sounds desperate. "I'm giving you what you want."

I flip onto my stomach and he pulls my hips in the air before he smacks my ass cheek, making me yelp. It leaves a pleasurable sting, causing a wave of goosebumps to rise across my skin.

He pushes his cock back inside me and I hiss at the roughness of it all, loving every minute of the stretch I feel.

"Isn't this what you wanted, Violet?" He spanks me hard a few more times in the same spot, and it sends a rush of arousal into my core, coating his cock in my excitement. I'm incoherent with want; I can't form words and don't answer him. "Oh, you're fucking soaked, which tells me you really *do* like that, huh?" He gives me one final sharp spank, making me arch my back, and I fully give myself to him, pushing my shoulders down into the mattress.

"Fucking stunning," he mumbles to himself, fucking me hard and digging his fingertips into my hips, which I know will leave bruises.

Over and over again, he goes fast, then slow, edging me until I'm almost crying and begging for him to let me come.

"I need to see you," I pant, desperate to be closer to him.

I whimper when he slides himself out of me, turns me back over faster than the crack of a whip and slides back in, deliciously filling me with his cock.

"You, Violet West, are very demanding. Now wrap your legs around me," Lincoln commands me and I lock my legs around his hips and he fucks me relentlessly. "I love how well you take my cock."

Every nerve ending switches on and the glimmer of my

orgasm morphs into a new form, building quickly. I look into his eyes, and through his clenched jaw he growls, "Let go and come for me. Now."

The fire burns hotter in my core and I know this is it. This is when he's going to give me everything he's got, everything I need.

I pull him down to me, and crash his lips to mine. Tongues dancing, teeth clashing, our slick bodies melt into one another, all the while he fucks me, his balls slap against my ass and with another thrust, warmth bursts in my core, shooting through my body as my orgasm explodes.

A fusion of multicolored stars appears behind my eyes and for a moment, I see everything as clear as day. A vivid moment of pure clarity, realizing how destined I am to find this incredible man.

My pussy clenches, my inner walls milking him as I cry, begging him to fuck me through my orgasm.

"Oh baby, that is the hottest thing I have ever seen," he roars.

Locking my legs tighter around him, I dig my nails into the hard flesh of his ass, urging him to come too.

Lincoln leans back slightly, and he looks at me as if he's looking deep into my soul.

"Come, Lincoln." I tilt my hips, panting.

His rough breathing builds as he continues to undulate his hips in hard thrusts into me. With one final loud grunt, he comes, filling me with his release.

"Violet, ah, fuck." He throws his head back, breaking our eye contact.

Deep satisfaction runs through me as my name drips off his tongue and my heart flutters at the enormity of what we just did and how it makes me feel.

Like he's the one.

A cocktail of sweet and sad emotions makes my stomach feel slightly queasy, and I don't like it.

Six weeks. Oh no.

I can't take my eyes off this incredible man above me. The one whose jaw hangs slack, his glistening chest moving with harsh breaths; the one who just called out my name like we've been doing this for years.

His thick length pulses inside of me as he descends from his high. Our heavy breathing is the only sound in the room.

I push my feelings way down. After all, I was the one who said it could just be fun.

So why does it not feel like that suddenly?

Lincoln's head falls forward. His mouth finds mine and he kisses me for what feels like forever.

"You feel like the part of me that's been missing." I'm not sure he meant to say that out loud and it makes my heart flutter in my chest.

It's then I realize, deep down within him, the little abandoned boy still lives there. My real-life lost boy. I want to spend every hour with him to keep him safe and heal those broken parts.

I keep my legs locked around his hips while he kisses my face, my cheeks, my temples and, in his strong arms, I feel so adored and completely treasured. I've never had anyone pay me such special attention after sex before.

When he slides himself out of me, I whimper at the loss, leaving me feeling empty.

He's so quiet when he talks, barely a whisper. "Let's have a shower, then I'm going to spend the rest of the night making you come with my mouth and my cock. I want to lick every part of you, my sweet Petal."

My sweet Petal.

My heart just gave out.

"I've been desperate to go home to Scotland. Now I don't want to leave," he mumbles as he nuzzles into my neck.

"Fate is messing with us."

"I hate fate. It's not my friend." He moves onto the mattress and lies on his side before urging me to face him. Moving closer, wrapping his arms around me, he engulfs me with his addictive scent.

"It's not mine either."

Six weeks.

14

VIOLET

I'm mad and stomp down the stairs while tying my pale-lilac dressing gown around my waist.

The morning sun beats through my glasshouse-style home. If this was my house, I would have half the amount of windows in it. It's already too hot, making me feel flustered.

At the bottom of the stairs, I turn the air-conditioning down a couple degrees and let out a *humph* sound.

He left?

Seriously? After what we did last night. In my bed. For hours.

I knew it was too good to be true. He was using me for sex. Pretending to be all, *oooh, I'm on a sex hiatus; you're different; oh, you're so hot...* What a load of baloney that was.

Waking up to an empty bed was not what I expected.

I thought he was better than that.

I'm madder at myself for believing he was different: a good man with a good heart.

Leaning against the wall, I close my eyes and bite my thumbnail.

"Are you sleeping standing up?" Lincoln's humored voice booms across the hallway and my eyes shoot open.

I was so consumed by my thoughts that I didn't hear the front door open.

My shoulders drop with relief.

He's here.

Lincoln is standing inside my opened front door, in last night's clothes with Pom-pom by his side. Silhouetted by the sun behind them, the two of them look comical together: tall and short.

"You took Pom-pom for a walk?" I'm so shocked. Shocked he's here, shocked I didn't notice my dog wasn't here. *I'm a bad dog-mom.* Also shocked he took my dog he hardly knows for a walk and shocked Pom-pom went with him.

"Yeah, he was whining, so I took him out. Turns out teacup dogs need little walking. Within fifty steps, he was shattered. I had to carry him most of the time." He looks down at Pom-pom. "I'm definitely taking him out later. He's a proper chick magnet." Lincoln's megawatt smile lights up his entire face.

He bends down to unclip Pom-pom's black leather lead from his collar and gives him a good rub behind his ear. Pom-pom tries to jump up onto his bent knee, but he's too short to reach. They are so cute together.

Visions of Lincoln walking my tiny white fluffy pup make me snort out loud.

"What's so funny?"

"Nothing." I shake my head and push myself off the wall.

Pom-pom scuttles over to me and I scoop him up and give him lots of cuddles. He smells of Lincoln's aftershave. I need to ask him what that is. It's oddly addictive.

"You look shocked to see me." Lincoln stands to his full towering height, crossing his arms over his chest.

I bite my lip, feeling silly now, and keep quiet, embarrassed for doubting him.

"Ah, you thought I'd left. Did a runner." He nods his head up and down. "I would never do that to you."

"It's just—"

"It's okay. You don't have to explain. I should have left a note."

"You should have."

"I'm not going anywhere, sweet Petal."

Yes, you are. In just a few short weeks' time, you are leaving.

Obviously sensing my doubt, he strides over to me and stands at my toes. With no heels on, I'm much shorter than him. His hands I'm now obsessed with cup my face, then he kisses me.

"You look freshly fucked and utterly adorable this morning, Petal." He kisses me again, much longer this time. "I went to get breakfast and a toothbrush." He lifts a brown paper sack in the air to show me. *Huh, I didn't notice he was holding that.*

"Hungry?" he asks.

"Starving."

He takes my hand and guides me through the house to the kitchen, appearing to know where everything is.

"You took a tour of my house while I was sleeping, didn't you?"

"Yeah. You have your code for your electric gate on the wall. You should change that. And I found the key to your front door on the console table in the hall. You make it too easy for burglars. I considered stealing your great-great-great-aunt Brenda's sapphire engagement ring, the keys to your Mercedes E Class drop top, and your dog, but then thought..." He places the brown bag on my stainless-steel kitchen island and turns himself into a set of human balancing scales. "All-you-can-eat pretty pussy for six weeks or prison." He tilts from side to side like he's weighing up his options. "It was a tough decision. But I figured I'm too pretty for prison." He holds his pointer finger up in the air. "It would be sex on tap, but not in a good way." He shudders.

A chuckle leaves my chest. He *is* way too pretty for prison. "You are so strange sometimes. And crass." But he makes me laugh and I love a man who can make me laugh and keep me on my toes. Placing Pom-pom back on the floor, I hop myself onto one of my baby-blue velvet bar stools.

"You weren't complaining about how crass I was last night. You ain't fooling no one, Ms. *Oh, Lincoln, Fuck Me Harder.*" He raises his voice in a high pitch, mimicking me from last night.

My cheeks grow faintly pink.

"Nothing to be embarrassed about, Violet. I fucking loved it." He pulls his wallet out of his back pocket—Prada, *nice*—along with his phone and places them on the counter.

"I'm glad you didn't steal my stuff. Great-Great-Great-Aunt Brenda would haunt you from her grave if you took her ring."

He looks at me in amazement. "Do you really have an Aunt Brenda? I was joking."

I burst out laughing. "I'm messing with you."

He rolls his eyes. "Very good. I would give anything to have a shot in your car, though. It looks wicked in that pearlescent white color. My dad collects cars."

"Does he? What does he have?"

Lincoln fills his cheeks with air and then reels off at least ten cars.

Holy shit.

"Your dad drives a P1 McLaren as an everyday car?" I know that supercar costs at least a cool two million dollars.

"Yup."

"And what do you drive?"

His voice goes all romantic and gooey as he says, "Porsche 911 GT, in black." He sighs. "I love her."

"Miss her?"

"Yeah. Castleview Cove has the best countryside roads. Sweeping curves, quiet cliffside, narrow hills. Perfect for throwing her around." I think he's missing home. "Nothing like your big freeways, and our rush hour consists of getting stuck behind a tractor. If that holds you up for at least five minutes, that's your whole day ruined." He huffs with fake annoyance, then smiles.

Five-minute rush hour sounds like paradise.

He pulls two fresh ham and cheese omelets out of the bag and hands me one.

"Where did you get these from?" They are still warm.

"Sunrise Snacks, round the corner."

"I've never been there before."

"You need to get out more. They do amazing pancakes and bacon. So good." He goes all starry-eyed and proceeds to casually pull out knives and forks from the drawer he's standing beside.

How did he know they were there?

"Oh, I checked before I left to make sure you had cutlery. You boss-bitch types don't tend to eat in your homes and work all the time, ain't that right?" He winks at me teasingly.

"Spot-on. You know me so well."

Stunned, I stay seated as he hands me a plate and we plate up our omelets together. He places cream and sugar in front of me, then pulls two coffees out of the bag too before he settles beside me.

"I checked your fridge before I left. You had eggs and ham

and milk in there, so I am assuming you have no allergies." He points at my omelet.

I haven't picked up my silverware yet. I'm too stunned.

"Are you not eating?" He digs into his food.

"Eh, yeah. You are just, well, here, in my kitchen. You walked my dog, and you got me breakfast." He's looking after me. No one looks after me. I take care of myself. All the time.

"And…"

"You're not like other guys."

"I'm special." He grins.

He's not wrong.

I pour a little cream and two sugars into my coffee.

"I have a sweet tooth," I defend myself automatically.

"Who cares? Eat what you want. Do what you want. Life is too short." He takes a mouthful of his black coffee. "Eat." He points his fork at my food. "You'll need all the strength you can get. I have plans to do naughty things to you all day. Once I pick up my car, drive back to my hotel, shower, and come back here, that is. I hope you don't have plans."

I take a bite of my omelet, then another. Wow, that's delicious. I may have found my new breakfast place.

We eat together comfortably like we have been doing this for months.

How can I have only known him for a few short days?

"I have no plans today. Are you staying at a hotel?" I'm pretty sure Rio said he was renting his spare room.

"Yeah, just one of the cheaper ones. Do you know The Blue View?"

"I do." And it's around five hundred dollars a night. "For six more weeks?" My jaw falls to the floor, but he doesn't pick up how shocked I am.

"Yeah. I'm a man who likes luxury. I couldn't rent Rio's spare room anymore. I moved out two days ago. He's not the cleanest, and he was bringing different women back night after night, and then there were the parties. I like my space." He swivels his head to look at me, surprise written all over my face. "What?"

"You are spending over twenty-two thousand dollars on accommodation for the next few weeks."

"You're quick at math."

"It's my strength."

"It's not as much as that. They gave me a deal as my dad knows the guy who owns it. I've barely spent any money while traveling because I've worked a few jobs here and there and that paid for my hostels, motels, and stuff. My plane ticket is already paid for, and I bought my first clothes in months yesterday." He indicates to what he is wearing. "My car doesn't count. That was an investment." He winks. "Oh, and my haircut and shave." He scratches his now-short scruff and goatee beard.

"I like it. It makes you look even more handsome."

"Am I handsome?"

"You know you are."

He shakes his head as if I told a lie. He may laugh and joke, but I sense he has his insecurities too.

"I like you with no makeup." He puts his cutlery down, then takes a sip of his steaming hot coffee. "You really have no idea how pretty you are, do you?" He runs his tongue across his teeth.

"Is it self-love Saturday?" I quirk a brow.

"Come." Lincoln pushes his stool backward and jumps off, swivels my seat around, and I hop off mine in the most unlady-like manner. "Your place is really cool, by the way. I love your kitchen. That soft blue color is wicked. I might remodel my kitchen when I get back," he says casually, pulling me by my hand through the house.

Lincoln pulls me up the first flight of stairs and stops when we get to the top. He maneuvers me around, my back to his chest, so we are now standing in front of the mirrored wall on the second floor.

"What are we doing?"

He unties my robe, letting it fall, so it pools around my feet, exposing me in all my naked glory.

I suck my lips into my mouth and fidget. *Oh, this feels uncomfortable.*

"Look at yourself, Violet," he purrs in my ear from behind me. "This right here…" He shapes his hand into the curve of my waist. "It's tiny and I love it. My hands fit perfectly." He circles both his hands around it. "Your hips are so sexy." He smooths over my hips that I've always considered too big. "You have a body most women would die for." His fingertips brush my skin and butterflies dance in my belly. "Your skin is smooth and toned; I can tell you work out." I flinch when he lays his palm over my tummy. "You have a belly. Most women have a belly, Violet, but you seem to think you are different. I saw you looking around last night, doubting yourself, second-guessing your outfit because people *were* looking at you last night. You got that right; they were staring at you." He kisses my shoulder. "Do you know why?"

I shake my head, unable to speak.

"Because you were the hottest woman in the club last night. Look at yourself."

His eyes hit mine in the mirror.

"Your hair is silky smooth; your eyes sparkle when you get excited. I saw the joy in them yesterday when we threw ourselves off that pole. You were so proud of yourself. I was proud of you."

"You threw me off."

"Potayto, potahto." He ignores me. "Your skin glows and you

are immaculate from head to toe. Your smile sucks all the air out of my lungs, and this bit here." He pushes my hair off my shoulder, leans in, and steals a kiss behind my ear, making me gasp. "I love this bit. And this bit." He kisses my shoulder. Another kiss.

He moves around to face me, and a small tear runs down my cheek. For the first time in my life I feel accepted.

I'm accepting myself for all that I am.

"This bit." He bends to kiss my clavicle and keeps moving south. He gently pulls my breast into his mouth and kisses my nipple. "Your nipples are the perfect shade of rosy pink and it makes me want to bite them like they are fucking gummy candies." He nibbles one and a deep ache burns in my core for him to touch me there again. Everything he does makes my body light up like the Fourth of July. "I really wanna suck it hard."

I want him to do that too.

Standing back to his full height, he kisses my forehead. "I never lie. Every day, I want you to stand in front of that mirror and tell yourself four things you love about yourself. You'll become less self-critical, your brain will create new neural pathways to self-belief, and you'll be happier in yourself. It works. I know because I have done it myself."

"You have?"

"Yes. When I was about eighteen, I went for therapy. It didn't matter how many times my father told me my mom leaving wasn't my fault or his, I didn't believe it. I thought there was something wrong with me and that she didn't like me. But after following some simple exercises and a few sessions at therapy, some things changed for me. But it began with me. I had to put the work in, figuring out who I was inside and out. Now look in the mirror and tell me what you see."

I roll my shoulders back, making my boobs pop, and take a

deep breath. "I have nice ankles." I lift my foot up, pointing my toes.

"They look sexy as hell in heels. Next."

"I like the length of my legs."

"Mm-hmm. You have great legs. What else?"

"I do actually like my waist. I think it looks smaller today." I lift my arms out and twist back and forth, checking it out in the mirror.

"And I like my teeth. I have no fillings." I bare my teeth, displaying my perfect rows of pearly whites.

"You missed one."

"You said four." I mentally count again: ankles, legs, waist, teeth. I did four.

"You missed this." Lincoln slides his hand between my cleavage.

"Trust you to say 'boobs.'" I tilt my head to the side so he can drape his arm over my shoulder.

"Not that. Your heart, sweet Petal. You, Violet West, have a beautiful heart."

Hot tears well in my eyes. "I think we met for a reason." I focus intently on his face.

He nods his head in agreement.

"Does your visa really expire in just six weeks?"

"Yeah."

"I want to spend all of my spare time with you." I turn around in his arms and rise on my tiptoes to kiss him.

"Same."

"Take me to bed, Lincoln. Show me how much you love my body."

He lifts me into his arms and carries me up to my bedroom where, for the rest of the day, he proves to me just how much he appreciates my body—with his tongue, his mouth.

Everything.

15

VIOLET

"Hold on to the headboard." His pants become more rapid against my neck.

I wrap my hands around the white metal bars as Lincoln drives himself into me from behind.

Our moans and wispy breaths fill the hot air.

Holding me firmly against his chest, he fucks me into oblivion. As I twist my head, he tips my chin upward so he can kiss me and when I part my lips his tongue assaults my mouth. Mine welcomes his and they swirl round one another as if dancing together in perfect timing.

"I could do this all day," he rasps against my mouth.

Incomprehensible words leave my lungs when his skilled fingertips find my clit.

He pinches, then circles it gently and repeats this until I can't take it anymore. I reach back to find his ass, pull him closer, and clench my inner walls to draw him deeper into my body.

"Oh, fuck." His muscles tense. I know he's close.

Lincoln continues to trace delicate circles around my clit

with his fingertips; it's the complete opposite of his movements behind me, rotating his hips frantically in a hypnotizing rhythm.

He fucks me toward my point of release. "Oh God, Linc. I'm coming. Come with me," I gasp.

Sparks turn into volcanic heat as I come hard in quivering waves.

Pushing myself back onto his thick cock, I urge him to come too, desperate for us to share this moment.

"Aw, fuck, Violet." His unashamed groans fill the bedroom.

His hot breath douses my skin, and his fingers dig deep into my hips as he jerks into me and holds himself deep inside of me.

My orgasm explodes through my body, and I'm shuddering and moaning his name in pleasure as I ride out my orgasm.

Pulling his cock out a little, he pushes back in, causing him to let out another groan as my inner walls hold on to him in a vise-like grip. Wrapping himself around me, his lean body envelops me with his warm embrace as he escorts me down from my high.

Lincoln pants softly behind me with an open mouth now resting on my shoulder and he kisses my shoulder with such tenderness it makes my heart do a weird flip.

After what feels like forever, he slides himself out of my hot core. My body now feels like Jell-O, and my hands are shaking from my orgasm comedown.

"I should body-cast this ass, paint it metallic violet to match your name, and display it on my living room wall. Fuck me, you have a fine ass. This bit here..." He smooths his hands down the tilt of my waist where my hips widen. "I'm obsessed with it. It's like living art." He circles my waist with both hands. "It's so tiny."

I marvel at the power my body has over this strong, gentle giant of a man behind me.

In perfect harmony, we both move off the bed together.

I'm so tired, and after a much-needed shower, we curl up together under the covers and sleep for most of the afternoon.

16

VIOLET

Sleepily, I hug my bedcovers and watch Lincoln redress in last night's clothes.

"I'm sorry I have to take off, but I do this thing on Saturday nights. I help Rio's friend out and I can't get out of it."

"That's okay." I yawn. "We didn't make plans for tonight, you and me. I'm supposed to be going out with my girlfriends." I stretch, feeling sore all over. It's a pleasurable pain, evidence of our bedroom gymnastics marathon.

Lincoln pushes his phone into the pocket of his black jeans and grabs his car keys off the side.

"Christ, I need to get a move on." He checks his wristwatch.

"I ordered you a cab but remember I did offer to take you."

"I know, but you can have a nap before you go out tonight. Are you going out with your two friends you have plastered all over social media?"

"Yes, Hannah and Ruby," I confirm.

He throws himself on top of me playfully. "Well, I hope you tell Hannah and Ruby all about me. How good I am in the sack, how I have a massive dick, and—"

"How much you like me fingering your ass?"

He drops his forehead to my shoulder. "Please don't tell them about that." His voice is muffled.

As if he has a sudden thought, he flings his head back to meet my gaze. "Where the hell did you even learn to do that?"

I run my hands through his hair. "I have never done it before. I read a how-to guide in a sex column in a magazine. It stuck, and I remembered. You loved it."

He groans, as if too embarrassed to admit he did.

"Okay, I feel better now knowing you've only tried that on me." He double-checks the time. "Argh." He smacks an urgent kiss against my lips and catapults backward off the bed. "I really have to go. Have fun tonight. Remember to tell your friends I have a big dick." He winks. "See you tomorrow, yeah? Can you surf?" He hits the elevator button on the wall.

"You'll be quicker walking."

"But it means I get to spend an extra twenty seconds with you. Can you?"

"Nope."

"Great, me and you tomorrow. We're going surfing."

I almost mention the thought of squeezing into a tight wetsuit makes me feel sick, but I bite my tongue.

My body is beautiful.

The elevator pings open.

"See you tomorrow." He waves goodbye.

"Oh, Lincoln," I call out to him just as the doors almost close. His fingers appear between the two stainless-steel doors, prying them apart.

"Yes."

"You're fired."

"What?" he exclaims.

I turn onto my side, push myself up, and rest my head on my

hand. "You heard me; you're fired. I checked our employment policy. We can't date."

"You can't fire me."

"I just did. Your temporary contract is now void and your services are no longer required at Urban Soul Studios."

"I've never been fired in my life."

"You're a director of your own hotel. You can't fire yourself."

With his hands on either side of the doors, his dark frame fills the entire space of the entrance, his mouth agape.

I sit up and continue my reasoning, mimicking his earlier balancing scales analogy. "It was either mind-blowing sex for six weeks or working together. It was a tough choice. Sex or no sex." I tip my arms back and forth like I'm juggling an invisible ball.

"You are wicked cruel." He narrows his eyes.

"And you are the biggest weirdo I know, wanting to work when you are supposed to be having time out to travel. I should call your dad. Does he even know you have a *job*?"

"I knew it, you are a ball-breaker, and are we having our first fight?"

"Yes."

"I hate you." His eyes twinkle with mischief, not meaning what he says.

"I hate you too." I let the covers wrapped around me lower slightly, exposing my boobs.

Just as expected, his eyes drop to his other new obsession.

He licks his lips and steps back into my room. "You made a good choice. Well done. Yup, I want more of those."

He's completely distracted as the elevator begins to shut behind him. "Aw, shit." He squeezes himself between the closing doors.

"See you tomorrow." I laugh as the doors shut.

When he finally hits the ground floor, he calls back up the stairwell. "Can we have angry make up sex tomorrow?"

"Yes," I shout back.

"And can I still help you at the gym? Not as an employee, but as a volunteer. If I don't, I won't see you as much."

"Yes." I can't figure him out. Actually, I can. He enjoys working, more than me it would appear.

"Pom-pom has pooped in the hallway. That's what you get for firing me." Lincoln's laughter fills my house then the sound of the door closing signifies his exit.

Wow, Lincoln Black.

He was most definitely not on my agenda this month, but it looks like he's just become my priority.

17

LINCOLN

I'm in the cab on my way to pick up my car.

Fiddling with my phone, I decide to drop a group text to my two friends back in Scotland.

ME

> Has a girl ever fingered your ass while giving you a blow job?

I receive an instant reply. I knew I would.

OWEN

> We haven't heard from you in two weeks and that's your opening text to start our conversation?

JACOB

> What happened to... Hey, how are you? Or a simple I miss you. I need you to limber up, a little warmth and a cuddle, a bit of foreplay.

OWEN

> You just fucked me up the ass with no lube with that one sentence. Most unexpected.

JACOB

Raw.

OWEN

It hurts.

I laugh to myself.

ME

I'm being serious. Have they?

Neither of them answers me.

ME

I'm asking a serious question here, lads. I need your advice.

OWEN

Aw, fuck it, yes, and if the question is, did I enjoy it? That's a big yes too.

JACOB

It's not for me, boys, I'm afraid. The girl who did that to me didn't lube me up, and I wasn't expecting it. A bit like this conversation.

OWEN

Yowsers.

JACOB

Feel the burn.

Jacob and Owen have been my friends since junior school and I love them like they are my brothers. They may not be blood brothers, but I spent every day with them growing up.

We even went to the same university.

OWEN

Wait, hold that thought. Did you break your sabbatical?

JACOB

Jesus Christ, I pity the girl who took your newfound virginity. You must have fucking exploded.

OWEN

Is she still alive?

JACOB

You're due me one hundred pounds, Owen. I knew he wouldn't last.

OWEN

Fuck off, we didn't shake on it.

JACOB

Asshole.

ME

Shut up, you two. So it's all good, right? The finger up the butt thing. I don't know what the hell she did to me, but it was fucking epic. I can't stop thinking about it and her.

JACOB

Sounds like one hell of a one-night stand.

ME

She's not a one-night stand.

OWEN

Shit, did you catch "the feelings"?

JACOB

No fucking way.

OWEN

Mr. I'm Going to be Lonely Forever caught
feelings, didn't you? Or you wouldn't be asking.

ME

She's different.

JACOB

Explain.

I find a photo from her social media account. There's one
that stood out for me the most when I was doing my research
the other night. Long wavy dark hair, to-the-floor Cadbury-
purple silk evening dress, blackcurrant lips, and she's wearing
black patent mile-high heels. I screenshot it and send it to them.
That photo makes my dick twitch. Her smile might just be my
ruination.

OWEN

Where the hell did you meet her?

JACOB

She's beautiful.

OWEN

Way out of your league.

I chuckle to myself. She really is.

ME

I met her at the gym.

It's a lie by omission.

JACOB

You're punching.

OWEN

She's dream girl material.

JACOB

Better delete the chat afterward. I'm sure Skye would flip out if she read that.

I don't know why I've always thought this, but I'm pretty sure Jacob has a thing for Owen's girlfriend, Skye. Ever since the night I caught them huddled together on the beach. I could be wrong, though.

I brush off my suspicious thoughts.

OWEN

Noted.

JACOB

So you like her?

ME

A lot. That connection I've been looking for. I think this is it.

OWEN

But she lives in California.

ME

You think I don't know that?

OWEN

Christ, please tell me you are coming home or you're going to break my heart.

JACOB

We miss you, buddy.

ME

Of course I'm coming home. I don't have a say in the matter. My visa expires, and that is it for me. I am flying home.

OWEN

Only you would finally find someone you
actually like and she lives thousands of miles
away.

I run over my brow with my fingertips.

ME

Trust me. I am fully aware.

OWEN

What's her name?

ME

Violet.

OWEN

That's a pretty name.

JACOB

You realize if you get married she'll be Violet
Black.

Jesus fucking Christ. That didn't even cross my mind.

ME

We're not getting married! I've only known her
for a few days.

OWEN

Yeah, but when you know, you know.

JACOB

Do you feel like that about Skye, Owen? Do you
know?

I knew it.

He's asked Owen this before. He's testing the water.

You just gave yourself away, Jacob. He does like Skye. I can't
blame him. She is beautiful, all space buns and quirky clothes,

but she's not my type. This is messed up. I need to have a word with Jacob when I return to Scotland.

> **OWEN**
>
> I honestly can't answer that. Ask me again in a few months.

> **JACOB**
>
> You're going to lose her. She's talked about marriage and kids. You know that's what she wants.

> **OWEN**
>
> She's mentioned nothing to me before. What about you and Erin? Do you feel that way about her, Jacob?

> **JACOB**
>
> We split up three days ago.

> **OWEN**
>
> Hell, man, you never said.

> **ME**
>
> I'm sorry to hear that. Erin was tops.

> **JACOB**
>
> I just wasn't digging it, to be honest.

> **OWEN**
>
> We need to go out for a beer this week, Jacob. Wish you were here, Linc.

> **ME**
>
> Not long until I'm home.

> **JACOB**
>
> Cheers, guys. I'm okay and actually fine about it all.

I need to steer this ship in a different direction.

ME

What do I do? Enjoy the next few weeks then see what happens? She's a manager for her father's business. She would never leave the company, and I can never leave the hotel and spa. It'll never work.

JACOB

So basically you're fucked if you fall in love and fucked if you don't explore the possibilities of what might be your future?

Jacob is always the levelheaded one out of all of us.

ME

I'm so confused.

JACOB

Why not just have fun? If you last six weeks, it will be a record for you.

OWEN

I've never heard you like this before.

ME

Maybe I'm overthinking it all.

JACOB

Well, stop thinking at all, Linc. Just see what happens. Enjoy the next few weeks of your visa and see how everything plays out. No pressure.

OWEN

Jacob is right. And if it still feels the same in six weeks' time, then you can figure it out then. Not now though. Okay?

ME

Okay.

OWEN

She's got a fucking cracking body.

ME

You can delete that photo now!

JACOB

Or I will tell Skye!

OWEN

Snitch.

ME

Right, I need to go. Off to get my car, then start my shift for tonight's event.

JACOB

I can't believe you still do that. I thought it was only for a couple of Saturday nights. Is this your third week?

ME

Yeah, it's great fun.

OWEN

Enjoy and remember to hold on to your boxers tonight.

ME

Will do. Cheers, lads.

JACOB

Keep in touch. We are having a big night out as soon as you're back.

ME

Sounds like a plan. Adios.

OWEN

Later, dude.

Only a few minutes away from my car, I close my eyes and

rest my head against the headrest.

Part of me wishes I had dropped a text Rio's mate, Dylan, and told him that I couldn't work tonight. I would much prefer to be wrapped around Violet instead.

I'm looking forward to tomorrow.

Surfing with Violet sounds like fun. I can't wait to see her in a wetsuit.

18

VIOLET

"What the hell is this place?" I look up at the colossal building before me, all the while trying to navigate my heels over the cobblestone pathway leading up to it.

Streams of cheerful people, mainly women, funnel in through the entrance.

Hannah hooks her arm into mine and we teeter together, watching Ruby sway her sexy ass confidently in front of us. She met someone she knew as we climbed out of our cab—typical. Our infamous party girl knows everyone.

"According to Ruby, this is the place to be on a Saturday night. It's only been open for two months, but it's so difficult to get into and you know Ruby."

"She knows everyone," we both say at the same time and burst out laughing.

Hannah's gray eyes meet mine. "Yup, so we got ourselves some tickets, baby, and VIP seats. It's gonna be wild. Have you not heard of this place at all?"

"Nope. I've been busy."

"Again." Hannah flicks her blonde locks over her shoulder.

"Yup."

"Well, tonight we are going to have some fun." Hannah whoops, alerting Ruby. She turns around, flings her hands in the air, and shakes her boobs at us.

"Hell, yeah," Ruby hollers. If she's not careful, her boobs may pop out of her black strapless dress. Or it might flash her panties. It's that short. She might as well have worn a hairband. I know for a fact Ruby doesn't own a hemline below the equator.

"Oh, God. It's going to be one of those nights and I'm tired already," I confess.

"Well, if you weren't up fucking a sexy Scotsman all night, you would be okay. So buckle up, baby." Hannah unhooks her arm from mine.

"Sleep is for losers anyway, and it was totally worth it." I bump shoulders with hers.

Hannah pulls the hem of her short silver sequined dress down. "Atta girl. It's been way too long since you got some."

"Made up for it last night and all day today." It was the most fun I've ever had with a guy.

"Please find me one of those, Violet?" She pouts her big glossy lips at me.

"I've only just found one for myself. You can find your own." Hannah and I step inside the grand entrance and we both tilt our heads back in awe at the big sign above the door, *Confessions*.

"Was this originally a church?"

"Yes, it was. This place is awesome." Ruby slaps our asses, making me jolt and Hannah squeal. "I've brought you here to repent for all of your sins. Especially you, Violet, following last night's events." She slaps my ass again.

I'm grateful we have seats booked. "Wow, it's crazy busy." The place is buzzing with beautiful people.

Ruby stops us from entering. "Before we go in. There aren't a lot of men here, but the ones who are, well, they are supreme. Top shelf." She chef-kisses her fingertips. "Just remember to have fun and you can thank me later."

"You are acting more secretive tonight. More than usual." Hannah pulls her lip gloss out of her black sequin-encrusted clutch and smothers her lips until they look like glass. She's obsessed with reapplication. She snaps her purse shut and smacks her lips together. "Shall we go in?"

"Hell, yeah." Ruby whips around in a flash, her deep-red hair swishing as she moves swiftly toward the towering wooden church-style doors leading to the body of the club.

"I hope you brought lots of dollar bills like I told you for tonight. Saturday nights here are all for charity. And I just know how charitable you girls are." She flings her head back, laughing, and finger-waves across at someone else she knows.

Charity night? At a nightclub?

"What the hell have we gotten ourselves into, Hannah?" I smooth down my deep-purple front-zip dress. It's riskier and more figure-hugging than I would normally wear, but I bought this ages ago and have never had the courage to wear it. I consider pulling the zipper up further to hide my cleavage but stop myself. Screw it, the girls are getting their monthly airing tonight. I push my boobs together and lower my zipper an inch. After all the soul-deep thoughts Lincoln told me earlier, I have never felt so sexy.

The main doors part for us and we're hit by a wall of soul-shaking beats. It vibrates through my entire body. It's going to be a great night.

I look up as we are ushered to our seats through a sea of excitable women, eyeing row upon row of wooden arches above. Both sides of the nightclub are lined with alcoves, all fitted with modern racing-green leather banquette seating.

The entire club is a complete contrast. At eye level it's dark, but the ceiling is lit with strings adorned with thousands of warm-yellow firefly lights and giant LED starbursts. The lights bounce off the stained-glass windows, causing a kaleidoscope of colors overhead. I gasp at its beauty.

I gaze around the enormous space and realize the crowd is at least ninety percent women. I lean near Hannah's ear so she can hear me over the loud music. "You are never finding a man in here tonight." I laugh.

She nods her head in agreement as we finally reach our VIP seating right beside the bar.

"We have the best seats in the house, ladies." Ruby lays her purse on the table and checks the time. "We have about five minutes before the fun begins."

I do not know what *fun* she is talking about, but I quickly stand and offer to get our drinks.

The bar is so long it disappears up one side of the club with at least fifty guys serving. Mirrors line the entire bar, making it look even longer. Wooden shelving houses row upon row of brightly colored liquor bottles in every stone alcove. The inner interior designer part of me praises the person who sympathetically designed this. It's breathtaking.

Facing away from the bar, I'm too busy looking around the dance floor when a voice from behind me asks, "What can I get you?"

I snap my head around. I know that voice. "Lincoln?" I gasp.

His eyes bug out. "Shit. What the hell are you doing here?" He looks concerned.

"What the hell are *you* doing here and why are you standing behind the bar?"

And what is he wearing? White vest top exposing his bulging biceps and strong bronzed shoulders, baseball cap, and massive baggy jeans that hang low across his hips. He looks like Channing *fucking* Tatum, but ten times more handsome.

"I work here on Saturdays." He hangs his head, then lifts it again, turning his baseball cap backward so I can see his face. His jaws tics, once, then twice. He's so gorgeous.

"What's with you and these random-ass jobs?" I can't believe he's here.

"I don't get paid for tonight. None of the guys behind the bar do. It's all for charity and I've only been doing this for four weeks. I'm helping out, that's all." He bites his lip, then checks the giant clock that's being projected onto the wall above the bar. Three minutes to the hour. "Shit. You should go."

"Why?" I frown, confused.

He doesn't answer and we have a stare-off.

"So you're staying?" He drums his fingers on the bar top.

"Of course I'm staying. We just got here," I shrill.

He fills his cheeks with air, then exhales slowly. "Fuck it. What are you drinking?" It's the most serious I have ever seen him.

I give him my order.

Light-footed, he moves around behind the bar, quickly making our drinks then places them all carefully on the tray and robotically takes my money.

He bites his lip before asking, "Where are you sitting?"

I point over to the girls in our seating booth barely a few yards away, and both Hannah and Ruby are staring with their mouths hanging open at my interaction with Lincoln.

My heart sinks. He's different tonight and I don't like it. He grabs my hand when I lift the tray off the bar, making my drinks slosh about.

"Please promise me you won't judge me or like me any less after tonight."

Huh?

"Well, having spent almost twenty-four hours with you in my bed, I feel like I don't know you at all. You're acting like an asshole, like you don't even know me tonight. You just asked me to leave."

"That's not why I asked you to leave, Violet." He shakes his head, his eyes full of sadness.

A loud gong almost makes me drop the tray, and a hive of activity behind the bar breaks out. Whoops, whistles, and claps echo across the cavernous club.

Lincoln begins clearing the top of the bar. His eyes never leave mine.

"Just please promise me you won't judge, okay?" he begs.

The crowd begins counting down from twenty. The projection clock behind the bar keeps everyone in time.

"You should go back to your table," he shouts over the jeering and shakes his head again. Two guys, dressed similarly to him, slap him on the back, telling him it's showtime.

Annoyed with him, I don't reply as I stomp back to the table where Ruby and Hannah fire dozens of *Who is the mystery man?* questions at me.

In a daze, I take a sip of my cosmopolitan, unable to work out if I'm mad or sad.

"God, you are so secretive, Violet," Ruby huffs when I don't tell her what she wants to know.

"Nothing to tell."

"Nothing to tell us about the freaking Hollywood-looking movie star behind the bar, no? Not a thing. Nothing to tell, even though you just had a full conversation with him. Did you at least get his number?"

I don't have time to answer because the club plummets into darkness and the crowd goes wild.

UV lighting floods the place, highlighting a wall of men standing all along the top of the bar, their white tops glowing a luminous lilac-blue color.

Heads bowed, baseball caps covering their faces, hands behind their backs, they stand like soldiers waiting to be given their command.

My heart pounds and I don't know why, but the mood in the room changes when a gritty instrumental harpsichord booms through the speakers. The boys all stomp their right foot in time to the music.

The intro of the song builds and when the beat kicks in, they all march, raise their heads, and salute.

Oh, dear Lord. Is Lincoln going to dance?

I search for him and find him three away from the end of the bar, right beside our table.

Holy shit, I think he is.

The bass booms, making the club vibrate. "If" by Janet Jackson picks up pace, and it springs the guys into action. Half of them jump off the bar and run through the club as the heavy metal intro gets louder. They jump onto the tabletops in every alcove and pick up the routine.

"Why do we not have a dancer?" Ruby screams across the noise.

My eyes are glued to Lincoln, who's still dancing on top of the bar.

Perfectly synchronized, the guys all move in time, one hand on top of their heads, chins to chests, while they have one hand over their crotches and hip-thrust, then grip their belts and dip up and down. The crowd goes crazy.

They move together in the perfectly practiced routine. Every new hip thrust makes the women scream louder. The guys all raise their heads together as the chorus reaches its peak, then fling their baseball caps into the crowd. Scantily clad women search the air, jump around, and dive to catch one. You would think they were trying to catch a bride's bouquet.

The crowd fades away and all I can see is Lincoln. Undulating his body in waves, he moves about the bar like a professional hip-hop dancer with hip isolations and body pops. I can't draw my eyes away from him.

On fast, nimble feet, he spins on his crisp white chunky sneakers and just as he comes to a stop, he rips the neckline of his shirt, pulling it off his body like he's the goddamn Hulk.

My mouth falls open.

Please tell me he's taking all his clothes off.

A warm flush of heat starting at my toes rises through my body. I've licked those abs and sucked his nipples, and holy hell balls, I've sucked his divine dick.

I fan my face with my hand. "Hot as hell," I mumble to myself.

Hannah and Ruby are too distracted watching the guys to notice how turned on I am.

He drops to his knees and, as if by magic, water pours from the ceiling. The ultraviolet lighting hits it, making it look like streams of diamonds. He flings his head back, letting the water soak his skin, and runs his hands all over his upper body as he slides his knees back and forth, gyrating his hips and pelvis.

I pat the side of my mouth to check I'm not visibly salivating over his droolworthy body.

He shakes his head, and droplets of water spray through the air, making the people nearest the bar scream for more.

He looks up and his eyes catch mine. He looks solemn, as if he's worried I will be mad at him for doing this. This is why he asked me to leave. He didn't want me to know.

I throw him my biggest megawatt smile, throw my hands in the air, and cheer as loud as I can. "More."

Relief washes across his face. As he shows his white teeth in a shit-eating smile, they glow under the ultraviolet lights.

He springs off the bar and sprints toward me.

Ruby and Hannah let out excitable yelps as Lincoln leaps onto our tabletop.

He continues to do a few routine moves along with the other guys, but then they begin to freestyle.

Lincoln drops on all fours and focuses on me. "Hi." His eyes dance with amusement. "It's for charity." He raises his voice over the loud music and crowd. "You okay with this?" His brows crease.

"Hell, yeah." I can't nod fast enough. "Now dance for me."

He leans forward and smacks a kiss against my lips.

Hannah and Ruby point at the projected rules on the back wall, which I didn't notice before.

1. Thou shalt not touch (unless instructed and given permission by a dancer).
2. Thou shalt not kiss, lick, or grope.
3. Thou shalt not dance on the tabletops (dancers only).
4. Thou shalt give to charity.
5. Thou shalt enjoy the show.

"Girls." Through a wide grin, I shout as loud as I can over the music, so they can hear me. "This is Lincoln."

Ruby's legs give way and she drops in shock to her seat, her mouth agape.

"*This* is Lincoln?" Hannah points to him while looking at me.

I nod.

"Our girl won the freakin' lotto." She throws her hands in the air and cheers.

Lincoln flings his head back, laughing, then he jumps onto his feet and dances for me on top of the table. His eyes lock with mine throughout every second of his routine, and I'm sure I'm panting as he moves his body in ways I can only dream about.

Hannah and Ruby skim their eyes around the room, watching the other guys. I think they are trying to be polite, but their eyes keep moving back to Lincoln.

Yup, my boy's got game.

His skin glistens in the provocative light, and I wish it was just the two of us. I'm desperate to touch him.

In one swift motion, he sits down on the edge of the table and straddles his legs on either side of me, his delicious abs right in front of my face.

"Take my jeans off." He shoots me a roguish grin.

"What? Here?" I squeal.

"Yes. Part of the show." He lies back flat against the table, unbuckles his belt, and pushes his hips in the air.

I'm going to hell doing this to a guy in a church.

I pull his wet baggy pants down over his carved hips and reveal a pair of white and blue Scottish flag boxers.

His cock looks massive in them, and I have to rub my thighs together to stop the warmth burning there.

Clumsily, I remove his wide-legged jeans over his sneakers and throw them onto the leather seating.

Lincoln pushes his hips into the air, his crotch right in my face, and thrusts himself up and down, causing my nipples to pebble against the fabric of my bra.

A guy appears at the end of the table with what looks like a wooden church collection box. He gives Lincoln a fist pump as

Hannah and Ruby drop dollar bills into the cut-out slot on top of the offering box.

Unable to move or watch, Hannah finds my clutch and makes my donation for me.

I'd happily pay triple.

Almost at the end, the gritty beats of the song are lowered slightly and the DJ thanks everyone for the donations and informs them this week it's going to the local charity to help homeless veterans. Lincoln sits up and leans forward. "Two more songs to do. You can donate more later, naughty girl." His eyes drop to my cleavage. "Does that zipper work?"

"Yes." I smirk.

"All the way down to the hem?"

"Uh-huh." I lean forward. "You can zip it off me later. I'm so turned on right now." I wiggle against the seat, trying to relieve the pressure building. If only we were alone.

"That so?" He licks his lips, his gaze dropping to my mouth.

I tilt my body toward his and he casually rests his elbows on his knees.

"This is the perfect height for you to fuck my cleavage, Lincoln."

His chest rises and falls and his eyes turn darker. "Aw, fuck. Grab my jeans. You are making me hard, and that's not appropriate here." He clenches his eyes shut.

I pass him his wet jeans. "Later."

"That's a promise." He covers his crotch with the denim. "Now behave for the rest of the evening. You're coming home with me."

"I can't."

"Why not?" He raises an eyebrow questioningly.

"Because I have to get back for Pom-pom. You're coming home with me."

His lips curl into a smile. "I finish at eleven."

My heart leaps with joy at the prospect of him spending another night with me.

"Perfect."

"You two are so hot together." Hannah interrupts our moment. "I'm Hannah, by the way." She shakes his hand as Lincoln continues to cover his hard-for-me cock with the other.

"You are ripped," Ruby counters as she examines Lincoln's brawny body. "Can you get us more drinks?" She gives him a flirty finger-wave. "I'm Ruby."

Lincoln spins around on his ass before he leaps off the table. "Coming right up. Same again?"

Hannah tilts her head, clearly checking out Lincoln's abs. "Yes, please, sir."

I give Hannah a nudge, making her jolt.

"Girls. Nice to meet you." He winks, runs his fingers through his wet hair, and strides toward the bar.

Our eyes follow his otherworldly physique until he's out of sight. The pair of them whip their heads to face me.

"I honestly did not know he was going to be here." I raise my glass to my lips.

They fire a dozen questions at me at a million miles per hour. They are relentless.

And the question I hate the most is: "How long is he here for?" Hannah's big gray eyes narrow.

"Six weeks," I say.

"Shit," they both say in unison.

Yeah, shit is right.

19

LINCOLN

Walking across the parking lot, we huddle together, my hand resting on Violet's hip. It's so natural to be with her. She fits perfectly by my side.

I can't push down this feeling of completeness when I'm around her. Everything feels good. Right.

As if the earth stopped spinning, she grounded me, and became my gravity.

And she's worlds apart from other girls I've dated—er, slept with—and this new infatuation I have for her is foreign to me. It's so strange to feel more for this girl in two days than I have with anyone. Ever.

Unaware of my thoughts, Violet hasn't stopped tweeting away about what an amazing night she's had and how much she loves my dancing. She asked me dozens of questions.

I taught myself to dance by watching hundreds of hip-hop videos on social media when I was a kid. Then I begged my dad to pay for online classes for me to follow. I picked it up quickly and loved it, but it was always just a hobby for me and something I did in the privacy of my own bedroom.

But when I heard the bar was looking for staff for their charity evenings, I jumped at the chance, and it gave me something to do on a Saturday night while here in Santa Monica. Plus no one knows me here.

I look down at Violet, who looks up at me at the same time. She's shorter because she trapped a heel in the cobblestones as we were leaving, and her broken shoe is currently swinging in her hand back and forth gleefully as she walks. She's right, she is accident-prone.

"Give me those. I'll carry them."

She passes me her broken shoes.

On tippy-toes, she smacks a kiss to my lips as she continues to wiggle her hips against my other hand.

Something weird happens in my chest when she lays her hand over my heart. Something I can't describe. But it's nice, warm. Like home.

Like I belong.

There has always been a gnawing sensation in my gut when I think about my mom leaving me when I was a baby. A small part of me that feels not good enough or imperfect.

Flawed.

Like a wonky tip of a hand-drawn five-point star.

It's not something I have ever spoken about with my dad, because he did a fantastic job raising me and I know he worried about me when I was growing up without a mother, but he went above and beyond to ensure he was always there for me—school plays, football games, swimming lessons, everything. He showed up for me, physically and emotionally.

He was the best father, but my mom was not someone we spoke about, not in depth anyway, because my mom and dad weren't together that long and separated not long after they got married, so I'm guessing he didn't know her that well.

Although my dad was always a silent and thoughtful man. Deep.

He also struggled with his own feelings too. It must have been difficult for him. Eighteen years old, divorced with a baby. I can't comprehend how he did that as well as working at the hotel and studying for his degree via distance learning. That still blows my mind. What a guy.

He framed a photo of my mom for me and it sat by my bedside my entire life until I came here. It's now tucked safely inside my wallet.

I used to stare at it, wondering what my mom was like.

If she loved me.

I guess I will never know.

While my father loved me harder and deeper than any love I have ever known, that little one percent of me, the little boy who looked on at friends surrounded by their mothers, he seeks the warmth, a hug, and the love of his mommy. Still.

I don't need it, but that one percent would like to know how it feels.

Traveling, however, has given me the perspective I needed. To see that I need to open my heart to hope and possibility and to stop pushing people away. To stop thinking everyone is going to leave, because they don't.

I know all too well, Violet and I have an expiration date and that guts me to my core.

Nothing makes any sense and my head has been reeling all day.

Violet cuts through my sad thoughts. "Want to live life on the edge?" She swings her passenger door open.

"What are you thinking?" Christ, I'm so tired. I'm fucked if I know where she gets her energy from. I'm pretty sure she pulls it from the sun.

As soon as we jump into my car, she places her purse on the floor, and just as I'm about to press the start button, she clumsily climbs across the center console and straddles me.

"I can't wait any longer. You've been teasing me all night." She pulls the front zipper of her dress down a little.

"People will see in." I grab her waist to stop her and look around the dark expanse outside the car.

"No, they won't. You're parked at the furthest point in the parking lot and you have blacked-out windows." She pulls the zipper right down to her waist.

Her large, pert breasts are my undoing. "Aw, fuck it."

She kneels up slightly to allow me to unzip her dress fully. "Best dress ever." I ease down the lace cup of her bra and suck a rosy-colored nipple into my mouth.

She clasps the back of my head when I lash my tongue around her pebbled nub.

Violet desperately scrambles with the waistband of my sweatpants, pushing them down to pull my cock free, stroking it, which pulls a moan from my throat.

She's almost telling me off when she says, "You've been teasing me all night, you naughty boy. You act like a nineteen-year-old, have the body of a god, and you fuck like a king. Now fuck me like I'm your queen, Lincoln."

Her filthy words from her sweet mouth make my cock grow harder for her.

We've had sex at least five times today, but she wants more.

I may have met my match. She is ravenous.

Her hand moves up and down my shaft. No woman has ever made me so hard and pre-cum weeps from the tip in anticipation of what's to come.

When she rubs her thumb across my glistening tip, I let out a long moan. "I need to be inside of you now." I struggle to form words and slip her soaked lace panties to the side to slide home.

She flings her head back, pushing her breasts into my face.

"I am fucking these later." I bite her succulent skin, making her gasp.

"Promise?"

"Pinky promise," I mumble against her nipple. "Shit, I'm not going to last." I pump her up and down my cock. "You are fucking soaked, Petal."

Violet grabs on to the back of the seat and begins fucking me faster.

I let her do all the work because she knows exactly what she needs to chase her orgasm. She tilts her hips, clenching her pussy, and I have to hold back my impending climax.

As she braces one hand against the roof to fuck me harder, I circle her clit just the way I've discovered she likes it. Gentle flicks mixed with subtle pinches and fast taps.

She lets out a pleasurable cry as I tease her bud between my fingertips, and I watch in awe as she lets herself unravel in front of me.

Lacing my fingers into the back of her hair with my other hand, I pull her forehead to mine. "Come for me, sweet girl."

Her soft voice rings out as she fucks herself on my rock-hard cock, her heavy tits bouncing.

My name on her lips and her soaking wet pussy are my downfall and the tingling sensation that's been building coils through my spine and into my balls.

My balls tighten and I cry out in pure pleasure as her body milks me of every drop.

How can it be possible for sex to be this good with someone you've just met? My brain can't comprehend what's happening between us.

"So good." Violet leans forward, kissing me with hungry lips, and sucking my tongue into her mouth, making my cock twitch again.

I've never had a woman who knows what she needs in the bedroom. But Violet knows exactly what she needs and how to get it.

She leans back slightly, all dopey-eyed and lust-drunk.

"Feel better?" I say, out of breath.

She pushes her long dark locks out of her face.

"I do. Now take me home. You have a pinky promise to make good on." She pushes her boobs together.

"You are going to fuck me raw, aren't you? I don't know if I can manage again." Still inside of her, I tilt my hips upward, making her moan.

That's a lie. My dick is always ready to go where she's concerned. She's a fucking dream come true.

That old part of me tells me to walk away because I already feel like I'm going to get hurt and the new part of me wants to wrap her up so I can keep her forever.

Another first for me.

"I need my beauty sleep." I pout.

"Not happening. Now take me home."

20

LINCOLN

It's another beautiful day in Santa Monica.

Sunshine is my new love. It makes me bounce out of bed in the morning.

I love Scotland, but Christ, it's depressing when it's cold. However, cozy days spent by the fire with Violet would make them less blue and dreary.

Never going to happen, Lincoln.

"What are you thinking about?" Violet breaks my daydream.

"Nothing." With my hands against the sand, I prop myself up and cross my ankles, watching hundreds of people and kids splash about in the sparkling sea and play in the hot sand.

"You're quiet today." Violet pushes her sunglasses onto the top of her head.

"I'm just tired." I yawn.

"Oh, I know how tired you are. When I came up to the bedroom last night expecting to find you ready to fulfill your pinky promise fantasy, you were passed out."

She lets out a squeal when I launch myself on top of her and push her hands above her head. "Well, this sex-crazed woman I only met a few days ago has been pogoing up and down my dick since I met her. I've got friction burns on my friction burns."

She shakes her head against her lilac towel. "You have no stamina." Her voice is barely a whisper. "And I'm always so wet for you that you have no friction burns." She licks her lips.

I roll off her and back onto my towel and groan at her honesty. I convinced her to wear a two-piece today, and she looks good enough to eat in the skimpy black fabric. She has drawers of the things but says she never wears them on the beach, opting for one-piece swimsuits instead. *One-piece, be gone.*

I ping the string of her bottoms. "Fancy a dip?"

She sits up and looks around.

"What are you doing?"

She chews her lip. "I'm sorry. It's a habit of mine, okay? I just sometimes have to check around. I don't want anyone seeing me." Her hand finds her tummy.

"You look beautiful, Violet." I look over at a group of girls standing and chatting. I point to them. "See those girls there? What do you see?"

She tilts her head to the side. "Pretty. Bronzed bodies. Proportional."

"And the girl in the yellow two-piece." I jut my chin out. "What does she look like to you?"

"Slim, toned, blonde hair, great skin."

"For the record and stating facts, you are the same size as that girl, but you are way sexier. She doesn't have your curves or your glossy hair."

She gasps in protest. "I do not look like that."

"Yes, you fucking do. But you are next level, Violet West. You have some fucked-up, skewed perception of how you look. Now, get up on those pretty little toes of yours and fucking walk across the sand like the queen you are, in the boardroom and the bedroom." I stand up and hold my hand out for her to take.

She doesn't move but continues to look at the girl in the yellow. "Am I really the same size as her?"

"I wouldn't say it if I didn't mean it. Now get up."

"You are so bossy." She huffs, standing to her full height, and fixes her swimsuit bottoms, then makes sure her boobs are secure.

"Also, you have much bigger tits than her." I kiss her balm-covered lips.

"I have bigger boobs than everyone."

"Fucking heaven." I go all starry-eyed.

"Not so heavenly that you fell asleep on a promise you made to me last night."

"Tonight, I double promise."

There are few women who would let you titty fuck them, but Violet seems to love the idea. My cock twitches in my swim shorts and I have to adjust myself discreetly. "And anyway, I was tired, up all night with a woman who can't get enough of me, she then spent the next day fucking my brains out, and then I was dancing last night on barely two hours' sleep, and then she fucked me again in my car and then in her bed again this morning. That was a nice way to wake up. Thanks for that." I awoke to Violet's warm and wet mouth wrapped around my cock this morning. Best wake-up call. Ever.

"Be quiet. People will hear you." Her eyes dart around the busy beach.

"No one cares. They're all too interested in themselves." I look around. I'm right; no one is paying us any attention.

"Let's go, Petal." I take the first step down the boiling sand, hoping Violet will follow. In a flash, she's by my side and grabs my hand.

"Good girl." I give her a wink.

I catch a few guys checking Violet out. They can fuck off. She's mine.

The need to kiss her in front of them licks flames around my self-control. I pull her closer to me. "There are a few guys checking you out."

"They are not. You are just saying that to be kind and anyway, they can't have me. I'm yours."

For now.

I scoop her up and fling her over my shoulder and run toward the water. She screams as we hit the cool waves.

After half an hour of larking about, kissing and teasing each other in the salty water, hand in hand, we slowly make our way back up the golden sand to our towels.

"Violet? Is that you?"

Violet tenses beside me, then lets out an irritated groan.

Just ahead of us is a tall wisp of a woman, dressed from head to toe in white, looking in Violet's direction.

"I've been looking for you." The woman before us crosses her arms. Even her oversized sunglasses are white too. She looks like a movie star.

"What do you want, Francesca?" As quick as a bolt of lightning, Violet's entire demeanor changes.

Oh, so this is *the* sister.

"Daddy offered to sell us the beach house. Having only ever been in it twice, I thought I would drop by, have a look around first, then decide if we want to buy it."

"It's Dad, Francesca, not Daddy. You're thirty-five years old. He's selling the house I'm currently living in?" Violet shrills, pointing at her house across the road.

"Yes. Why? Did he not say anything to you?" Her voice is laced with innocence, but the way a smirk pulls her mouth, she gives herself away.

Their polite conversation goes from zero to one hundred in a millisecond.

Violet stomps past her on the way to her beach towel. "No. I mean, why would he? I'm only his tenant, after all." She sounds so defeated. "It's not like I don't talk to him every day—" Violet stops stuffing her beach towel and suntan lotion into her transparent beach bag mid-sentence. "Ah. I see." She shakes her head back and forth. "You decided you want the beach house and talked him into selling it to you."

Francesca doesn't confirm or deny, which screams volumes.

Violet continues, "Or you hoped he would say, '*Here you go, Franny, you can have it.*'"

"Well, he gave it to you."

"He didn't *give* it to me," Violet spits back. "I rent it. He takes it off my wages every month. I pay my own way."

Violet rambles incoherent words under her breath that I can't make out.

"You can come back another day. When Pom-pom isn't here. I would hate for him to trigger your allergies." Violet's insincere words are apparent.

Angrily, she pulls on her black cover-up and stuffs her feet into her flip-flops. "I've had such a great day today, dancing last night, surfing this morning—"

"You went surfing?" her sister splutters.

"Yes, and it turns out I'm pretty great, actually. Isn't that right, Lincoln?" She pulls me into their verbal combat.

"Incredible. You're a natural." She looked sexy as hell in a wetsuit, too. She was amazing today. Every time she fell off, she got back up, and within an hour, she was surfing. She's good at everything. She clunked her head, sending her under the water, but she got back on the board and was determined to master her technique.

"I'm assuming you wore a wetsuit too; how uncouth, Violet." Her sister flares her nostrils in disgust. "Do they make them in your size?" Francesca snickers at her poor attempt at what she thinks is a joke.

I narrow my eyes. *Who does she think she is?*

I jump in to defend Violet. "They make them in all sizes, actually. But they don't make them in rude, ugly soul size. It would appear you're out of luck."

Violet bursts out laughing while Francesca's mouth hangs open in shock. "Excuse me?"

"You heard," Violet says, deadpan.

"Who is he?" She points at me while looking at Violet. "And who does he think he is speaking to?" Francesca's voice raises an octave.

"He's speaking to the bitch who has done nothing but belittle me my entire life." Violet stands tall and then hands me my sneakers. "He's speaking to the bitch who just implied I was too fat for a wetsuit. And the bitch that had to get her *daddy* to find her a husband because she was too lazy to work." Violet stuffs our belongings into her beach bag. "Now, if you don't mind, my boyfriend and I were just leaving."

Boyfriend.

"And in the words of my handsome Scottish boyfriend, piss off, Francesca."

Yes. My girl's found her fighting spirit.

My girl.

Violet grabs my hand and marches past her.

I don't say another word or mention the fact that my feet are currently receiving second-degree burns as I haven't had the chance to put my shoes on, and the droplets of water running from my shorts aren't doing a very good job to cool them down either.

I turn back to look over my shoulder and Francesca is still standing in the same place we left her. I don't think she can believe Violet stood up for herself.

I don't know Violet very well yet, but what I can guarantee is that she's never had the courage to speak to her sister like that.

"My sister is like Gizmo from *Gremlins*. She looks harmless, just add water, and she's truly ugly beneath that cute exterior. That's why she never swims in the sea; it would reveal the real monster within. God, she truly is an awful person. I'm sorry you had to witness that."

As we cross the road, I ask, "Did you get a dog to keep your sister away?"

She snorts. "Maybe."

"Brilliant." I give her hand a reassuring squeeze.

Back in the house, I let Violet process the events at the beach and leave her to have a shower and freshen up.

When she appears back downstairs, I'm lying on her large white leather sectional sofa with Pom-pom curled up on my chest, fast asleep.

He's like a living snowball.

"You found fresh towels, then?" She eyes the crisp white towel wrapped around my waist.

"Yeah, my shorts were soaked through. I've hung them outside. I still need a shower, though." I had to dash out this morning and buy swim shorts and new clothes for today. I wasn't prepared for bumping into Violet last night or staying over here again. I could have nipped back to my hotel, but it was quicker to hit the shops a couple of blocks over.

Violet places two fresh coffees on the white gloss table, then sits down with an enormous sigh.

"You must have accidentally sat on Pom-pom before. He's camouflaged against your white leather."

She rests her head on the back of the low couch. "He's too short to jump up. He needs me to lift him on top."

I chuckle. "I never thought of that. He's a funny-looking wee thing." He's so soft and light, his weight barely registers on my chest.

"He's cute, though." Violet rolls her head to look at me. "But he costs a fortune in vet bills and he was very expensive."

"How much did he cost?"

"You don't want to know." She rolls her eyes.

"Ouch."

"Ouch, alright," she says softly.

I reach for her hand and knit our fingers together. "Are you okay?"

"I'm fine."

"You're not, though, are you? You feel bad for saying what you did to Francesca because you have a heart. In the moment, you wanted to finally defend yourself, but the afterglow is not what you expected. You feel worse now. Am I correct?"

She cringes. "Yes. God, I was awful."

"You weren't. You were brave today and finally said what you've been holding in for years. And maybe it's time for a change, Violet. As beautiful as this house is, it doesn't reflect you. It's all straight lines and stark. You're more warm and welcoming than this place. Also, I noticed you have hardly any ornaments or soft furnishings in here. It's like you haven't moved in."

She looks around. "You're right. I haven't. Being by the beach is so nice, though."

"I'll grant you that, but maybe your sister is doing you a favor. This is just a house. It doesn't suit your personality. It suits

Francesca's, though—cold, white, sharp edges." I shudder dramatically, making Pom-pom flinch.

This makes Violet laugh.

I bolster her confidence. "You were nothing but articulate when you stood up for yourself, especially when you told her to piss off. You should have also told her she was a bawbag. Now I would have paid money to see that."

"A what?" Violet looks confused.

"A bawbag. It's Scottish for an idiot."

"I love that." She giggles, then whispers the word back to herself. "You don't say many Scottish words like that. I thought I would find it difficult to understand you, but you don't use a lot of slang words."

"I live on the east coast of Scotland, so our accent is not as strong as other parts of Scotland. But none of us really go about saying your stereotypical words like, *och, aye, the noo*. We don't speak like that. We subtly drop in a Scots word or two into what you would class as a normal sentence."

"Like what? Give me an example."

I do an easy one. "You're a blether."

She scrunches her nose up. "What does that mean?"

"You are talking nonsense."

She giggles. "Give me another."

"It's braw out today."

"Meaning?"

"It's a pleasant or nice day today."

She nods her head.

"It's more common for the older generations to speak broadly but me and my friends don't tend to. It's a subtle word here and there. I think it's a generational thing."

"That makes sense, I suppose, as more and more people travel."

"My grandfather has a very strong Scottish accent. My *yaya* still finds it hard to understand him sometimes." I laugh at visions of her shouting profanities in Greek when she gets frustrated.

"And your *yaya* is your grandmother, correct?"

"Yeah, you remembered. She's Greek. Short. Elegant. Feisty and wow, can she cook. Her baklava is the best." My mouth waters at the thought of flaky pastry layers drizzled in honey, syrup, and nuts.

"I do not know what that is. You'll have to find a place that does it here so I can taste it."

"Deal." New mission: find a Greek bakery.

Violet stays silent for a few moments, sipping her coffee, and I can tell she's gearing up to ask me something.

"Can I ask you about your mom?"

I knew it.

"Yeah, but there isn't much to tell. I told you pretty much everything I know at our team-building day."

She turns around to face me, tucking her bronzed legs underneath herself on the couch.

Her wet hair is plastered back, and she's wearing an over-sized pastel lilac tee shirt and booty shorts. I like how she can be her natural self around me, and I love how she always wears loads of purple clothes to match her name. It's cute.

"So you have never met your mom? Ever?"

"Nope. I don't know where she lives, and she might not even be alive." That's the first time it's crossed my mind, and it doesn't sit well with me. "Can you pass my coffee, please?" I don't want to disturb Pom-pom.

Our fingers touch as she carefully places the mug in my hand, and when she rests back against the sofa, a puff of her fresh scent of pear fills the air. I must ask her what perfume she wears.

I take a large sip of the hot nectar and rest the mug under my chin. I need all the caffeine courage I can get if we are having *this* conversation.

"Have you ever thought about finding her?"

"I have." But it was a fleeting moment. "She traveled a lot. I'm not sure she would be easy to locate."

"Do you want to locate her?"

I shake my head. "That's a hard question to answer. I feel like I would be betraying my father."

"Have you told him you might like to find her?"

"Never."

"Do you think he would object?"

"My father is a very levelheaded guy. He would be hurt, I think, but he wouldn't hold me back if that's what I wanted to do." I find the next part very difficult to say. "You also have to remember that she never returned to Scotland to visit me. Not once. I'm not sure she wants to be found."

Violet's hand finds my shoulder, and she gives it a gentle rub.

"But like I said before, I'm fine." An episode of heartburn is coming on. I touch my chest.

"Like me with my sister. *Fine.*"

I roll my head to meet her gaze. "Straight-up, no-nonsense talk? Can I share something that I haven't shared with anyone before?"

"Yeah." Her eyes flash with curiosity.

"Deep down, I would like to find her and talk to her and perhaps discover where she went after she left us. What she did with her life, what her passion is, her hobbies. I'd love to know where she is now. Sit her down and honestly ask her if she ever loved me at all. Ask her if she ever thinks about me." That hurts to say out loud and nerves slam against the walls of my stomach. "But what if she rejects me again? What if I find her and she didn't want to be found? I'm not sure my heart could take it." I don't mean to say the last part out loud.

"Oh, Linc." Violet moves in closer and cups my face. "I'm so sorry."

"If I went looking for her, it would either make or break me. I'm not prepared either way. It's best left alone, I think."

"Would you not want to make peace or find closure?"

"Yes and no. It seems like the easier choice to keep everything as is and not to go looking for unanswered questions. There is this niggle inside of me, though, that tells me to find her. Almost like she's the missing key to this unsettled feeling I often have. It comes in waves. I've never told anyone about it. You're the first." I don't know why I am telling her.

"What kind of feeling?"

"Like a knot that needs to be untied in my stomach. It's all coiled up with tension. I don't know. Maybe my mom is the one who holds the key to untying it. Sometimes I feel like there is a missing piece of my jigsaw puzzle out there, making it hard for me to see the complete picture of myself. I know you don't know me very well, but I hide my fuckery well, and I have bad days sometimes. I've become an expert at hiding it, though. I do everything in my willpower to push those feelings down. *I* don't even understand what I am saying, so how can you? Sorry." I pull Violet's hand away from my face. Trying not to show how uncomfortable I am, I give the palm of her hand a quick kiss. I fucking hate that look of pity she's currently displaying. "I need a shower."

Violet picks up Pom-pom off my chest. He opens his small mouth and lets out a whimpered yawn. "Are we going out for dinner?" I ask.

"I was going to order in for us."

"Okay." I need to kick myself out of the solemnity. "You pick, Petal. You know this city better than I do."

"I'm not so sure. You've introduced me to places I have never been or heard of before all weekend. Maybe I should let you pick."

I jump over the back of the sofa. "What about Sea & Soul?"

"Never heard of it." She laughs.

"Look it up and we'll order when I'm out of the shower."

"Great idea."

Violet's curious voice calls out to me as my foot hits the first stair. "What was your mom's name, Lincoln?"

"Olivia. Olivia Grace Black. She took my dad's name." I haven't said her name out loud for a very long time.

"Pretty name."

I grab on to the handrail and make my way up the stairs, now feeling like the weight of the two floors above me is on my shoulders.

As I reach Violet's bedroom, a text comes through on my phone. I grab it off the bed.

DAD

Do you fancy having some visitors?

ME

What do you mean?

DAD

We're coming to Santa Monica.

ME

Who?

DAD

All of us. Eva, your brothers, and sister. Eden, Hunter, and their three boys. Ella, Fraser, and little Mason. You up for that?

ME

Are you serious?

I would love to see them.

DAD

Yes! Fraser's stepson doesn't live too far away. It was his excuse to vacation there. We got chatting. One thing led to another, and we all booked.

ME

For real?

DAD

Yes. Flying out in four weeks and we'll all fly back together two weeks later with you coming back with us.

ME

Who will look after the hotel?

DAD

We have managers for that, Linc. Calm your pants.

ME

But I'm home in a few weeks.

DAD

I know, but we can spend some time together, catch up properly; otherwise, you'll come straight home, dive into work, and we won't get the chance to hear all of your stories from your travels.

ME

I can't wait to see you.

DAD

Me too. We're staying at the same hotel as you. We have the presidential suite, so we'll all be together. Can you imagine six adults and seven kids under the same roof? It's giving me a headache just thinking about it.

ME

You love it, really.

DAD

I do.

ME

I'm setting a countdown for your arrival on my phone.

DAD

Already done mine. *smiley face* Twenty-eight days.

ME

Can't wait.

21

LINCOLN

"Are you working?" I lean against the office door on the second floor of Violet's house.

She lifts her head from her laptop screen and scrunches her nose, making her look cute but flustered. Her hair is tied up in a messy bun, tendrils spilling from it haphazardly, and she's wearing an oversized pair of luminous lilac thick-rimmed glasses.

"You wear glasses?" I'm surprised.

She pushes them up on top of her head and rests back against the office chair. "For screen work only." She presses her fingertips into her eyes. "I thought I would catch up on the four hundred and thirty-two emails that have dropped into my inbox over the weekend. Interestingly, not one from my father to tell me about the house. I'm sure Francesca is pulling my leg."

"I wouldn't be able to work if this was the view from my office." I push my hands into my pockets and walk over to the floor-to-ceiling windows, my bare feet slapping against the white-tiled flooring.

"It's a little distracting." Violet catches my eye. "Could you not find a tee shirt to wear, Lincoln?"

"I was hot and I'm half-dressed." I point to the navy sweatpants I bought this morning.

She pulls her glasses down on her face, then uses her pointer finger to slide them back up her nose. "You need to go. You are too much of..." Her eyes zone in on my abs. I flex them to tease her. She groans. "Just too much." She focuses back on her laptop screen. "My morning will be chaotic tomorrow if I don't do this now. I have contractors to meet first thing. This is the first weekend I haven't worked in months. Now I know why." She seems tense. I remember that feeling and have that all to look forward to again on my return to my job.

"Is that your stationery cabinet?" I walk over to the opened unit on the other side of the office. It's stacked high with dozens of planners, all in different colors.

"Don't touch anything. I know where everything is. Don't mess up my system." She jumps out of her chair.

Labeled clear-lidded boxes are filled to the brim with rainbow-colored stickers, inserts, highlighter pens, page markers, and washi tape. What the fuck is washi tape? I laugh in confusion.

She closes the door and pushes my chest, moving me away from her coveted planner stash.

"No touching." She waggles her pointer finger at me.

I hold my hands up in surrender. "Got it."

She moves back to her chair.

"Can I help with anything?"

"Nope. I'm good. I just need an hour, then I am all yours." She's already distracted, reading something on her screen. "I don't think I like my job anymore."

"No?"

"It's the same crap, every day and night. It used to excite me."

"And now?"

"Mundane, expected, and recently I've been asking myself, is this all there is to my life? Last night was the first time I have been out on a Saturday in months that wasn't in a work capacity."

"Maybe you need a vacation?"

"Or a new job." She sighs. "Ignore me. I get like this from time to time." Her expert fingers glide across her keyboard, creating a pandemonium of tapping sounds.

"I'll take Pom-pom for a walk, then."

"I'm not sure what I am ordering tonight to eat. You pick."

"Or I could fuck you on this desk," I say, aware she's not listening to me.

"Sounds like a good choice to me. Do they do chili prawns? I love them. But extra hot."

"Or lick your lovely pussy under the desk while you're sorting out your emails."

She taps angrily on her keyboard. "Jennifer, there is no more money left in the budget for a new ergonomic chair for your home office."

And she hasn't noticed I'm now standing by her side. I spin the chair around and lean over her.

She sucks in a breath. "What are you doing?"

"Helping you relax." I slide my hands up her thighs, which look bronzed by today's sun.

"But I am work—"

I cup my hand over her mouth. "Shhhhh. Will you stop talking?" I raise my eyebrows.

She nods her head.

"Good girl. And keep the glasses on; they make you look like a sexy secretary." I remove my hand.

I trace my fingertips to the hem of her booty shorts.

"Lift your hips for me."

"Bu—"

I give her a *don't question me* look.

Willingly, she tilts her hips off the chair, allowing me to slide her shorts off.

"Tee shirt too," I command.

She removes it without being asked twice and flips her lilac top up over her head, revealing she's braless.

I drop to my knees. She looks down at me as I spread her thighs wide. Our eyes lock and the force of a hurricane pounds against my chest. I never want this *thing* we have to end.

Violet reaches down and cups my cheek. "What are we going to do?" she asks, as if she's speaking to herself.

Does she mean now or in the future?

I can't answer that question, so I don't. Instead, I lean forward, drag her hips to the edge of the seat, and kiss her clit.

She hooks her legs over the arms of the chair, giving herself to me.

With deft fingers, I tease her now-swollen lips, before parting them gently, then suck her clit into my mouth.

There is no force, no rush. Just soft and careful licks and flicks needed to soothe her stress away.

I spread her lips wider, and flatten my tongue against her wet core, making her cry out. Drawing small circles around her hole, I then insert my rigid tongue into her wet center, and push it in and out over and over, edging her until she's writhing and panting my name.

Violet lets out a soft, "Oooh." Grinding her pussy into my mouth to find her own release. "I need to come, Linc."

I pull back slightly to get a good look at her now pink and

soaked-for-me pussy. "I know, sweet Petal. I know." I trace my fingertips over her clit, then flick it with more force.

She arches her back and I know I've found her sweet spot. She's almost there.

"You're so sexy when you come. Give yourself to me and come. Let all your stress go, Petal."

I kiss her inner thigh.

When I look up, she's staring at me. She smiles and I can't stop the grin forming on my lips before I focus my attention back on her clit as I slide two fingers into her hot heat and hold them there, deep.

Her moans become more prominent and wild.

I push my fingers against her inner walls, curving my fingers, teasing her insides and beckoning for her to come while lavishing licks at her clit. I go faster, finger-fucking her until she comes all over my fingers, coating them with her arousal.

"Oh, you're so good at that," she coos, sweeping her fingers through my hair, sending shivers down my spine. Every touch of hers turns me on so bad.

I remove my fingers and suck them into my mouth. "You taste like heaven."

With hooded eyes, she watches and licks her lips. "I wouldn't know. I've never been." She sighs.

"I've just taken you there."

"What we do together feels more like hell. Hot. Unquenchable. I'm certain there is always something trying to eat you up." She giggles.

I love it when she laughs.

Unhooking her legs from the arms of the chair, she places her feet flat on the floor. "Thank you." She kisses my lips. "I needed that."

"I know. Now put your clothes back on and work. We have a dinner date down the stairs in an hour."

"Done. I'll be able to concentrate much better now."

"Thought it would help." I rise to my full height. "And you can help me with my concentration later on." I point at my full-mast erection through my trousers.

"I can do that now." She licks her plump lips.

"Nope. Work." I rub my pounding cock. Christ, that is painful. "Fun later. I'm off to walk Pom-pom then I'll order dinner."

"You know, if you keep doing nice things for me, I might just ask you to marry me and you could be my personal assistant in every way." She half laughs, and then her eyes go wide and her cheeks blush pink as she realizes what she said.

Our eyes bore through each other.

In a fully vulnerable moment, completely naked, Violet pulls herself up from her chair and walks over to me. She looks up at me with her big dark doe eyes. "You know I'm kidding, don't you?"

Was she?

"And honestly, Lincoln, I don't know why I met you, but there is a reason. I'm not stupid and I am fully aware you can't make me any promises past a few weeks. But promise me this, please. Tell me if you want out because although I asked you to take a leap of faith with me, I know that it's also okay to take a step back too, when it all becomes too much. To protect this." She lays her delicate hand against my chest.

Fuck. My heart beats more rapidly because I want to jump into the abyss with her, but the only words that leave my mouth are, "Okay. It's only been a few days. We'll take a day at a time."

Okay? We'll take a day at a time?

I'm an idiot.

"Okay." She pats my chest twice. Her bountiful ass jiggles as she rushes back to her desk and puts her clothes back on.

It's only been a few days?

I flee from the room and roll my eyes at my stupidity.

"Remember to put a top on. Those abs are for my eyes only, Lincoln Black."

I stop at the bottom of the stairs so I can hear what she's saying as she talks to herself.

"Oh, nice one, Violet. What an absolute ass I am. Oh, I might just ask you to marry me." She puts on a warbled, low voice. *"Idiot. It's been three days, you silly woman.* What an utterly stupid thing to say. It just slipped out. New rule, think before you speak. Way to lose all your coolness. Christ, who am I kidding? I was never cool. Right, emails." I hear her pulling her chair back to her desk. "And who the hell wants to be called Violet Black? That's a stupid goddamn name if ever I heard it. Violet West-Black. Violet Black-West." She groans.

So she's thought about her name.

"That name will never work. I will sound like a color swatch. Why did my parents not call me something like Jane or Monica, but oh no, '*We called you Violet because violets were your grandmother's favorite*'?" She mimics a high-pitched posh voice. "Could she not have picked a flower called Susan?"

I have a little chuckle at the bottom of the stairs.

She's funny.

I'm in so much trouble.

22

LINCOLN

"Wow, that was delicious. I am ordering from them again." Violet licks the remnants of her chili prawn kebabs off her fingertips. Turns out she likes them extra hot and super spicy.

Just like her.

"So good." I pat my stomach. "You will have to roll me to bed."

"You decided you're staying over, then?"

"I figured I would drive back to my hotel tomorrow morning, shower, and change there, and I will meet you at the gym."

"Are you sure you don't have anything else to do? Do you seriously want to help out? I'm not pushing you away or anything." She prevents me from saying anything with the flash of her palms in a stop gesture. "But you only have a few weeks left here. Are you sure you want to spend it in a gym with me bossing you around?"

"Yes, I want to. I have nothing else to do. I'm just marching time at the moment and it means I get to see you. If you have nothing for me to do, though, I can always be your personal assistant. I don't mind fetching coffee. I've made beds, helped in the spa, assembled gym equipment, and worked in every part of the hotel, oh and the restaurant."

"What was your least favorite job?"

"Oh, that's easy. Reception. I can only speak two languages and one of those is English, but we have guests from all over the world. Speaking at least two or three additional languages is a requirement for the job, so all of our concierges and receptionists speak at least ten different languages between them. I should make learning a new language my new goal." I dip my finger into Violet's chili sauce and have a taste. It catches in my throat, making me cough. Holy shit, that is hot. I take a sip of my ice-cold water, then ask her the same question. "What about you? If you would work in any department or function of your dad's business, what would you do?" My mouth is on fire.

"That's easy for me to answer, too. My father invested in a cosmetic company years ago, but he's never grown the business. It has so much potential." Her whole face lights up. "It's manufactured, distributed, and sold in the UK. You may have heard of it, Nkd by Nature?"

I shake my head.

"Never mind." She moves on. "But the packaging is on point, as are the formulas. It's vegan-friendly, not tested on animals. It ticks all the boxes." She becomes more animated as she continues. "I would love to get my hands on it. It needs a rebrand to appeal to a younger target market. He's often talked about launching it globally, but he never has."

"Sounds like fun."

"It would be. But I can only dream. Also, a project like that means more work, which means less time off, and I already work lots of overtime. You'll see what I mean over the next few weeks. I will apologize right now for the amount of time I work. But I promise I will also make time for you, too." She sighs. "I think you're right about me needing a vacation."

She pops her last extra-spicy prawn into her mouth. "So, the first day tomorrow as a *volunteer*?" she mumbles around her food.

"I was never working for the money, Violet."

"Treading water, I know, you said." She smiles cheekily. "Weirdo."

"I can't wait to work with you. Do you wear skirts and dresses to work, even when you're on site?" I slide my dinner plate onto the white coffee table.

"Every day, as I bounce between the office, meetings, and numerous premises."

"Got any more of those zipper dresses, like last night?" I wink suggestively.

A confetti of laughter leaves her chest. "That won't happen at work. You are so naughty, Lincoln Black."

I test her after the mention of my surname. "Do you know *if* we did get married, you would become Violet Black?"

She looks at me innocently. "Oh yeah, I never thought about that." Her cheeks grow pink. "What a stupid name. I would sound like a paint swatch chart. Just as well, that's *never* going to happen." Her voice sounds strained. "Let's clean up."

That tells me everything I need to know. She likes me. More than she wants to openly admit.

I pull the plate she is holding out of her hands and lay it on the table beside mine.

"What are you doing?"

"I want to kiss you."

She pulls herself onto her knees and instructs me to lie back on the sofa. "Nope. Me first."

She's always eager to please and moves faster than a panther.

Christ, this woman is going to destroy my dick.

Going from no sex for months to this, I'm struggling to keep up with her, but she's always horny as shit. Although I'm not going to fill out a customer complaint slip anytime soon.

Wasting no time, she pulls my dick free from my easy-access elastic sweatpants and licks me from shaft to tip. I hiss at her getting-straight-to-it tactic as blood pumps into my cock, making me hard in an instant.

"Oh fuck, Violet."

She pulls my pants down to my ankles to position herself better.

It feels incredible when she covers her plump lips over my crown; she runs her tongue around it, making pre-cum leak from my tip. Moving her hand up and down my now achingly hard cock, she's making a tunnel for me to fuck, and I grow thicker and, harder for her, and when she sucks me deep into her mouth, I almost come there and then.

Her cheeks hollow out as she sucks me harder. "Oh yeah, keep doing th—" Uh-oh, that doesn't feel so nice anymore. A stinging sensation pierces hot barbs in my skin.

A blaze hotter than the sun heats my dick, and it's getting hotter.

What the hell?

I reach down to stop her sucking me, but she takes this as a sign to suck me harder.

"*Oh, my God,*" I roar when the heat kicks up a notch, and it feels like someone has poured molten lava over my cock. "Stop, fucking stop."

In the distance, I can hear Pom-pom barking his head off.

"Get off," I bellow.

She finally pulls back, and I reach for my dick and pull my knees to my chest. I can't fucking think straight or breathe.

"What did I do wrong? Did I hurt you?" She's shouting over my loud moans.

"My fucking dick is on fire." I clench my eyes shut.

The dog continues to bark.

I'm wailing like a banshee now and my cock is getting hotter by the second. I feel like I might pass out.

"Motherfucker." I continue to roll around. I want to get up, but I'm in excruciating pain.

"What do you mean... Oh my God. I ate chili," she exclaims. "It's in my mouth and on my hands. It was extra hot," she shrills.

"And now it's on my dick. I need ice." I leap up, fall over, forgetting my pants are around my ankles, and smack my head on the edge of the white gloss coffee table. I hear Violet scream, and that's the last thing I remember.

23

VIOLET

"I'm only going to say this once, and then we are never speaking about this again. Okay?"

I suck my lips into my mouth, trying not to laugh, as Lincoln stands facing me, legs spread as wide as a cowboy.

"Okay." I snort.

He narrows his eyes at me. "Once we leave the hospital parking lot this evening, we never, *ever* speak about this again and you can't tell anyone." He holds the ice pack against his crotch.

"There could be an issue with that. I may have accidentally dropped a group text to Hannah and Ruby."

"Jesus Christ." He hisses as he rearranges his dick. "Why the fuck is it still burning like Satan's anus?" He grits his teeth. "I need a cold bath." He's on the verge of crying.

"The nurse said to try dipping it in cold milk when we get home. But it might make the milk taste funny if we do that." I snort again.

"Oh, isn't this just hilarious?" He widens his stance. "I have a chili stick for a dick, a superglued forehead, which is going to leave a mark and a mild concussion. Although I'm guessing the real kick in the crotch, and I am sure you find this part even more hysterical, is having two female paramedics find me unconscious with my dick in my hand, bleeding to death on your living-room floor."

I can't hold it in any longer. A wild cackle of giggles leaves my throat and I almost pee myself from laughing so hard. I've been so good at keeping it together all night.

After a few minutes, I stand up and wipe my eyes with the hem of my tee shirt. The nurse warned me not to touch my eyes or mouth for a good couple of hours.

"Are you finished, Ms. West?"

I put my hands on my hips and tip my head back to try and keep it together. I let out a few breaths and fan my face with my hand to calm me down.

"Continue." I have to tuck my lips back into my mouth because I keep getting flashbacks of this evening's events. I think I'm either high off the adrenaline of it all or the chili. It would appear it is quite potent. It could very well be that.

Lincoln continues to hold the ice pack against his crotch. "Repeat after me. I, Violet West."

"I, Violet West," I reply, placing my hand over my heart like I'm taking an oath on the witness stand.

"Do solemnly promise."

"Do solemnly promise."

"To always wash my hands and brush my teeth after consuming extra-hot chili before giving Lincoln a blow job."

"To always wash my hands and brush my teeth after consuming extra-hot chili before giving Lincoln a blow job." I have to cover my mouth with my tee shirt as more giggles threaten to take over.

"You are such a child."

"You are such a child."

"Oh, stop it."

"Oh, stop it."

He groans.

"Okay, I'm sorry." I try to compose myself again. "Let's just get in the car and go home. It's been a long night."

"You know, Ms. West, earlier this evening, I was thinking to myself about how you were slightly older than me and how I thought you were trying to destroy my dick. Mission accomplished. You fucking broke him. I dub thee Violet 'Dick Destroyer' West."

I walk toward him, roaring with laughter, and he continues to tell me off, grumbling about his broken dick and his bruised ego.

Between the laughter and his incessant moaning, I manage to coax him into the car.

I push the start button, and my sports engine purrs. Lincoln rests his head back against the head support. I know it's been funny and all, but I do have to watch him tonight as he did suffer a head injury. The nurse gave me a leaflet that outlines all the symptoms that need emergent care and what to look out for.

I'm not sure I'm a very good nurse, to be honest. I'm not very levelheaded when it comes to emergency situations of the human kind. Buildings, spreadsheets, and logistics? Yes. A giant Scotsman bleeding on my living-room floor? Nope.

I wasn't sure what to do first. Put the dog away, call 911, cover him in a blanket, stop the bleeding, resuscitate him? Everything was swirling in my head and I couldn't think straight.

I'll never forget the cracking noise when he smacked his head on the coffee table or what followed after. Blood. So much blood. The vision of his vibrant poppy-red color spilling across my stark white marble still makes my stomach churn.

Before the paramedics arrived, I did at least think to cover him up. He was still wedged between the coffee table and the sofa so I couldn't move him. I tried but he was too heavy. So what could I do? I had to leave him there, unconscious on the floor, cover him up to hide his dick, and press a towel to his head to stop the bleeding.

It's a clean slice, but he bruises so easily and it turned purple and black in places instantly. The nurse said the redness and swelling around the edges of his cut should reduce over the next couple of days.

I feel so bad.

What a night.

"I'm so sorry, Lincoln."

"You have so much making up to do," he grumbles.

"I could kiss your dick again."

He rolls his head my way as we stop at the traffic light and looks at me as if to say *never again*, but his eyes are warm and glint with mischief.

24

VIOLET

"You stay here today and rest." I sit on the edge of the bed and give Lincoln a kiss. "Lots of water. No driving and absolutely no chili."

His eyes sparkle with laughter at my chili joke. He knows I'm never going to let it go. He finally says, "I'm fine."

"You are not fine. You were dizzy when you stood up earlier and you have a headache. Nurse West says, stay in bed today."

"I would feel so much better if you had a PVC nurse's outfit on, Nurse West." He dramatically pouts.

"Oh yeah. Let me just pull one out of my magician's hat for you."

"Fantastic. I'll lie here while you get changed into it." He lets out a sigh. He is still teasing today but he is not his usual quick, smart-ass self I've come to know and adore.

"If you are well in a few days, you can come to the gym with me, but today I am giving you strict orders to watch a series on television. I have made your lunch. I put it in the fridge and you need to rest. No strenuous tasks for you today and Pom-pom doesn't need a walk; he's done several laps of my swimming-pool-sized bed today already." I laugh when Lincoln sits Pom-pom on top of his head.

"He can heal my head today."

"Good plan. He's a good therapy dog."

With his giant hand, Lincoln removes his little white fluffy body from his dark locks and places him on his lap on top of the bedcovers.

"Are you okay with me staying in your house all day by myself? You barely know me." He leisurely strokes Pom-pom.

"Oh, I know you, Lincoln. I've spent more time with you in these past few days and found out things about you I never even came close to with my last boyfriend. I trust you. However, I hid my great-great-great-aunt Brenda's sapphire engagement ring just in case."

"Wise decision." He props himself up against the bed pillows. "Thank you."

"For?"

"Looking after me last night. I know you got little sleep because of worrying about me and that you have a busy today ahead, but I'm very grateful."

I run my fingers down his cheek and stare into his big brown eyes.

He's worth it.

"Just promise me you will rest today."

"Okay, Mom."

Not knowing if this is the right time or not, I figure there is never a right time for this type of conversation, so I say, "Speaking of moms. Last night when I couldn't sleep, I did a bit of research online and discovered a UK agency who can find long-lost family members."

He pulls his head back slightly. "You did that for me?"

I nod my head. "I'm not saying you *should* go searching, but I wanted you to know that you *can* if you want to, that's all. It's a possibility." I dip my gaze and play with my pastel-colored abstract floral bedding. "I just thought maybe you would like to find that missing part of you that's out there somewhere when you are ready."

He tips my chin up. "I think I might have already found it."

"You're clearly concussed."

"I'm not. You look beautiful today." His lips curl slowly into a smile.

"Definitely delirious," I whisper.

He leans forward and kisses me with such heartfelt emotion. It's a soft ghost of a kiss, barely a kiss at all, but it sets off a tornado of sparks swirling in my lower belly. Not ideal before heading into a full day of work, but the things this man does to me.

"Can you send me the details so I can at least have a look?" He kisses my cheek. "I kind of made my decision in my head yesterday that I wouldn't go searching." He kisses my forehead. "Because I think I'm starting to see the full picture." He kisses my temple before he leans back. "Right there." He closes one eye, then makes a picture frame with his fingers, framing my face as if he's a photographer. "Perfect."

A feeling I can't describe hits my chest and whatever he asks of me, I'm in. All in.

I'm completely smitten.

He smiles back at me, knowing I can't form words. "You need to go to work or you'll never make it in time to meet the contractors this morning. Traffic in that part of the city is horrific, especially if you don't leave…" He checks the time on his phone. "Now."

I don't want to go. I want to stay here with him.

"You be good for Lincoln today, my happy canine cloud." I

bend to kiss Pom-pom, but he doesn't move. Lincoln is his new best friend. Traitor.

"We'll be fine. Now go before the traffic takes on a new meaning to 'frozen in time'."

Reluctantly, I remove myself from the edge of the bed. "Text me if you need anything." I smooth my dress over my hips. "Okay. I need to go." I stand by the bed.

Lincoln reaches out and takes my hand. "You don't want to go today, do you?"

I let out a long sigh. "I've been feeling more and more like that recently."

"I'll be here waiting for you when you come home." He pulls my hand to his mouth and kisses my fingers.

I bob my head. "Right." It takes everything within me not to jump back into bed with him. I let go of his hand unwillingly. "Unfortunately, I am meeting my father for dinner after work today, so order food for yourself. I've been summoned to meet his new girlfriend. I arranged it last week and I can't change it. My dad does not like anyone messing with his schedule."

"Sounds like fun."

"Girlfriend number seven so far this year."

"He's had seven girlfriends in seven months?" Lincoln's mouth hangs open.

"It's exhausting and every one of them is *the one*."

"*He* must be exhausted. What a stud."

I screw my face up. I don't want to think about him in *that* way.

Squeezing my toes into my black patent heels, I make my way to the elevator, then sling my purse over my shoulder and push the call button, instructing the doors to open.

"Use this today. Do not use the stairs. Promise?" I stall in the doorway of the stainless-steel box.

"Promise."

Removing my foot to allow the doors to finally close, the last thing I see is Lincoln's bronzed body lying in my bed as he pets Pom-pom. I hold my hand up and give him a finger-wave.

"Think of me." The words fade on his lips when the doors close.

I can't stop thinking about you, Lincoln.

25

VIOLET

I walk around the enormous space, looking around the remodeling work that's begun in the gym. I'm always the first one to arrive.

This is my favorite part of the day. The check-ins, updates, problem solving. Every day in my job pretty much starts the same way.

Today, I have multiple location checks to make and it's already scorching outside. I'm relieved I wore my thin summer dress. I would've melted otherwise.

Although Lincoln said I look better naked. I smile at his beautiful words.

Tearing myself away from Lincoln every morning while he continued to rest this week was very difficult.

I dreaded the last four working days, something I have never felt before. Boredom, yes, but not dread. However, today I'm excited as he's meeting me at the gym this morning.

Today is the first morning he's not been dizzy and felt good enough to drive, so he left my house early to go back to his hotel to shower and change. It's the first time he's been back there since Saturday.

Having him living in my home has been oddly natural, and coming home to a warm hug, welcoming smile, and someone who cares about me is a novel experience for me.

When I was growing up, my mom and dad never saw eye to eye, so he stayed away when she was around, making the excuse that he was *working late.* To be honest, my mother wasn't around much either; she was always too busy shopping, dining, or cocktailing with God knows who, doing God knows what, and it's not as if Francesca and I were ever close, so most of my childhood and teenage years were spent by myself in that big, empty, loveless home. Why my mother and father had me, I will never fully understand. While Francesca was an accident, I was an even bigger one.

As awful as it was, when my mom and dad divorced, it was also such a relief. Like a weight had been lifted off my shoulders. While Francesca continued living in our tomb of a home with Mom, I moved in with my dad and the peace and normality I craved happened overnight. And I finally had a father. The change in him was remarkable.

That's when my father and I became very close. He shared his days with me and it's where I learned all the ins and outs of West Oracle Corporations. I decided, over all our many dinners, that I wanted to work for him.

It was the best decision I ever made. As soon as I left college, I joined West Oracle and worked my way up the ranks. I love my job, but I've been doing the same role now for six years and I'm feeling an itch for change.

I've felt restless in my job for a while. I still want to work for the family business, but I can do my job in my sleep and it's becoming a bit like *Groundhog Day* for me. A new challenge is what I think I need.

And for the first time, all I have wanted to do is stay at home. *With Lincoln.*

The times I haven't been at work, we've spent every waking moment with each other, and he keeps surprising me.

On Monday, he did all my laundry. Tuesday, I returned from work to discover he had cleaned my pool and made a three-course meal for dinner. Wednesday, he cleaned my house, and all day Thursday he texted me telling me how much he missed me and all the things he wanted to do to me when I got in from work.

I've never met anyone like him.

I know he craves the love of a woman. Every morning I wake up with him wrapped around me. He cuddles me every chance he can and all week he's asked me what time I was going to be home.

It's almost like he needs to know I will return to him.

To reassure him, every night this week, I sent him a text message to let him know I was on my way back, and every night butterflies danced in my stomach as I drove closer to him.

His warm Scottish voice awakens my lucid dreaming: "Morning, Petal." Familiar hands skim my waist and his soft lips trace the back of my neck. "I like when you wear your hair up." I lean back against him as his zesty scent floods my senses. Lincoln kisses the pleasure patch he found behind my ear, and it sends a wave of goosebumps across my body, making me shiver. I love that he likes my body so much and enjoys kissing every part.

I want to go back home with him.

A needy moan escapes my lips.

"I think my girl needs me," he mumbles.

"She does." I turn myself around in his enormous arms and

loop mine around his neck. "It's been a few days; I've been letting you rest." I check his glued-back-together head. "It looks so much better today."

"It does and I feel great today too. Plus, this little dress of yours makes me feel even better still." He grabs my ample ass.

"Easy access." I giggle. I've become a giddy schoolgirl around him.

"You had better have panties on today."

"That's for you to find out." I rise on my tiptoes and give him a kiss. "But first, work."

"Show me everything you've been up to this week." His eyes light up.

I go over the dozens of architectural plans with him that plaster one of the walls and show him the final phase, the new gym layout. He studies it in great detail, shuffling left and right and back again, then he frowns. "Who did these?"

"The architect." I thought that was obvious.

"What do they normally design?"

"Bars, clubs, restaurants, hotels. This was a new project for them." We've never used them before.

"You can tell." He points to an area on the plan. "Also, the person who designed these doesn't work out."

"How do you know that?" I look at what he is pointing to.

As the workmen filter in through the doors, Lincoln explains to me in fine detail how the new layout of the gym has no flow. Highlighting the lack of distance between the equipment, the areas aren't distinctive enough, how each zone should have a different vibe with lighting and flooring. He goes on and on, making incredible and valid points that no one else has picked up on, and when he stops, I realize he's drawn a crowd of workmen who all agree with him.

I push my fingers into my temples, feeling a headache

coming on. "I was trusting the interior designers to get this right. They assured me they knew what they were doing. We have never owned a health and fitness business before either, so this is all new territory for all of us and they knew that. How the hell did I miss this?" I look at the plans on the wall, getting more and more frustrated for not seeing this before.

I've been juggling multiple acquisition projects for months. It's no wonder I've dropped the ball recently. My father was right. I need an assistant.

The enormous space is so quiet you could hear a pin drop.

As pissed as I am, I refuse to fall apart in front of them. Shoulders back and head held high again, I turn to face them.

Jeremy is our site manager, and his face right now says it all. Lincoln is right.

"Okay, I'm on it." I hold my hands up.

Lincoln jumps in. "Hey, don't change the plans because of what I have said. This could cost a lot of money to redo the plans."

"But you're right, Lincoln, we need to change it." I pull the plans off the wall. "Lincoln, you're coming with me. Jeremy, can you do as much as you can today? I'm off to the architect's office with Lincoln, and can you rally all the other project managers together at the other sites and explain the situation?"

"On it." He salutes me.

"Thanks, Jeremy."

"Sounds like you have a busy day ahead of you now, Violet."

Oh, poop. I spin around when the deep voice of my father makes his presence known.

He does not look happy.

Around fifty burly men scamper faster than a mouse eying some cheese to begin their work for the day.

"And who are you?" Hands still in the pockets of his dress pants, he tilts his head at Lincoln.

World, swallow me up now.

Lincoln starts to answer, but I blurt, "This is Lincoln. Lincoln Black."

"And he is?"

"My boyfriend?"

"Was that a question or a definite answer, Letty?"

"Definite answer." I place the now-abandoned gym plans on the large wooden table beside me.

"You sure?"

"Oh, behave." I move toward him and throw my arms around his waist. "Morning, Mr. Grumpy." His mood changes in a heartbeat. He may be a big gruff bear with his workers, but with me, he's a big soft-hearted soul.

He kisses the top of my head. "Morning, Letty." He then whispers in my ear, "Boyfriend?"

I pinch his side. "Don't embarrass me, Dad." I pull out of our hug. "Lincoln, this is my father, Anthony West. Dad, this is Lincoln. My new boyfriend."

Lincoln strides forward with an outstretched hand. "Pleased to meet you, Mr. West." My father shakes his hand firmly.

My dad frowns. "Scottish? I recognize that accent. Did I not meet you at the team-building day?"

"You did. I don't work for S&M Gyms anymore. Your daughter fired me."

"She what?"

"She fired me. I was only on a temporary contract, but if we want to have a relationship, I can't work for the gym. Company policy."

A deep laugh fills my father's chest. "Oh boy, she must really like you, then." His eyebrows shoot up. "And you must be a glutton for punishment or have balls of steel to stick around after she fired you." He waggles his finger at him, smiling the entire time. "Although you Scots are brave, wearing kilts in the cold weather across the pond." My dad turns to me. "You fired him? This may be the funniest thing I have ever heard you do, Letty. Also, the silliest." He frowns at me. I know my father well enough to know what he's thinking—employee sexual harassment lawsuit.

I shake my head to let him know it's all fine.

Unaware of our unspoken conversation, Lincoln shoots back, "Oh no, when she fell over in the office last week—that was the funniest thing I've ever seen."

"You fell last week? Again? You seriously need to think about wearing flat pumps, Letty. Did you hurt yourself?" His voice is full of concern.

"I'm fine." I swipe my hand through the air.

"Did you do that too?" My dad points to Lincoln's cut forehead but asks me. He knows me so well.

"Yes."

"No."

Lincoln and I both say the opposite at the same time.

"Kinda." I twiddle my thumbs and Lincoln snorts.

My dad shakes his head. "I'm sorry I asked."

"You really do *not* want to know how it happened." Lincoln folds his arms across his chest.

I feel myself turning scarlet. "You really don't." I close my eyes. *Change the subject, Violet.* "So, did you hear all of that? What Lincoln was saying about the plans and layout?"

My dad sifts through the plans on top of the table. "I can see what you mean, Lincoln. Is this a new firm we are using?"

"Yes, but they reassured me they understood the project and

our vision." I go through a few pointers with them both. "I'm going straight to the architect's office now with Lincoln."

"Give them hell, Letty." My father smiles. He knows he never has to worry when I am project managing. I've never missed a deadline yet. "Right, well, nothing to see here until we get these new plans, so I had better go. I have three appointments this morning with finance, and then I'm meeting Viva for lunch." He smooths down his silver tie against this stark-white shirt. He looks very handsome today.

I met Viva, Dad's new girlfriend, at dinner on Monday. She seemed nice enough, but she was quite cold and closed-off. I'm guessing she's in her mid-forties as she has two teenage sons and works as an administrator at the high school her kids attend.

God only knows where he met her, as she seems way too normal for my dad. There has got to be something wrong with her.

"Walk me out, sweetheart." My father makes a teapot shape with his arm, and I thread mine into his. "Nice to meet you again, Lincoln."

"You too, sir." Lincoln politely waves goodbye.

When we reach my father's white Porsche Cayman, he jumps into the driver's seat and rolls his window down. "It's going to be a hot one today."

I look up at the sun. "A scorcher."

"You fired him? And he stayed with you?" He looks up at me.

I rest my hands on his driver's door. "What can I say? I'm very persuasive."

"Tell me about him."

"You need to go."

"Tell me about him, Violet."

I give in as I know he will only call me later. "He's Scottish.

He's twenty-nine years old. He's a director of a five-star hotel and spa that he co-owns with his father and grandfather. He's been traveling America for the last few months because his father wanted him to explore the world, making sure he wasn't working for the family business because he felt he had to." My father's eyebrows shoot up into his hairline. "He was only on a short-term contract with S&M Gyms because he decided to stay here for the last six weeks of his work travel visa and was bored suntanning and surfing. He leaves in just over five weeks. Anything else?"

"Nope, I think that covers it." He's thinking. "Have you ever felt like that?"

"Like what?"

"Like you only work for the family business because it was the natural thing to do?" He puts his sunglasses on.

"No."

"Are you sure? You would tell me if you were unhappy, wouldn't you?"

"Yes."

"Great." He throws me a beaming smile.

"I'm not unhappy, but..."

"But?" He pushes his sunglasses back on top of his head and his eyes narrow as the blazing sun dazzles him.

"But I would like to speak to you about the possibility of moving to a new role."

"What's up, sweetheart?"

I sigh. "I... I'm... Oh, I don't know. I think I would like to do something different. This job takes up all my time, Dad. Last weekend was the first weekend I have had off in months and it made me think about all the time I might be missing out on. I haven't had a vacation in three years and well, I'm—"

"Tired." He finishes my sentence.

I let out a huge sigh of relief. "Yeah."

"Do you think I don't know how hard you work?"

I'm unaware how my dad will take this, but I say it, anyway. "Since meeting Lincoln, he's made me realize I don't have much of a life. He introduced me to all these new places in town I never knew existed. I realized I'm not living. All I do is work. How on earth could I ever consider having a family? Not that I am saying I'm getting married and starting a family today or anything..."

"Thank goodness for that. I'm still too young to be a grandfather."

He makes me laugh.

"But I'm not exactly getting any younger, though, Dad. My biological clock is ticking. Even if I had a family, where would they fit in?" It's a rhetorical question. "And *if* I do move to a new position, I don't want to work around the clock. Yes, I want a new challenge, but I also need balance." I chew my lip. "I've also decided, since I'm the only manager without one, I need an assistant."

"Finally." He holds his hands up to the heavens.

"Stop it." I swat his shoulder playfully.

"Have you given any thought as to what you would like to do or what department you would like to work in?" He looks up at me with hopeful eyes.

"Yes, actually. You know the cosmetics brand you purchased?"

"Nkd by Nature?"

"Yes."

"I should have told you, Violet, but I'm actually selling it. Negotiations are already underway."

Oh, well, isn't that just peachy?

"Right." That's that then.

"Anywhere else?"

"Nope."

"Okay, well, give it some thought, and let's have dinner after all the gym sites are finished." He points back at the gym. "Then you are going to go on vacation, young lady. No arguments. And when you come back, you can move to whichever department you want."

Trying to stay positive, I focus on the vacation part of his offer. "Sounds good," I say with a half-heavy heart. I really wanted to work for Nkd by Nature. I need something, anything, to break up the monotony of my current role. The other half of my heart sighs with relief; I'm finally going to have a vacation for the first time in years. Except who will I go with if Lincoln is gone?

Maybe I should spend it overseas. I can do that as my passport is up to date, or there is always Hawaii; I've always wanted to go, or perhaps Cancún. Riviera Maya is supposed to be incredible. I could always surprise Lincoln in Scotland. Forget that. No one ever comes back from a British vacation and says the weather was great. I'm not sure my Californian bones would survive the cold.

And would Lincoln mind if I visited him?

I'm jumping the gun.

It's only been a week since we met. Is it really only a week? It seems longer.

"Violet?" My father's voice makes me jump.

"Sorry. What were you saying?"

"We're not expecting a lawsuit, are we?"

I screw up my face in confusion.

"With Lincoln," my dad blurts out.

"Oh God, no."

"You fired him?" He shakes his head again in amusement. "He must like you if he stuck around."

"I think he does."

You feel like the part of me that's been missing. His words, after the first time we had sex, spiral through my thoughts.

"Right. I need to go." He checks the time on the digital screen of his car.

"Before you run off. Did you tell Francesca she could buy the beach house?"

"Your house?" His lips hitch up in an Elvis curl and he frowns.

"It's not my house, Dad, it's yours."

"No, never. Why? Is that what she said?"

I sigh.

He reaches out for me to take his hand. "That house is yours and Pom-pom's until the end of time. She's not getting your house, sweetheart. Also, there is not a hope in hell Richard could afford it." He scoffs. "That girl is a dreamer and an opportunist."

I knew she was lying.

He winks. "We'll catch up later, okay? Call me when you leave the architect's. I want to know what they have to say. Take no bullshit from them today and demand they redo the plans within the next twenty-four hours at their expense or we take our business elsewhere."

"That was already my plan."

"That's my girl." He slips his sunglasses back on. "He had some great ideas." My dad nods his head at Lincoln, who has just stepped out of the building holding all the neatly folded plans and my black leather purse. "I might steal him from you.

We could use another analytical and practical mind in acquisitions. You sure he's only here for another few weeks?"

"Yeah." Bile rises in my throat.

"Shame."

"I know."

26

LINCOLN

Since my dad texted me twenty-eight days ago, those days have zipped by in a flash. Violet and I have spent every day together, and every night wrapped up in each other's arms. We've become inseparable and I've practically moved in with her.

Our days begin with me fetching her coffee, sorting out her schedule for the day, walking Pom-pom, and making sure she eats.

I've basically been Violet's right-hand man. Anything she needs, I do it. During the day, Violet is a badass. She knows how to motivate people and get the job done. She whipped the architects into shape and she had new updated plans couriered to her by midnight that same night.

Since then she's been checking and triple-checking emails, plans, paperwork, spreadsheets. She is going to run herself into the ground if she's not careful.

My dad and the rest of the motley crew will be here in less than two hours.

I haven't told Violet they are coming. I didn't want her overthinking their impending arrival. She's a little twitchy where family is concerned as I don't think she had the best childhood before she moved in with her father. My father built me a house at the bottom of the garden of his estate many years ago and it's perfect because my family can drop in all the time. But what I wouldn't give to have a mom who lived in the same town as me. My *yaya*'s hugs were always the best when I was growing up. She used to call me the cuddle monster because I clung to her. Thinking about it now, I'm guessing, subliminally, I missed having a mother in my life, and that's why I loved staying with her. Admittedly, she still gives the best hugs.

"Who are you texting now?" Violet rolls her naked body on top of me, and I place my phone, facedown, on the nightstand.

"None of your business, Mrs. Noseypants." I bop her nose.

"You've been glued to that thing for days."

"I know. I've had a few emails to sort out back home for my return." It's not that. My dad got Wi-Fi on the plane and that was him texting to say they were on schedule and they would see me at the hotel.

I run my hands up the soft skin of her cinched waist when she straddles her legs on either side of me.

She looks sad when I mention the word "home." I can't even bear to think about it anymore. I never want to leave her.

"Will you fit inside my suitcase so you can come back with me?"

"Funny you should mention that because as soon as Urban Soul Studios have their opening day tomorrow, I have been instructed by my father that I am to take a vacation."

Making it very difficult for me to concentrate, she rubs her pussy against my now-hard cock. "So, Mr. Black, I thought, after tomorrow, I would take the next couple of weeks off so we can spend your final two weeks together, and then maybe once you're settled back in Scotland, I could come and visit you for three weeks."

A lump forms in my throat. *She's coming to visit me in Scotland.* I'm like a puppy with a new toy. "I would love that."

"Me too." Her eyes suddenly become glazed. "I don't want you to go." Her voice cracks.

Dread rolls into the pit of my stomach and the words I want to say get stuck in my throat. Every part of me wants to stay with her, glued in her arms forever, because nothing and no one has ever made me feel this happy before. No one has ever made me feel like I belong to them, but she does. She is my missing piece, and she fits perfectly into my heart.

Instead, I wrap myself around her and turn her over onto her back, kissing her with every part of my being, pouring my feelings into her through her skin.

She spreads her legs wide for me, letting me know she needs me. Wants me.

All the blood rushes to my cock, making me thicker and longer just for her.

I slide into her wet core and she moans as I drive myself slowly in and out.

Unlike all the other times we've had sex, this is different. There's no rush or urgency and we aren't strangers anymore. This is us, connecting on a new level where neither of us has ever been before.

Our eyes fuse as I continue to gyrate my hips, then stop and hold myself deep inside of her.

For me, in the past, sex has been just that, sex. Nothing more and nothing less. A means to get a release, but this is not anything like I've ever experienced before. It makes my heart bloom in my chest.

It's not a feeling I'm familiar with as she stares deep into my eyes. For a moment, time stops; she holds her breath, and I know this is it. She's my person.

The one.

Her hands find mine and she entwines our fingers. I push her arms above her head and squeeze her hands tight against the mattress.

I never want to let her go.

I begin to move again, and she lets out a small whimper as I slide my throbbing cock leisurely in and out. Her eyes never leave mine. They magnetize us to one another as we cross an intangible milestone.

The surrounding air becomes thick with lust and our unspoken words.

I work my hips, aligning my pelvic bone with her clit and in infinitesimal movements, hit her delectable spot deep inside that I know drives her to a point of no return. I don't even care if I come; I want to make sure all her needs are met, and I'm the one to give it to her, because I think I've fallen in love with her, and I want her to feel it. Hope she does.

Violet takes a deep breath and then lets out short, quick moans. It's not her usual feral noises she makes when we fuck each other hard; it's sweet and soft and fucking addictive.

I tilt my hips and push in even further.

Unblinking, as if not knowing what is happening, she comes, and it's so fucking beautiful.

Her warm walls flutter around my cock, contracting in such a gentle way, my balls tighten up close to my body, and the deep intensity of her stare is my undoing as I come too, spilling inside her.

I want to prolong this level of intimacy with her forever.

Like I've run a marathon, I breathe deep, my chest heaving.

It's the most pure and honest orgasm I have ever had. Just pure love.

Her eyes well up and a small tear escapes.

She blows my chest wide open with her next words. "I love you, Linc."

The words I want to say in reply get stuck and I can't say them back because it's all too much. Too real and so unfair.

I can't be in love with someone who lives an entire ocean away from me.

I already feel heartbroken.

Instead, I bow down and kiss her, and I know I probably just fucking broke her heart too.

27

LINCOLN

"Where are you going again?" Violet asks as I jump into my car, very aware that I'm currently coming across as a fucking douche canoe.

The evidence of a heartbroken woman standing in her doorway, holding her miniature dog, questioning my every move, proves exactly that. After we both had a shower—in complete silence, I might add—she said things like...

Who are you having lunch with?

No, it's fine if you go.

You don't have to come back.

You don't have to stay the night.

Don't bother coming here later. I have plans with my friends.

When I know she doesn't.

I messed up.

And to add to my shitty behavior, I am now leaving her, straight after she told me she loved me, as I'm about to meet my family, who I wanted to surprise Violet with.

Meeting my raucous family in an all-at-once, impromptu, surprise, get it over and done with, is what she needs—no buildup, just a full-on surprise. *Here's my family.* Or she'd be fretting over what to wear and question her hair and ask me several hundred questions about them and if they will like her or not.

It's a big fat yes.

They will love her.

Like I do.

Just say the words, Linc.

"I am going back to the hotel to pick up Rio's keys for his house. I forgot to give them to him when I moved out, and then I am meeting Rio for lunch so we can catch up," I lie.

"So, you're going to the hotel first?"

"Yes, Violet. You can track me on your phone?" I try to tease. She doesn't laugh.

My phone dings and I check the screen.

DAD

We're twenty minutes from the hotel.

ME

Just leaving Violet's.

Violet eyes me suspiciously. She looks gorgeous in a little lilac summer dress and she's waved her hair today. No make-up needed. She's pure perfection.

"I'll see you tonight," I call out to her through my lowered window, but she shouts back:

"Don't bother. I'll see you tomorrow." Her front door slams shut.

"Shit," I hiss and slam the palm of my hand against the steering wheel then I drop my dad a text.

ME

What does love feel like?

DAD

I'm jet-lagged. Have a very grumpy eighteen-month-old daughter and two small boys who need to be peeled from the ceiling because they are excited to see you and that's what you go with?

ME

Yes.

My dad moans about having three young kids now, but he secretly loves it. Eva and the children run circles around him, but he would also do anything for them all, and me.

DAD

Okay, I'll give it my best shot...

DAD

When all you can think about is them. That it doesn't matter if they do something silly or stupid, you simply like them for being them. You can't wait to go home to them. Your heart feels like it is going to explode when they smile. When all you want to do is spend every minute of every hour of every day with them. They make you feel better. They feel like it's what you've been searching for, and you finally find them. And you don't mind sharing your food with them.

That's exactly how I feel, but I think I've blown it.

DAD

The jury's still out on the last one.

ME

Thanks for that.

DAD

Now get your ass to the hotel before I have to
medicate the boys.

I let out a chuckle, then reverse out of Violet's driveway. I'm
fucking coming back here later whether or not she likes it
because once my family has settled in, freshened up, and have
rested, she's meeting them later for dinner; she just doesn't know
it yet.

28

VIOLET

I peek out of the window, paying attention to what direction Lincoln drives in, and as soon as he's out of sight, I push my feet into my sandals and jump into my car with Pom-pom.

He's lying. He's not meeting Rio today because Rio is currently at the gym doing all the last-minute prep for tomorrow's opening.

I know a quicker way to his hotel and when I pull out of my drive, I head in the opposite direction he went in.

What is he hiding?

He must take me for a fool.

What was I thinking, telling him I love him? I've never said those words to any other man before, and then he didn't say them back, and then he left.

I let out a frustrated huff through clenched teeth.

I'm embarrassed that I told him.

But the way he looked at me as we made love—because that's what we did—it was the most incredible thing I have experienced. I thought he was going to say it too.

And then boom... *Titanic* meets iceberg-style catastrophe.

I pull up in the hotel parking lot and find the farthest spot away so he won't see my car. From where I parked, I have the perfect view of the entrance.

No sooner have I arrived than Lincoln pulls in.

He bounces out of his car, looking giddy. And runs straight into the arms of a tall, blonde gazelle, er, I mean, woman holding a beautiful baby.

My pulse beats faster than a two-step beat and my hand finds my chest.

I can't breathe as I watch Lincoln scoop the baby out of her arms, spinning her around before he kisses her chubby cheeks.

Two little boys appear by their side, almost tackling him to the ground as they throw their tiny arms around his legs and waist.

My blood boils hotter than the sun in my veins as a realization dawns on me and it all makes perfect sense.

I grab Pom-pom and fly out of my car, slamming the door behind me, and stomp over to Lincoln.

Let the battle commence.

29

LINCOLN

"I can't believe you're here." I give Eva a quick hug and pull Thea out of her arms. My baby sister grants me a huge smile as I spin her around and she lets out a high-pitched squeal. Her green eyes are even more emerald than I remember. She's so cute with her little blonde pigtails. She's adorable and could be a lot of trouble for me as she gets older. I may turn into the Hulk if a boy comes anywhere near her.

"I've missed you, little one." I give her chubby cheeks a kiss.

"Everyone else is checking in. It's carnage in there, so I came out here for some fresh air." Eva scrunches her nose up and pulls her statement green fedora hat down to protect her face from the high sun. "Traveling with three kids was a challenge. Oh, and then of course my sisters' four, too. Not great."

"Lincoln!" Archie and Hamish scream with excitement and when I bend down, they almost bowl me over.

"Look how big you've gotten."

They both throw their arms around me and Thea.

"I've missed you both."

"I've missed you too," Archie whispers back, melting my heart.

"I miss the sandcastle competitions." Hamish leans out of our hug and smiles. "Your boo-boo is all better." He points at my forehead.

"Like magic, Hamish."

"We have a present for you." Archie pulls something from his pocket. "Close your eyes."

I clench my eyes tight.

"Now open." Cupped in Archie's two hands is a gray-colored heart-shaped rock.

"Is that for me?" I choke up.

Archie and Hamish bounce their heads enthusiastically. "We found it on the beach."

"It's to show you we love you, Linc, and we missed you." Hamish throws his little arms around me again. "Are you coming home with us?"

"I am." I gaze up at Eva. "Thank you."

"They seem to like you for some reason." Her eyes are now glassy.

I take the heart rock from Archie's hand. "I will treasure this forever."

"Promise?" Hamish's big brown eyes look at me.

"Promise." I clench the stone tight.

"Can I look after it for you, just for now?" Archie's crystal-blue eyes are full of hope.

"Yes, please. Put it in your pocket and I will get it later. Thank you."

Trying to pull myself back together, I ask Eva, "How was the flig—"

"Eh, excuse me, Mrs. Black, is it?" Violet's sweet American voice interrupts us and I shoot up to my full height.

What the hell is she doing here? She looks mad. Crazed, even, as she places Pom-pom on the ground.

"Yes," Eva replies.

I don't get the chance to introduce Eva as Violet jumps in, "Did you know your husband has been sleeping with me for the past thirty days? Not that I've been counting or anything."

Yes, she has.

But wait... "What?" Eva and I both shriek at the same time.

"I like sleeping. I'm tired, Mommy." Hamish yawns.

It suddenly dawns on me; she thinks Eva is my wife.

I feel my face paling. "Oh no, Vio—"

"Don't you dare speak to me, ever again." An angry blotchy-looking rash forms on the bronzed skin of her chest.

I pass Thea back to Eva.

Violet looks so upset. "You've been lying to me this whole time," she says, her words sounding pained. "You said that I was your missing piece. And now I know why I've never been back to your hotel. Because you have a secret family. I've been such a fool." She sucks in a breath. I think she's on the verge of tears. This isn't good. My poor girl thinks I cheated on her, have lied, and I'm married.

"Is that a real doggie?" Archie asks and plays with Pom-pom.

"It's very cute," Hamish tweets. "Does it belong to the crazy lady? She talks funny."

"Hamish, be quiet," Eva scorns.

"Don't come near me." Violet raises her hand to stop me as I try walking to her. "You have a family, and all the things you told me about how beautiful I was..." She looks directly at Eva. "I knew you were lying. I look nothing like her."

"No, you don't. She's not my type." I take a slow step forward.

She shakes her head. "You are disgusting and why is your wife not upset?"

"Because I'm not his wife," Eva says from behind me.

"What?" Violet looks like a deer caught in the headlights.

"I'm not her husband."

"I am." The voice of my father suddenly appears. I haven't seen him in months, but I don't turn around to greet him. I need to calm Violet down and reassure her.

"Those two rascals are mine." I can only imagine my dad is pointing at Hamish and Archie. "As is the blonde terror in Eva's arms and Eva, here, is my wife. And the big lump in front of you..." He must point to me last. "Is also mine. Eva is Lincoln's stepmom."

"Shit," she mutters under her breath, her face turning a bright raspberry color.

"Surprise." I try to lighten the mood, but I'm nervous she might knee me in the balls.

"But you didn't tell me you loved me today when I told you. You left, and I thought..."

What a fuck-up.

"Violet, look at me."

When she does, she's chewing the side of her mouth.

"I didn't tell you I loved you this morning because I was stupid, a complete idiot." I don't take my eyes off her pretty face. I pluck up the courage to tell her how I feel. "But I am scared. I've never been in love before and I usually mess everything up." I point to my family. "Case in point, like this now." I cup her face. "I wanted to say those words to you so badly, but I couldn't get them out. You scare me and the distance thing scares me too. I don't want to ever not be with you, but in two weeks' time, everything changes, and I don't get the choice to stay. It's completely out of my hands. I'm the guy who fixes everything, but the ocean between us? I can't solve that." I take a deep breath in. "I love you, Violet, *your-mom-should-have-called-you-Susan*, West."

She snorts. "You heard that?"

"I heard that and I wouldn't change your name for the world because I love it. I love you." I bend down to kiss her.

"I love you too, Lincoln, *your-dad-has-a-crap-surname-and-makes-me-sound-like-a-color-palette-if-we-get-married*, Black."

Against her lips, I smile.

"Eww, Lincoln is kissing the crazy girl that speaks funny," Hamish says, drawing out his words as if disgusted.

A cacophony of laughter breaks out.

I give Violet another kiss, then take her hand in mine, and when we fully face my family, we find Eva fanning her face. "I feel teary; that was beautiful."

"I think I need to pump some iron or chop some wood because I've come over all emotional too." My dad pretends to dab his eyes, making us giggle.

"Oh my God, what is wrong with you two? Can you not try to be normal for once?" I look at Eva then my dad and they shake their heads.

"We'll give you two a minute." Eva lifts Pom-pom into her arms.

They all start chatting among themselves and coo over Pom-pom.

I lean into Violet. "I should have told you they were coming. I'm sorry. But my family is a lot to get used to. They have enormous personalities and collectively they are, the only word for it is, *extra*."

She smirks. "Oh, I don't know. Your wife seems nice."

I squeeze her waist.

"A little heads-up on that would have been good, Lincoln," she says and steals a gaze at my family. "When you said you had brothers and a sister, I thought they were older."

"If I was to tell you my sister is almost three decades younger than me, it would sound weird, but when you see my dad, Eva, and the kids together, it's not. It was easier to show you than tell you."

"That makes sense. They look incredibly happy together."

I bring her up to speed. "Hamish and Archie are from Eva's first marriage, but the boys don't see their father. And Thea is my dad and Eva's."

"Blended family." She continues to gaze at them.

"And Eva has two sisters. She's a triplet. And their husbands and children are all here too."

"Wow."

"I've made such a fool of myself."

"No, you didn't. It was very Violet." She hides her face in my chest and I hold on to her tighter. "I would never cheat on you, Petal. Never."

"I'm sorry I doubted you," she says, her words muffled.

I kiss the top of her head. "The reason we have never stayed over at the hotel is because your whole life is at your house. It's your home. Your clothes, office, files, stationery cabinet."

She laughs.

"Me, I am currently living out of a suitcase, plus you have Pom-pom, *and* you live near the beach. It made sense for me to stay over at your place."

"It was a stupid thing to say."

"It wasn't. It's okay to have doubts. You haven't been here, and we have only been dating for thirty days. Have you been counting?"

"Maybe," she mumbles as if she's embarrassed.

"We'll chat later about the distance thing, okay? We will work it out."

"I'd like that."

I kiss Violet again before leaning out of our embrace.

"Can I interrupt?" My dad walks to me, and Violet moves away to find herself in Eva's arms. Eva tells her to forget whatever happened before asking her about Pom-pom.

"Christ, I've missed you so much." His eyes become glazed, then he wraps me in a tight, fierce bear hug.

I choke up and pat his back. "Me too," is all I can say.

He clasps either side of my face. "Violet is beautiful."

"I know." I look over at Violet, who is now crouched down, deep in a conversation with Hamish and Archie about Pom-pom. Poor dog won't know what's hit him these next two weeks. Those boys already think he's a toy.

My dad's eyes glint with amusement. "So you went for a strong, confident, outspoken woman, then? Because we don't have enough feisty females in this family already." My dad punches the top of my arm. "You're a glutton for punishment."

I am where my heart is concerned.

I hope I'm not setting us up for a fall somehow.

No matter what happens between me and Violet, I'm sure a swift kick to the nuts would be less painful than the thought of leaving her in two weeks' time.

Fourteen days.

30

VIOLET

After our wonderful dinner in the hotel restaurant, we're now having evening drinks on the rooftop patio of the presidential suite.

Lincoln's father has booked the whole top floor for the family for two weeks.

When Lincoln showed me around the place, I may have dropped more than a few *wows* and I'm pretty sure at one point Lincoln had to lift my jaw off the marble floor when I walked into the bathroom and saw the floor-to-ceiling window that looks out over the entire city. "I've had such a lovely evening." I sigh, resting my back against the enormous semicircle outdoor sofa as I stare at the stunning view across my hometown and take a sip of my crisp white wine.

"Me too." Lincoln lays his hands on my exposed thigh.

I like that I didn't have to go back to my house to change or put make-up on. This family is all about keeping it real and being natural around each other.

I really like them.

Eva's sister Eden and her husband, Hunter, have triplet boys while Ella, her other sister, and her husband, Fraser, have one boy, and they've made me feel incredibly welcome tonight, like I am already part of the family.

With the atmosphere combined with Lincoln's incredibly loving family, it's as if I've been wrapped up in an enormous hug this evening. My own family doesn't hold a candle to this one.

Lincoln gives my leg a quick squeeze and then heads off to sit beside his father on the other side of the sofa.

Curling my knee underneath me, I turn to speak to Hunter King; he's a famous pro golfer and originally from the US. I've seen him on billboards, advertising men's underwear, and on the television, but he's even more handsome up close, and he's cut. Very, *very* cut.

"Was moving from America to Scotland a big decision for you, Hunter?" I ask.

He looks over at his adorably cute wife and smiles. "Never. I just knew. The great thing about my job is that it allows me to stay anywhere in the world because we travel so much and it makes no difference where my base is."

"Yeah, I can't do that," I mumble under my breath, then take a long sip of wine.

"What do you do?"

"I work for my father as an operations manager. All of my work is based in the US."

"Ah. So that could be a problem if you wanted to, say, move to Scotland, for instance?" He gives me a knowing look.

"Yeah." I glance over at Lincoln, who's deep in conversation with his father.

Hunter stretches his long legs out in front of him and crosses them at the ankles. "Before Eden and I got married and had kids, Eden's mother once told her this great story about how you don't have to see or know your final destination. You only have to take one junction at a time. A bit like traveling, you never know what you will find when you do." He looks from Lincoln to me, then back again. "She was right."

What a wise woman. "What do you love most about living in Scotland?" I take another sip of wine and place my glass on the table.

"They use the word 'shag' a lot. It's a great word." He smiles. *"Fancy a shag; want to shag; let's have a shag; they are shagging."*

I almost snort my wine through my nose.

He adds, "And I like how excited they get about a cup of tea, especially in the morning and..." Hunter looks across at his half-asleep wife. "Eden is there, and my boys. I wouldn't change the four of them for the world."

"Do you miss America?"

"I did in the beginning. But I don't anymore. Even if I did, it's only twelve hours on a flight."

"Twelve hours?"

"Trust me, I know. We did that with seven kids." He shakes his head. "And we have to return home. Maybe we should leave them all here. Or I will go home separately." I think he's seriously considering that as an option.

Twelve hours.

That's a lot of distance between Lincoln and me.

Could we make it work?

31

LINCOLN

"You'd like to find your mother, Linc?"

"I've been thinking about it," I say, trying not to sound nervous.

"If that's what you want to do, I won't stop you." My father frowns.

In the pit of my stomach lies a little boy who's all curled up and is not prepared if his long-lost mother rejects him again.

"What if she doesn't want to be found?" *And what if she doesn't like me?*

His expression softens. "You won't know if you don't try."

I evade his sad stare and quietly say, "If she'd wanted to know me, I think she would have contacted me by now. Don't you?"

"Linc, you know I can't answer that without sounding biased." He sighs. "Part of me wants to tell you maybe she's changed and the other half of me wants to tell you to prepare yourself for heartbreak."

I've thought about that myself.

"What if she's dead?" I don't want to think about that as an option.

A shadow of dismay crosses his face. "I never thought about that."

We both go quiet.

My dad finally breaks our silence. "Do you want me to help find her?"

"I think I need to do this myself. I'm still undecided."

"Well, Linc, if you decide to trace your mother, please tell me. Don't keep any secrets from me because I am always here for you, regardless of the outcome. If you want to have a relationship with her, then I will fully support you, and if the opposite of that transpires…" He doesn't finish his sentence.

Yeah, I don't want to think about that either. I do, however, have a big decision to make; do I want to find her?

"Thanks, Dad."

"Whatever you decide to do, you have us. Eva, me, your brothers and sister, we will stand by you."

My dad is a man of his word. I know they will.

"Do you need any information from me about your mom?"

I take a deep breath in. "I have everything I need if I want to make a start and Violet found me an agency in the UK who finds lost relatives."

"Did she?" He looks over at Violet. "She must really care about you."

"She loves me." Wow, saying that out loud freaks me out somewhat. "I'm very lovable," I joke, brushing off how much those three little words have changed everything between us.

"It will all work out, Lincoln."

"Will it, though?"

"If it's meant to be, it will."

"And how do you know if it's meant to be?" This is all new to me. I've never wanted to make it work with a girl before and now I have this incredible woman in my life and I don't know what to do or how to solve our distance problem.

My dad clears his throat but doesn't answer my question. "Can I ask *you* something? And you have to answer me honestly." My dad takes a sip of his beer.

I bob my head.

He licks his lips. "Do you still want to work at the hotel? Is it what you want to do for the rest of your life?"

"What?" He should have slapped me across the face. I think that would have been less painful. "Yes. Always. Never ask me that again."

He holds his hands up in surrender. "I just thought, maybe, *if* you wanted to move here, permanently—" His eyes focus intently on Violet across the rooftop terrace.

"Don't say it." I cut him off.

"Then I wouldn't stop you." He finishes his sentence anyway.

"Seriously?" I'm angrier than I need to be. I feel like he's pushing me away.

"Don't be mad at me, Linc. I'm setting you free. That's if you want to be. The hotel will be there for years to come. But she..." He looks at Violet again. "Won't wait forever." He stands from his chair and pats my shoulder. "Think about it."

I don't know how long I sit there, but Violet appears next to me and breaks my jumbled thoughts. "Everything okay?" The touch of her hand against mine soothes me.

"Yeah." I pull her sideways onto my lap and loop my arms around her waist.

I don't mention what my dad said about me leaving the hotel, and instead, I say, "I was asking if he was okay with me tracing my mom. He said he was."

"Oh, that's great, Lincoln."

"I haven't decided yet."

"You don't have to. Fate and destiny will do its job."

"Like it did for us?"

"Just like us." She wiggles her bountiful ass against my clothed cock.

I hold her hips still. "Not here."

She bites her lip seductively. "I enjoy teasing you."

"I know you do."

The soft thrum of a piano from John Legend's "All of Me" tinkles through the outdoor speakers. Automatically, and no words needed, the three couples I love and adore most in the world rise to their feet, couple up, and sway together. Each is lost in their own little bubble as they hold each other close, whispering sweet nothings to one another.

Violet watches them with fascination. "What are they doing?"

"Dancing."

"I know that." She swats my hand playfully. "But why?"

"This is what they do: food, drinks, banter, and the night always ends with them dancing. They love each other." The sight of the three happy couples is inspiring. "I normally leave now or I dance with the kids if they are still up."

A sudden look of emotion passes across her face. "You have me now." She slips off my lap and pulls me to my feet. "Dance with me, Lincoln Black."

We huddle together, swaying, understanding all the lyrics to the love song playing across the airwaves.

The fierce and dynamic woman is so small and delicate in my arms and, with no shoes on, she's shorter than normal.

My father looks over Eva's shoulder and winks at me.

He knows.

I do too.

I want to do this with Violet forever.

32

LINCOLN

I look down at Violet kneeling on the floor of the shower as she fucks my cock between her huge breasts.

My heart is about to fucking explode, as is my hard dick.

"You're so hard for me, Lincoln, and I'm so wet for you."

Plus, there is the fucking dirty talk. My sweet-mouthed girl has become a dirty talker as she's become more confident and comfortable with me.

"Fuck my tits, Linc." She squeezes her soap-covered boobs together and sucks my crown into her expert pouty mouth with every hip thrust.

"I fucking love your mouth on me." She's like a drug I can't get enough of.

The warm water splashes over her body, making the perfect lubricated tunnel for me to fuck.

Her deep and hypnotic, pure sex-filled eyes look up at me, and that's it; I'm done for.

My hands cover hers, squeezing them together, and I fuck her tits faster, chasing my climax.

"Oh fuck, I'm coming," I roar, my eyes rolling back, my blood pumping hot through my veins. I blow my load, coating her chest with my cum.

I'm almost paralyzed by pleasure and when I finally open my eyes, Violet has risen to her feet and is now standing in front of me.

She smiles and then slants her mouth over mine and I don't care that I can taste myself. I'd do anything with this woman who has me by the balls, figuratively speaking.

"You need to wash me now."

"That's all we are doing. I can't fuck in the shower. Shower sex is shit."

"No one said anything about fucking. There are other things we can do." She pulls her pink vibrator wand down off the shelf and passes it to me.

"This"—I hold it up—"is going to be your new BFF for the next couple of weeks until you come to Scotland and when you use it, I want a video call. No fucking questions asked. Doesn't matter what time of day it is. Call me. I want to watch." I wiggle my eyebrows.

Violet washes the remnants of my orgasm off her chest, then turns her attention to my dick, making me hard again.

I leave tomorrow evening. I shipped my car back today too, so that was another thing off the list. So much shit to do before it can be made road legal in the UK, but that's not my concern anymore. It's in the safe hands of the shipping company who are car export specialists.

The last two weeks have gone too quickly, but we've created memories together I will remember forever, with her and with my family.

I only have two weeks to wait for her to visit me in Scotland. Her flights are booked and an odd peacefulness at knowing I'll be seeing her again settles over me.

We belong together and I can't remember a time now when I didn't love her.

We've agreed to take turns visiting each other because we were overthinking it all, but it's really not that complicated. I will miss her so much, but we are going to see how the first year goes and take it from there.

I spoke to my dad and we've agreed that we could take on a new manager. Another version of me, basically, so I can have time off when I want to. And Violet spoke to her father and now she is getting an assistant who will become her mini-me too.

We might actually make this work.

"Turn around," I instruct her. She never needs to be asked twice.

"Switch it on, Linc." She's almost fucking panting when she wiggles her ass against my thick cock.

She spreads her legs wide and braces herself against the tiled shower wall.

"Fuck, you are a sight for sore eyes." I spank her ass and she gasps. I do it again a few times. My hand makes her round ass pink up nicely. I smooth my hand over her soft skin to soothe it.

I switch the wand on and press it gently against her inner thigh at first and move it slowly to her pussy, which I know without even touching her will be fucking soaked.

She gasps and throws her head back against my chest when I press the wand over her tender bud.

"Make me come."

"Fast or slow, Petal?" I whisper against the shell of her ear.

"Fast." She gyrates her hips.

With my other hand, I part her lips and rub the wand down to her wet pussy and move it back up, coating her clit with her own arousal.

"Press it harder, Linc." Her hips move faster.

Fuck, I love this woman.

I grab her hip, rub her clit harder with the vibrating wand, and, without warning, slam my hard cock inside of her, making her cry out a ramble of unintelligible words.

If she wants it fast and hard, she's getting fast and hard.

I jackhammer myself with punishing thrusts. My balls slap off her wet pussy as I bury my cock deep inside her.

Pleasure begins to pool in my balls.

The water splashes all around us and the sounds of our pleasure fill the air.

Her hand covers mine, pushing the wand even harder against her clit, and within seconds she lets out an almighty cry and comes all over my cock, taking me with her.

My fingertips dig into her hips as I unforgivingly jerk myself into her. Our gasps and groans echo together as we both lose control.

I kiss her shoulder and wrap my arms around waist.

"Yeah, shower sex is totally shit." She gets her words out before tilting her head back in laughter. Her smile is fucking hypnotizing.

I let out a deep, heartfelt laugh. "We need to get ready."

She groans. "Do we have to?"

"It was your idea."

"It was a stupid one."

I slide myself out of her and slap her ass one last time for good measure. "C'mon, shower, get dressed, dinner with your father and his new girlfriend, my dad and Eva, then home. I want to do more stuff with you." I tickle her sides. "Then tomorrow is our last day together."

"Don't say any more or I will cry."

"You won't cry. You are seeing me again in two weeks."

"I will not cry," she affirms to herself. "I will not cry."

I have a better affirmation for her. "You will take Lincoln's cock like a good girl at least twenty times before he leaves."

She spins around with a soap-covered face. "Twenty? I was thinking more like thirty."

I burst out laughing.

Violet West, the dick destroyer.

33

LINCOLN

"Sorry we are late; we sort of got waylaid." I push Violet's dining chair into the table and take the seat next to her.

"Or just laid," my dad mumbles under his breath.

He knows me so well.

My dad's Greek skin is so dark. He's caught up with me on the tanning.

"It's not like my dad to be late." Violet checks the time on her phone.

"Maybe he's waylaid too?" I josh.

She screws her face up. "Oh wow, no, I don't want to have that vision of him and Viva. Thank you."

"This is a cool place," I say, making everyone look around. It's a giant glass box that suspends over the cliffs. "We should do this." I lock eyes with my dad. "Fish restaurant. Suspended above the cliffs with the wild North Sea below?"

"I'm all for that." My dad looks excited.

"Let's do it. Better than this, though," I whisper. "Fish-tank walls. Low-level lighting."

"Long nights, I won't see you, you'll be grumpy. Sounds great." Eva smiles. I know she is only joking, but she's not wrong. When Dad throws himself into a project, he gives it one hundred and ten percent.

"Done," my dad decides.

"Is that how quickly you guys decide?" Violet looks shocked.

"Pretty much." My dad takes a sip of his water.

"We have to draft plans first, obviously, and take it to the board, work out the budget, but I guarantee they'll agree because there is nothing like it in the area. We own the surrounding ten miles of field one way and then thirty miles on the other. The hotel sits high on the cliffs. This would be awesome to do." I feel excitement bubbling in my chest.

"Sounds like fun," Violet tweets. I love her accent. I can't get enough of her or of that.

"It is. I do all the refurbs." I take a sip of water too.

"That will be a great project to work on. Oh, here's my dad now." Violet rises to her feet, and we all join her.

Violet's father strides in, apologizing with a giant smile on his face. "I'm sorry we are late. Viva had to return her two sons to their father's first. She's just visiting the ladies' room." He kisses Violet on the cheek.

"Dad, this is Knox, Lincoln's father, and this is Eva, his wife." Violet introduces everyone and they all shake hands. "Knox, Eva, this is my father, Anthony."

"Pleasure to meet you, Anthony." My dad cups his elbow at the same time in a friendly gesture.

"It would seem these two are smitten." Anthony tilts his head in our direction.

"It would appear that way." My dad smiles.

I place a quick peck on Violet's cheek and she snuggles into me. She looks great tonight in a black fitted dress. My girl has dangerous curves. She's spent the last two weeks relaxing with my family and tanning herself; she's so bronzed and she looks like she's glowing.

"Good evening, Lincoln." Anthony shakes my hand. "Going back home tomorrow?"

"Yeah," I say with a heavy heart.

"You'll be back." He winks. "But I will look after her while you're gone."

That's a lie. No one looks after Violet. Not one of her family members has called in two weeks. The only reason we are here is because Violet organized this so our parents could meet each other. If it wasn't for her two friends, Hannah and Ruby, she wouldn't have anyone.

We all settle into our seats, and Anthony is the first to speak. "Now I haven't exactly been truthful with Viva. I said it was just dinner out." He looks like a naughty schoolboy as he tells us. "She shies away from meeting people, especially bigger groups." He looks straight ahead. "Oh, here she is now."

A beautiful, familiar-looking woman walks in our direction. She's looking toward Anthony with a smile on her face. I tilt my head. For the life of me, I can't think where I have seen her before.

My dad and Eva both turn at the same time, and Viva's face falls and turns ashen when she sees my dad and stops dead in her tracks.

"What did you say your girlfriend's name was, Anthony?" my dad asks in a steady voice.

"Viva," he says.

"And would that be a nickname for Olivia?"

My mind is reeling with confusion, and then the penny drops.

"Why, yes," he answers cheerfully.

"Oh, no." I hear Eva's muffled voice.

I stand up faster than I realize, sending my chair flying, and it lands with a loud bang against the floor behind me.

"Mom?"

34

LINCOLN

"This has got to be a joke?" I spit.

The woman standing across from me looks like she's in agony, but not for me, not for my pain, but for hers.

"Did you do this? Is this a setup?" My dad is almost shouting at me when he rises to his feet. "You said if you found her, you would tell me."

"I didn't find her." My heart batters against my chest.

"Did you do this?" I glare at Violet. "Did you know? Have you known her all along?"

She opens her mouth, but no words come out.

"Sorry, what's going on?" Anthony asks, now confused. "Did you say *Mom*?"

Olivia covers her mouth with a shaking hand and mumbles words I can't hear behind her fingers.

"So what is this, then? And why is *she* here?" My father is raging now.

The whole restaurant goes quiet.

"I didn't do this. I promise." My eyes plead with him to calm down.

The manager appears at our table and tries to calm my dad down. "Please, sir, settle down or you'll have to leave."

"Oh, I am leaving, alright." I've never seen him so angry. "I cannot believe this."

Eva rises to her feet. "Knox, calm down."

"I will *not* calm down."

A slight movement from across the restaurant causes me to look over and just as I do, Olivia whirls around on her heel and runs out of the restaurant.

I run after her down the steps. "Wait. Please stop running," I plead.

I'm not expecting her to, but she does, and I stop only a few feet away from her.

My chest is heaving from my sudden sprint to get to her, but it also feels like I'm wearing a compression vest and it's trying to suffocate me.

When she turns, she has tears running down her face, her eyes full of fright, and her cheeks are already blotchy in places.

My mom is here. She's standing in front of me and I can't think of anything to say. What do you say to the woman who left you all those years ago so she could go travel to *find herself*? It's a hard thing to comprehend.

"It's just like you to run away, Olivia. Old habits never die," my father says sardonically as he appears by my side, causing a sob to break from Olivia's throat.

"Dad. Pop a cork in it so we can work out what's going on. Just back off for a minute."

He steps back, but his jaw is twitching. This is so out of character for him.

"Are you okay?" I look at Olivia, softening my gaze, trying to calm her. "I think this is a shock for us all."

I take a small step forward. The startled woman before me is beautiful, and I'd recognize those eyes anywhere. I've stared at that photo of me and my mom thousands of times.

Olivia finally speaks. "What are you doing here?" She's almost inaudible.

"I think that's my question," I say.

"I live here," she says shakily.

She almost doesn't seem real. I made her this big thing in my head, but she's nothing like how I imagined her to be.

She looks lost.

And scared. Like a trapped animal in a cage.

"I've been traveling, and then living in Santa Monica for a few months." I pause for a moment. "I can't believe I've been living in the same city as you." I'm stunned, and hysterical laughter bubbles in my throat. I can't work out if I should laugh or cry.

I explain why I am here tonight. "I'm dating Violet, Anthony's daughter. Violet wanted our parents to meet tonight before we returned home."

"You look so much like your father." Olivia's face is emotionless. Her voice isn't how I imagined, either. It's some weird intercontinental mix of accents. She sounds anything but Scottish.

"I hope that's a good thing." I try to summon a thread of emotion from her, but she doesn't give me anything in exchange.

"Look. I just want to talk. I know this wasn't planned, but could we sit down, maybe?" My heart fills with hope and dread all at the same time. I'm certain I know what she'll say, but my *yaya* always told me we have to remain hopeful if we want good things to happen.

I try taking a step closer, but she steps back, causing my gut to tighten. My hope is clinging on for dear life. It's holding on by its fingertips on the edge of my emotional cliffside, but as she shies away from me, I feel it slipping away into the abyss.

She doesn't want to know me.

"I have to go," she blurts.

Her words confirm my worst fear. "Do you not want to talk?"

"I don't," she stammers.

I shrink back from her.

She would have hurt me less if she'd driven a knife through my heart.

"I'm only here for another day. Can we please meet up? Just to talk."

"I hope you have a safe trip home."

Is that it? *Have a safe trip*? The blood pounds in my temples from sheer humiliation.

My dad finally loses it. "You haven't changed one bit, Olivia. Our son is standing in front of you, asking to speak to you, and you say you have to go. Christ, he even said please." His voice rises. "He's not asking for the moon on a stick. He's asking to speak to you. Just talk. And you can't even do that for him."

My dad keeps going with his verbal attack. "Can you see him in front of you now? Our boy. He's now a man. A good man, with a beautiful heart, not that you have one yourself to know what that's like. But our boy has one. He's smart, funny, caring, but he has demons because of you." He points his finger at Olivia vehemently. "He jokes and makes light of everything in life because all he wants is to be accepted, to be liked because he fears people will reject him. You did that to him. You made him feel like that, Olivia. And he never says how he really feels because he never wants to worry me. But I know. I know him. He's *my* son." He stabs his finger deep into his chest. "Not yours. You don't fucking deserve him." My dad paces. "I have defended you for years. Never once have I name-called or bitched about you, but you've fucking done it now. I won't hold back anymore. You're a pathetic excuse for a mother."

Olivia is sobbing now and my heart breaks for us all, and I want so badly to reach out and touch her, to confirm she's real, but I can't move.

She doesn't want me.

"And did I hear Anthony correctly? You have two other boys?"

My brain must be muddled because that didn't cross my mind. She started a family with someone else.

"You have two sons?" I shout, a savage edge to my voice clear as it echoes around the parking lot. "You have two other sons?" She turns a vivid red. "And do they live with you?" I have so many questions. "And do they even know about me?" Blood boils in my veins.

"I don't want them to find out." Her eyes widen with fear.

"I'm guessing their father doesn't know I exist either?"

She doesn't answer. Instead, she says, "I don't want to do this."

They don't know about me.

She grabs her chest as if she's in pain.

I point at her furiously. "*You* don't want to do this? You don't want *me* to make *you* feel guilty. Is that what you don't want me to do? Do you not want me to make you feel bad for abandoning me as a baby? Did you just think you could forget about me? Do you ever think of me?"

She stays silent.

I don't even register in her thoughts. I never have.

Fury takes over and I can't stop my words. "I realize that you don't care, but you caused so much pain and hurt for me and Dad. I used to wish that I had a mom, like all the other boys in my class, and when they asked me where my mom was, I used to tell them she was on vacation. Because that's what it was. Fucking traveling," I scoff. "I've been traveling, and you and I both know the grass isn't any greener on this side of the pond. It looks like you ran away from a life you didn't want and ended up with the exact same result somewhere else. Kids, house, stuck in the same place, and you don't exactly look to happy about that either. I hope to God you don't emotionally mess your other two sons up too. How old are they?"

"Fifteen and thirteen," she says through tears. "I wanted to make a fresh start," she cries.

"I'm so happy for you." I fake a smile. I didn't think I could feel any worse, but I do now. She's just opened my wound wide and poured salt in.

Olivia says the words I've always dreaded. "I felt trapped with you and your father. That is not the life I wanted." She wipes her nose with the back of her hand. "I didn't want to be stuck in a small town for the rest of my days. I wanted more. I wanted to see the world and make more of myself. Meet people, experience new things, and I could not have done that with a baby. I was seventeen. I was a baby myself and you cried all the time, and the sleepless nights," she grumbles, as if I was a burden. To her I was. "My friends went out partying when I was changing diapers. I wanted to be like them. I didn't want a baby back then." She looks disgusted.

Is this woman for real? She's a lifetime away from anything I ever imagined.

In fact, scratch that; she's fucking rotten to the core.

I can't take it anymore and fire back, "But the difference is you *did* have one. Me. And what I needed was a mom."

"And what I wanted was my freedom," she spits back.

"That's a pathetic excuse. My father was the same age as you and he may have been a boy, but he acted like a man. He stepped up while you fled." I rub my fingers into my temples. My head is thumping.

This is not how I thought the last evening of my trip would end. I wanted to spend a lovely evening with Violet, creating everlasting memories that we would cherish forever.

But this is just a fucking car crash.

I swing around to see if my girl is watching our wrecked reunion, and she is. She's standing next to Eva and her father, her face reflecting the pain I feel.

And she heard everything Olivia had to say. Heard how unhappy she was with me and Dad, so she left but has a new family and she's happy with them.

I'm so embarrassed.

I wasn't enough.

An explosion of pain fills my chest with sorrow.

My face feels wet and when I explore my cheeks with my fingertips, I discover I'm crying. I wipe my face angrily with the back of my hand.

I have to end this. I will not let her decide how we move our relationship forward. "Have it your way. You don't want to know me. That's fine." I suck in a breath. "I am such an idiot. There was a small part of me that believed, maybe, just maybe, you might have wanted to meet me, to find out how I was, what I became, know if I was healthy and well." I feel so stupid.

"And I had this picture-perfect idea of us meeting up, that you would hug me tight, share your stories with me of all you had experienced on your travels, then you'd tell me how sorry you were and I would forgive you for everything, and then we could move forward with our lives and maybe keep in contact." A pang of disappointment hits me with the force of a tsunami. "But you can barely even look at me. You stepped away when I moved closer to you, so I got the memo. You don't want to know me." Fuck, that hurts. I bow my head and my tears fall to the ground.

I add, "But here's the thing. All the shit you left behind. You got dealt the same cards here as back home. You just live in a different town. But it's the same shit. Two kids, a home you probably hate, and an ex-husband to boot. Your life is no different. You didn't change the world or go on to do great things. You became a reflection of everything you didn't want." My chest hurts so much, but I keep going, knowing I need to get it all out.

"I was going to visit an agency back in the UK to see if they could find you for me. Part of me was excited. But after meeting you and the things you've just said, you've made me feel like such a fool." I throw my head back and look up at the now orange and pink sky. "Fuck this and fuck you. You are dead to me." I pull my wallet out of my pocket, angrily remove the photo of me in her arms as a baby, scrunch it up, and throw it on the ground.

I storm off, not knowing where I am going.

"Lincoln," my dad shouts after me and I hear Violet calling my name at the same time.

But I don't look back.

Heels behind me ricochet off the asphalt and grow closer. "Lincoln, please, stop," Violet begs and I stop walking.

Her concerned face appears in front of me. "Please know I didn't do this." Brows wrinkled, she looks worried as hell that I don't believe her.

"I know that now. I'm so sorry." I can't think straight.

She takes my hand in hers. "I am here for you."

For less than a day she is.

Caustic grief cripples me inside at the thought of being without Violet every day. I need her. But a vast expanse of sea will separate us come tomorrow, and what will a few weeks here and there be like? All of this is so overwhelming, and my chest feels heavy, as if I can't breathe.

"I need some time alone, Violet."

"Where will you go?"

"I don't know. I want to be by myself. Just a walk to clear my head, but I will call you later."

Her beautiful face smiles back at me. "I love you, Lincoln."

I nod my head. "I know."

And I fucking love her so much it's unbearable.

She touches the softest of kisses to my lips, but I wrap her in my arms and give her the tightest of hugs.

"I will always love you, Violet." Then I let her go as I struggle to hold myself together, and for the next few hours, I walk around in a daze.

Alone.

35

VIOLET

I haven't been able to get a hold of Lincoln all night or this morning.

I'm on the verge of calling the hospitals.

"Good morning." I tap my fingers nervously against the hotel reception desk and force a smile at the receptionist.

I slide the key card for Lincoln's private hotel room across the black wooden desk.

"You kindly gave me a spare key for room 358 a couple of weeks ago. My boyfriend's father and his family are staying in the presidential suite here, but my key my boyfriend's room doesn't appear to be working this morning."

"Let me just check that for you." The cheerful gentleman picks up my card.

After a few moments, he says, "Ah, yes, Mr. Black checked out in the wee hours of this morning."

Panic climbs my throat and it feels like the devil's claws are scraping along the bottom of my gut.

"I'm sorry, say that again?" I blink a few times. He's got that wrong, surely. His flight doesn't leave until tonight.

"It says here he checked out at three this morning as his flight plans had changed." The receptionist lifts his head and when he sees my face, his smile disappears.

He knows I didn't know he'd left.

I try to remain calm. "Is his family still here?"

"Violet." Someone calls my name from behind me. "He's gone."

I slowly turn around to face the voice I know so well now—the voice that just confirmed my worst fear.

Knox.

He looks tired.

"I couldn't talk him into staying. He made up his mind. I'm so sorry, Violet." Knox holds out his hand for me to take. "Please come with me. We need to talk."

36

LINCOLN

Three weeks, five days, five hours, and thirty-six minutes.

That's how long it's been since I've seen Violet.

Since I've had a full night's sleep.

Since I held her.

Felt her warm skin on mine.

Since I saw her smile.

She's gone AWOL on social media following my departure and the last photo she posted was a selfie of her and me on the beach together. We were so happy and her eyes were sparkling with joy.

Fuck.

I left her.

I'm a fucking dumbass.

I didn't even leave a letter, and I did exactly what my mother did to me. I left without a word, leaving it up to my father to explain.

What a low-life asshole shitty thing to do.

And I can't even bring myself to call her. I don't know what I would say.

"Sorry" will never cut it.

I feel sick to my stomach with the way I have behaved and I've been avoiding my dad and my family because I'm so ashamed of what I did.

I fucking blew it all to hell.

And I miss her.

So fucking much.

I fucking hate goodbyes. So I didn't say it. What the fuck would she want with me? The broken boy rejected by his mother. Twice.

Nobody wants or deserves my fuckery. Violet deserves better. She deserves someone who lives close to her, in the same town —Christ, someone who lives in the same state. But I live in a completely different country.

She deserves more than I can give her.

After the showdown with my mother, I thought I knew best. I thought it would be easier to leave without a backward glance. My mom seemed to manage it just fine.

But I am not her and I have lived with so much regret since leaving Santa Monica.

I fucked up. Big-time.

I don't know what I was thinking.

Clearly, I wasn't, and I still can't think straight.

And now I am back to square one.

Back to feeling like I'm missing something in my life.

And nothing has changed here in Scotland. It's as if I never left.

Everything is the same.

But I have changed.

A sharp pain spears my chest. I've been getting shooting pains since I left Santa Monica. I went to see a doctor about them, but after running a few different tests, he gave me a clean bill of health and sent me on my way. But there is something wrong with me. I feel horrific.

Maybe I need a good home-cooked meal as I've barely eaten in the last few weeks either. I've lost my appetite for everything.

"You look like *skatá*." My *yaya* throws shade my way, telling me I look like shit in Greek.

I hunch myself over her wooden kitchen table. I feel like *skatá*.

"When did you last eat?" Her accent is a mix of Greek and Scottish. It's a fucked-up cocktail.

"*Chthés*." Yesterday.

She flies off the handle, throwing her wooden spoon into a sink full of water, making the soapy water splash everywhere.

Food is a big thing on the Greek side of my family. It's a huge part of our culture. Food for us is about celebrating and, more importantly, it's about family, friends, and socializing. Food for my *yaya* is about her keeping us content, warm, and happy. She feels better when she feeds us, and she sure loves to feed us.

"*Fáe*." Eat. She slams a heaped plate of moussaka in front of me. There is no elegance about her today. She's mad at me. Mad at me for not eating. Mad at me for throwing the love of a good woman away. Mad at me because I didn't speak to her about my predicament.

She's just mad.

She bunches her jet-black hair up on top of her head and wraps it in a bun. Dressed in a simple maroon wraparound dress, as always, she is effortlessly chic. However, it's the first time I have noticed that she's going gray as little white hairs poke out here and there through her dark locks. She's getting older.

She's going to leave me, too.

I dig into my food with a heavy heart. She rambles away to me in superspeed Greek, telling me about her and my grandfather and how it all seemed impossible, but how I am not like him and she's disappointed I didn't fight hard enough for Violet.

I could recite what she is saying to me word for word. She's been saying the same thing to me since I returned from overseas.

While on vacation in Athens, my grandfather fell in love with my *yaya* and he did everything he could to bring her back here to Scotland. He swept her off her feet and literally changed her life.

He promised her mother and father he would look after her and boy, did he do that. She has a bountiful life here. They live in the biggest house in all of Castleview Cove. She has several staff who take care of everything besides the cooking, and my grandfather tells her every day how much he loves her. He's forever leaving love notes for her everywhere. He's such a big soft-hearted soul.

Pulling a chair out from the table, she sits down beside me.

She tells me off for slouching and whacks me across the back of the head with the palm of her hand. She's a stickler for manners.

I pull my shoulders back and sit up straight.

"So what are you doing tonight, huh?" Her nose takes a scornful tilt.

"Going home."

"But it's a Saturday night. Are you not going out with the boys?"

I sigh. "Not tonight."

"Lincoln, my darling boy." I've always loved how she rolls her *R*s when she calls me her darling boy. "What are we going to do with you?" She ruffles my hair.

I shake my head and throw my fork down on the plate. It makes an almighty clatter when it hits the fine china.

"I can't do this." I push the palms of my hands into my eyes as an odd rush of emotion I've been holding in finally breaks the dam. "I feel so lost."

Warm arms envelop me as she pulls me into her chest. "Let it all out, my boy. You have a heart and this is why you feel such true and pure emotion. Just let it all go."

"I don't want to feel like this anymore." I sob in her arms.

"You don't have to hide your pain." She rocks me slowly while I have my breakdown.

Violet was the first person I actually felt like I could be myself around. She didn't care about my flaws and she saw me for who I truly was. I miss the way she kissed me and the way she would hold me.

"I messed everything up."

"You did." My *yaya* is anything but subtle and she's always honest, sometimes too much.

Everything hurts. From my heart to my head, I feel exhausted. The weight of my heart feels too heavy to carry around.

But I only have myself to blame.

It's breaking over the self-inflicted loss of Violet and for losing my mother all over again. It's a double blow of grief I'm not emotionally equipped for. I need therapy.

Or Violet. I need her; she made me feel grounded and whole, a feeling I hadn't truly realized I was missing until I found her.

"Come now. Sit up and look at me." She cradles my face and wipes my wet cheeks.

I force a half smile.

"Stop pretending everything is okay, Lincoln." She pats my cheek twice. "My gorgeous boy. You are so very handsome. Just like your father."

"I'm so glad I don't look like my mom."

"Hey now. Stop that. It took two people to make you and you have her to thank for you being here. Even if she is not here now, part of her will live on in you forever. She is part of you, and you are part of her. You cannot rewrite history or your DNA."

I've never thought about it in that way before.

Although you would never know she was my blood mother after all her inconsiderate and hurtful words said to me weeks ago. I've replayed them every day in my head, looping around like CCTV.

Her eyes light up when she continues in her clipped accent. "You are so very special to us and when you were born, I loved you from the minute you arrived in our lives. When you were a little boy, you made me smile every day, and you thought it was so funny when I muddled up my Greek and Scottish words." She used to make me laugh and say stupid combinations of things that made no sense to me, but then I think she continued doing it on purpose because she knew how much I loved it. "Oh, how all of my friends loved you. You were so cute with those big brown Disney eyes and chocolate-brown hair. You were the most beautiful baby." She pinches my cheek like I am four years old again. "Just don't tell your father I said that."

I'll have great pleasure telling him that.

"Deep down, I am glad your mother left. You know why?"

Her confession is a complete surprise. "Why?"

"Because I am selfish and I got to spend every day with you." She's trying to make me feel better, but I also know she is telling the truth. "You made me feel happy all the time. You filled our lives with so much joy, fun, and laughter. Plus, I am a very possessive woman when it comes to the men in my world."

Her words make my heart seem better.

She tilts her head. "You are loved beyond measure. Your father is a great man. The best mom and dad all rolled into one.

And you know deep in your heart that it was more than you ever needed."

If she's not careful, I will cry again.

"And I know if you and Violet are meant to be together, love will find a way." She winks at me. "So no more carrying on like a zombie." She lets her mouth drop open as if she's making a zombie face.

"That is not an attractive face." I attempt a laugh.

"Exactly, but that's what we've had to look at since you returned. Now you know what we've had to put up with these past few weeks. So eat up. Go home. Sleep, my darling boy, and go to work on Monday. It will get better. I promise. But you come to me when you need to talk. Okay? Okay. That's settled. Eat." She tilts her head to my food. "You look like a skeleton."

I don't. I've done nothing but hit the gym; that's also why my body is sore. Not eating properly and working out relentlessly is not the smartest combination.

Come Monday, I will throw myself back into work.

My job was always my first love. Until Violet.

And as much as it pains me to think, I hope she finds someone who loves her better than I did.

She deserves better than me. Someone who doesn't walk away and someone who can make her happy.

She deserves someone who would fight for her.

But all my fight disappeared.

My tank is empty and even though the talk with my *yaya* has made me feel better, I am exhausted.

For the first time in weeks, I finally feel like I will sleep tonight, not from finding peace, but because I have nothing left.

37

VIOLET

"Goodbye, lovely beach house." I look around the empty space.

I pick up Pom-pom and tuck him under my arm. "Do you want to say goodbye too?" I hold on to Pom-pom's paw and wave it for him.

I've made some big life-changing decisions since Lincoln left Santa Monica almost a month ago. For some of which I am still not sure I have done the right thing.

Like leaving my house.

Selling all my furniture.

And the biggest one of all, changing my job.

My dad and I sat down and had a huge heart-to-heart. He understood where I was coming from. He knew I needed a fresh new challenge, so he helped me find one.

And as for Viva?

She is no longer in my father's life. Thankfully.

He visited her the day after Lincoln's family left, but he said she wasn't exactly forthcoming, and she knew they were over.

And guess what? My father has already moved on to somebody else, girlfriend number eight.

I'm yet to meet her but I'm pretty sure she'll be the *one*.

Hannah and Ruby have been so supportive and have checked in with me every day, especially on the days I couldn't get out of bed when my heart was breaking.

I've missed Lincoln every minute and every hour.

I've longed to reach out to him but I haven't because I have a new life plan.

"C'mon then, little fluff ball, let's go start our new adventure."

I take a deep breath in.

I hope I'm doing the right thing.

38

LINCOLN

"Afternoon." I yawn. It's been three nights since I visited my *yaya* and still sleep evades me.

My head is reeling.

I keep seeing flashes of purple everywhere. From the fresh flowers in reception this morning to the tie my father is currently wearing.

It's just a color, Linc. It doesn't mean anything.

I swear I'm losing my mind.

"Still not sleeping?" my dad asks as I amble into his office.

"Nope." I sit down on his black leather sofa and close my eyes.

A familiar scent that smells a lot like Violet's perfume assaults my nose.

"Well, you had better pull yourself together because we have a staff meeting at four this afternoon. All of the management team will be in the ballroom in an hour."

"Do we?" I pop one eye open.

"Yes. Did you not see the email I sent last night?" He leans against his desk and crosses his legs at his ankles. "You are a complete shit show."

He's right and I've mentally checked out. My dad was supportive at first when I returned to work, but he's losing his patience with me.

"I'm fine. I just need coffee."

Or a double shot of a California girl named Violet.

I pick up a cushion from the sofa and smell it.

"What are you doing?"

"Something smells nice." Like fresh pear and Violet. I'm fucking losing it.

I put the cushion down and pull my heavy frame off the couch. "See you in an hour, then."

"Get your shit together, Linc. And for the love of God, will you shave?"

I run my hands over my face. He's right. I don't suit a long straggly beard and I've not had a haircut or shave in almost four weeks. "I'll go do that now before the meeting."

"Good idea, and maybe brush your hair."

"Do you think Vincent will have time to cut it before our meeting?" I always use our in-house barber. He does the best job, but you have to book weeks in advance. He's very in demand.

"I will call him now and tell him you are on your way. Go."

"Thanks."

"And Linc?"

I turn back. "Yeah?"

"It won't always feel this bad."

"That's easy for you to say. Everything worked out for you and Eva."

"It wasn't always easy, though. Remember when her father broke my nose?"

"How could I forget?" That night was awful.

"But it worked out. Things always have a way of working out."

"You keep saying that, but my girl lives five thousand miles away." So that is never going to happen. "And she's not my girl anymore," I mumble.

"Go," my dad instructs.

I straighten my tie and smooth my suit jacket down.

"Have a good day, Lincoln." He winks at me with a twinkle in his eye.

He's been annoyingly happy since he married Eva.

"Yeah, whatever." I give a one-shoulder shrug and leave his office.

39

LINCOLN

I sneak into the ballroom and take a seat near the back, listening in for a moment to get an idea of what the meeting is about.

I didn't read the email, so I'm unaware of the agenda.

My father is rambling on about plans for the new staff onboarding software, employee responsibility, vacation booking... yadda yadda.

I take a large sip of my strong coffee. I've had around ten of these today to keep me fueled. A large waft of that familiar scent hits me again. I'm losing my mind.

"So without further ado..." My father rounds up the meeting.

Oh great, meeting over. I get ready to stand, holding on to my coffee like it's my life buoy.

"I would like to introduce you to our new operations manager." My father looks around the room.

My ears prick up. *Say what now?*

When the hell did we interview for one of those? And I'm the operations director—how the hell was I not privy to this?

He must have interviewed them when I was away. We talked about it briefly, but we never firmed up the plans.

I pull out my phone and check my emails, quickly locate today's meeting to check the agenda, and there it is. *Special Announcement.* That's all it says.

My dad runs everything past me.

Although maybe he mentioned it to me and my head has been so far up my ass, I wasn't paying attention.

My father continues. "This new role we have filled with a very special person. Someone who has vast experience in marketing, health and safety, policy, and procedure."

Fuck, they'll be after my job. I shuffle in my seat, moving left to right to get a better view over the sea of heads in front of me.

My dad continues, "They left a highly prestigious job to join our team, and I am delighted to say they are going to manage the new cliffside restaurant project we are planning to build on the east side of the hotel. It is going to be our biggest challenge yet. Having it suspended over the cliffs will be no mean feat, but we have the best person for the job. They have extensive experience in refurbishment, building, and managing contractors."

Wow, he really is going to be after my job.

My dad rounds up his introduction. "I hope you all give her..."

Her?

"... a big warm welcome from us all here at The Sanctuary. Ladies and gentlemen, I present to you Violet West, our new operations manager."

I spring onto my feet, spilling my remaining coffee all over my dress trousers. It makes me hiss, but I don't care about the scalding liquid currently seeping through the fabric.

All I care about is the girl who's now made her way to the front of the room, looking more gorgeous than I remember, and she's wearing our uniform of fitted black blazer with our gold logo embroidered on the left breast pocket and black fitted dress, highlighting all of her curves. Although she looks as if she's lost a lot of weight, which I don't like at all.

With shoulders back and head held high, she looks confident, but she gives herself away when she nervously tucks a little tendril of dark wavy hair behind her ear. It's something only I would notice.

Wait, what?

My heart is flipping out.

I am flipping out.

Why is she here?

"Because your father just said she was the new operations manager," Fredrick, our spa manager, replies and low laughs ripple through the team.

I didn't mean to ask that out loud.

My head bounces back and forth to my dad, then back to Violet, then back again at my dad. He winks at me.

Winks.

I'm being played.

And Violet has yet to look at me.

"She's hot." One of the managers in front of me makes his attraction to her known. If that was Adam, I'll fucking fire him. He can fuck right off. She's mine.

But she's not anymore, Linc. You fucked up, remember?

My dad closes the meeting with a quick thank you and over ninety of our managers, deputy managers, and supervisors stand up at the same time. My attempts to get out of my aisle are futile as my happy chattering employees pass by on their way toward the exit. Out of politeness, I wait for them all to leave while standing on my toes to see over their heads, trying to get a glimpse of Violet.

I must surely be dreaming. It's the only explanation for her being here.

As the last stragglers make their way up the aisle, I eye the front of the room, but there is no one there.

My dad is gone, as is Violet.

I run my hands through my freshly cut hair.

I don't know who I am anymore.

I clench my eyes shut and open them again. I am definitely awake.

Pulling out my phone from my jacket pocket, I hit my dad's name and call him.

But it just rings. I try again.

"Pick up, pick up, pick up." My eyes dart around the empty space.

Still no answer, so I drop him a text while running to the back of the room.

ME

What is going on?

They must have gone through the hidden pocket doors we have scattered throughout the hotel.

Sliding one open, I poke my head into the hidden staff corridor, frantically looking left and right. Nothing.

"Shit," I hiss.

I'm being played for a fool.

I check my phone. It glares back at me as my text message goes unanswered.

I pull up my dad's calendar and it has a dinner date at Eva's parents' house tonight.

I dash to the hotel entrance, where the receptionists are of no help either. It's official. I'm going mad and I'm seriously considering checking myself into an asylum.

Did it happen? She was here, wasn't she?

I slap my phone against the palm of my hand over and over,

questioning my sanity and contemplating what to do. I'm out of ideas, so I text Jacob and Owen.

> **ME**
> She's here. I saw her.

OWEN
Who?

JACOB
The Queen?

OWEN
Please tell me it's JLo.

JACOB
Beyoncé.

OWEN
Adele?

JACOB
She is the Queen.

> **ME**
> No! Violet.

And they don't reply to me either.

> **ME**
> Hello?

Nothing.

Where is everyone?

Figuring I'll catch my dad back at his house before he goes out for dinner, I dash down the hotel corridor in the direction of the back exit to get my car.

I think my body has gone into emotional overload. It can't

cope and I'm most definitely having a breakdown. Fatigue, memory loss, hallucinations, mood swings, and the sensation that I am detached from my body, I tick all the boxes.

40

LINCOLN

I slam the car door of my black Porsche and look up at my father's house. Darkness. No life to be seen, no cars, just one big nine-bedroom mansion looming over me.

I walk down the drive to my house at the back of the estate.

With every crunchy footstep closer down the gravel drive to my house, I start to feel better. I needed fresh air, that was all.

This afternoon was a hallucination. A momentary glitch.

And between seeing purple everywhere, smelling her, and then imagining she was in the ballroom earlier, I know I have to make an appointment to see the doctor again tomorrow. He can give me something to help me sleep. That's all that's wrong with me.

I just need to sleep.

Approaching my house, I realize I must have left the lights on this morning. My modest three-bedroom house is lit up like a lighthouse.

I go to put my key in the door, but it's already unlocked.

Shit, I must have forgotten to put the alarm on this morning too.

I really should start paying more attention.

I push the door open and I can hear a scratching noise and the soft thrum of someone in my house.

Have I caught the thief red-handed, taking all my worldly goods? They'd better not be taking my new gaming console. I queued for hours to get my hands on that fucking thing.

And that seems to be how I spend most nights now, shouting down my headset at sad fuckers like me to *cover me* and *get first aid*.

A faint hum of music hits my ears, then a tiny clicking noise alerts me to a little white fluffy ball scuttling across the gray wooden flooring of my hall in my direction.

I get the fright of my life and jump when it looks up at me cutely, then barks.

Pom-pom?

I shake my head, my mouth dropping open.

"Oh, sorry. I should have put him in his cage before you came home." Violet appears in the living-room doorway, still in her black Sanctuary dress with no shoes on. She scoops Pom-pom into her arms, then disappears into my kitchen.

I didn't make it up. I'm not going mad. She *is* here.

"What..." I hold my hands up, frozen to the spot, and discover I can't make words.

Violet reappears. "Your dinner is in the oven. Your *yaya* dropped off a moussaka for us. I've poured you a glass of wine and I am off to take a shower. It's been a long day." She jumps onto the first step of my stairs. "I smashed a glass in the kitchen earlier and I think I found all the shards, but just be careful in case I missed any." She pops her finger in the air. "Oh, I forgot." She jumps off the bottom step and skips across the hall toward me.

When she kisses me on the lips, she takes me by surprise.

"Welcome home." As quick as a flash, she disappears up the stairs.

I hear the bathroom door click shut and then a *snick* indicating she's locked it behind her.

The pitter-patter of water is what I hear next, and then she starts humming.

Fucking humming like everything is normal.

When in fact, since four o'clock this afternoon, nothing has been normal. Actually, since I left Santa Monica, nothing has been normal.

I appear to have walked into another dimension and I look back at my front door and then all around to confirm this is, in fact, my house.

Slowly making my way across the hall, I look inside the kitchen and sure enough, the warm glow from the oven confirms my dinner is in it. My glass dining table has one place set with a glass of wine poured and Pom-pom is rolled into a tight ball, already fast asleep.

Dazed, I walk up the stairs, the faint sound of Violet showering in the background.

Stepping into my bedroom, I discover a wall of bottles filled with perfume, potions, and lotions lining the top of my chest of drawers. Next to it, a new dresser that wasn't here this morning or *ever*, is littered with tiny black makeup pots, lipsticks, a small lilac leather jewelry box, and a vase full of fresh purple flowers.

She fucking moved herself in. When?

I'm so flabbergasted I can't do anything else but look around. I rub my hands down my face, as if to wake me up and open my eyes.

Nope, her stuff is still here.

On the nightstand is a thick rainbow design planner and resting on top is her pink vibrating wand.

Is this for real?

Double-checking her moving-in status, I fling open the double doors to my walk-in closet. Half of my suits have been replaced with an array of purple dresses. Leather handbags line the back wall that used to house my collection of designer sneakers.

I fall onto the black leather chair in the middle of the closet and look around.

I'm having a *Sliding Doors* moment and sit here for a while staring at all her things.

There's even a stack of multicolored planners lined up in one of the storage cubes.

Eventually, I get up and check a few drawers. When I pull out one of my underwear drawers, I'm startled when instead of picking up a pair of my boxers, I pull out a pair of the tiniest pink lace panties and hold them up to my face.

Motherfucker.

"Oh, thanks. I'll put them on." Violet grabs them out of my hand.

My mouth turns dry as she drops her towel in front of me and proceeds to lotion her naked sun-kissed skin with that fresh-as-fuck scent she wears.

I groan when she rubs the cream across her tits, making her nipples pebble. Her hands dip lower over her stomach, over her hips, and I know she's teasing me when she moisturizes her bare pussy lips, making them wet, inviting me to touch them.

"Enjoying the show?" she says seductively with that fucking sweet-as-honey California accent.

I swear someone stuffed my head full of cotton candy and for the first time in weeks my dick bounces in my boxers as he finally wakens up from his hibernation period.

Violet exits my closet, wiggling her plump ass into my

bedroom. My cock goes rock-hard in an instant as she jiggles about my bedroom.

Unable to move or take my eyes off her, I need something to prop me up and I lean against the doorjamb as I'm unable to comprehend what is happening.

She pulls on her lace panties, a pair of booty shorts, then slips a giant white tee shirt over her head.

"I'm going to watch some Netflix. Are you joining me?" She piles her long, wet locks up on the top of her head, making it look like a wild nest.

My confusion is beginning to fucking annoy me, as is Violet.

This is a fucking ambush.

I run my hands through my hair and pull it. "Sorry. Let me get this straight. You are in *my* house, using *my* shower, making yourself at home in *my* home, and you are asking me if I am joining *you* to watch Netflix? Using *my* login details and *my* password?" I'm feeling something other than confusion. It's more like mild irritation mixed with uneasiness. "Sorry. But what the fuck is going on?"

"Oh, I moved to Scotland and moved in with you," she says matter-of-factly.

No shit, Sherlock.

She moves out of the bedroom and skips back down the stairs.

It's then I notice, styled neatly in some sort of weird display, several decorative cushions now decorate my bed.

Unbelievable.

I run down after her and she's already got her ass parked on my black leather sofa, her feet up on my glass coffee table, and she's pointing the remote control at the television as she flicks through the menu.

"Are you joining me?" She pats the cushion beside her but

doesn't look my way. "There is supposed to be a new series of *Vikings* started. I know how much you love it."

Right, that's it. I'm done pussy-footing about. I storm across to the television and unplug it.

With my hands on my hips, I stand in front of the giant screen.

"Everything okay?" A soft smirk of mischief softens her owlish eyes.

"What?" I bellow. "Is everything okay? I haven't seen you in almost a month—"

"Because you left me," she interrupts me.

"Because I left you," I parrot. Christ, no. I correct myself. "Nope. That's not what happened." I draw a line through the air. "Because I didn't know how to say goodbye and tell you it was a terrible idea for us to have a long-distance relationship. It was easier to make a clean break."

"Oh, did I miss the memo? Did we break up? You never officially broke it off. Nice touch trying to lay that burden on your dad, by the way." She winks.

Fucking winks at me like she's fucking high-fiving the worst decision I ever made, but I see the pain in her eyes.

She keeps assaulting me with her words. "I get it. Your long-lost, emotionally detached, and messed-up mother broke your heart, and it was a huge shock for you meeting her the way you did, and then you didn't get the outcome you wanted. That night turned into possibly one of the shittiest days of your life, and instead of seeing the beautiful parts of your life you already had, you decided to mess all those other great parts up. You left because you felt like that was the right thing to do. For us. And I get it; having a long-distance relationship sounded horrible. I didn't want to do it either. But I was willing to give it a try and do it for *us* to see how it went. Because what we have is unique and special and so beautiful. But you didn't even let us test it out to see. So you left the girl you supposedly love. The *only* girl you've ever loved because you thought she would be better off without your fucked-up, rejected heart. When, in fact, she was the one who could heal it and make it better. But how would you know because you didn't stick around to find out."

I feel a stab of remorse as she assaults me with truth bombs I wasn't ready to face.

She keeps going. "And since then, you've been moping around. Feeling like shit. Dragging your body around like a zombie. And now you feel worse. But if you had chosen to speak to me before you left, you wouldn't feel this pain."

She's been speaking to my grandmother.

She sighs. "And now you feel blue. Pathetic. Lonely. Have a painful heart and the worst case of sadness you've ever felt, but you've been too stubborn to call or text me. Fearful I would reject you. Because everyone rejects you. You pigeonholed me into the same category as your mother. But newsflash, asshole, we aren't all the same."

She's pissed and has every right to be, but she's got me pegged and she's here. Even with me fucking up as I did, she still showed up for me.

"But I'm here for you now." She folds her arms across her body.

"You're staying?" After all the shit she's just said about me being an asshole.

"Oh, I'm staying." She's defiant.

"Here?"

"Yes. Here."

"In my house? With me?"

"In *our* house. Together. Isn't that what couples do?"

Couples?

She shakes her head, her brows pinching together. "You never broke up with me. We're still together unless you tell me otherwise." She rises to her feet. "I changed my mind. It's been a long day; I'm super jet-lagged. I think I'm going to go to bed. Are you coming?" She doesn't wait for my answer and toddles off up the stairs. "Can you let Pom-pom out before you come up? Eat something too. You look like shit," she shouts from the top floor.

I blink with bafflement.

She's a fucking firecracker—small, but she packs a punch.

But I'm that one who's about to explode with annoyance.

In complete dismay, I head back into the kitchen, unlock Pom-pom's cage, and take him outside for a pee.

What the hell am I doing? She's already bossing me about.

I head out to the garden shared with my father and follow closely behind Pom-pom to make sure he doesn't get lost in the huge grounds. The lights in my dad's kitchen flick on, signaling his return.

I grab Pom-pom and run across the grass.

Pom-pom's identity tag jingles around, alerting me to his new black leather collar.

I check out the metal tag. On one side it says *Pom-pom* and on the other, my home address.

"Holy shit," I hiss.

How long have they been planning this?

41

LINCOLN

Carrying Pom-pom under my arm like a football, I storm through the kitchen door at the side of my dad and Eva's house.

"I was wondering when you would arrive." My dad casually leans against the white marble kitchen island and takes a sip of his red wine. I bet he's been here all along.

"What are you playing at, Dad?"

"What do you mean?"

"Don't act the fool. You brought her here. She is living in my goddamn house. She's moved all of her shit in and she's even burning scented candles." They did smell quite nice, though, now I come to think of it.

"Is that to clear away the stench of pity and loneliness?" he says, his dark eyes full of amusement.

"Oh, isn't this hilarious? I bet you have been up for nights concocting this master plan."

"Nope. Just one."

"When?"

"First night you left Santa Monica."

"The first night?"

"Yes. But it's taken three full weeks for Violet's work visa to come through, and that was pushed through as a matter of urgency for us. Human resources have been sorting it out for me."

"She left her father's business?" I can't believe she would do that.

"Yes. For you."

"For me?"

"Yes, Lincoln. For you. Are you mad at me?"

"Yes, I am mad at you. You seem to think that I need molly-coddling or something. First you brought me up by yourself when Mom left, made life sacrifices to raise me, then you gave me a partnership in the hotel, then you built me a house at the bottom of your garden, and now this." I point at Pom-pom.

"The dog?" He leisurely takes another sip of wine.

"It's not just a dog, though, is it? It's the owner that comes with the dog and she's put my address on his name tag. Look." I flip it over and show him my address on his collar.

"Right, I don't see what the problem is." He chuckles.

"She's... you're..." I clench my jaw and growl.

"Lincoln." He places his goblet of wine on the marble countertop. "I looked after you because that's what parents do. It's not a chore or a burden. I brought you up because you are my son, my boy. As for the partnership. You weren't given it; you earned it and you know that. It was written into your partnership agreement that you had to meet several criteria to gain it. The house in the garden? Your grandfather gave me money from a trust fund he set up for you when you were a baby for that very reason."

He lets me absorb that information before continuing.

"Family look after one another, Linc. I look after you. I look after Archie, Hamish, Eva, Thea, and hell, when Fraser and

Hunter are away on tour, I look after both Eden and Ella and their kids too. That's what we do for each other." He pauses. "Stop pushing everyone away."

"I'm not."

"You are. Violet wants to be here. She came here for you. I didn't need to ask her twice. She loves you. Like Eva did for me, she tracked me down and followed me. Violet is doing the same. She's following her heart."

She followed me.

"She's too good for me."

"She's perfect for you. She is strong, confident, and she knows what she wants."

I arch my neck back and eye the ceiling. "So she's working for the Sanctuary?"

"Yes. You are her boss."

"I'm anything but that. She has taken over my house with perfume, pink panties, and a fucking pink vibrator." Not to mention the five framed photographs of us I counted scattered throughout the hall, bedroom, and living area.

A deep laugh leaves my dad's lungs.

"Shit, forget I said that last bit."

They've all got me by the balls.

"I'm leaving now, but I'm not happy with you. I may not speak to you at work tomorrow." My eyes narrow.

He nods slowly, smirking. "Okay. Would you like me to cancel Violet's visa?"

"No," I say petulantly. I honestly don't want that, but I don't tell him that. "You are so annoying."

And sneaky and clever, and I might just admire and love him more for it with his clever plan.

"I'm aware. Are we done here? Because my wife is currently

upstairs waiting for me." He winks. "The kids are at Eva's parents' tonight."

I screw my face up in disgust and move to leave.

"The dog suits you. Enjoy your first night together," he shouts as I exit his house.

I'm fucking sleeping in the spare room.

42

LINCOLN

I've been staring at the ceiling for hours. Sleep is not my friend, and it will be yet another long day of feeling like shit.

It's early and I can hear Violet moving about across the hall.

Other than living at Violet's house for a few weeks, I've never lived with a woman before, never had a woman live in my house, ever. And I never had a mom either.

I don't let girls stay here for more than one night. It implies I want more and I never have.

Until Violet.

The infuriating woman who has moved into my home and has used my shower this morning has been singing through the house and has the radio blasting through the sound system. It took me a month to work out how to use the fucking thing, but nothing seems like too much effort for her. It's weird having a woman around who makes the house smell and look homier. She even added scatter cushions to my couch, candles fucking everywhere, and fucking fresh flowers—four bunches in total downstairs. When did she have the time to buy all this shit?

Catching me off guard, Violet bursts through the spare bedroom door.

She scuttles fast across the floor to my bedside with her hands around her back. "Sorry, I'm in a rush. Your dad is taking me to work this morning. I need to go car shopping. Can you please help me with my zipper?"

She sucks all the air from my lungs when she turns around, displaying the skin of her back, all bronzed and exposed. And begging to be touched.

I want to touch her.

A triangle of her black lace thong panties at the base of her spine allows me a peek of what's beneath the low-zipped dress.

I place one foot on the floor, then the other, rise to my full height, and slowly slide the teeth of the zipper together.

She sweeps her long hair to the side, ensuring I don't snag her glossy locks.

My fingertips brush her soft skin, setting off a wave of goose-bumps on the back of her neck as I reach the neckline of her dress.

On impulse, my body has a mind of its own. I bend down and kiss her nape on the spot she loves me licking.

The tip of my tongue taps her skin, and she lets out a little whimper as I taste her for the first time in what feels like forever. I let out a heavy exhale of relief.

She tilts her neck to the side, reaches up, and runs her fingertips across the back of my shaved neck, making my whole body come alive. "I have to go." She moves away from me. Her soft body leaves a cold space between us and I'm hard. Rock-solid hard.

Not acknowledging our moment, she turns around before she exits the bedroom. "Am I allowed to take Pom-pom to work with me sometimes?"

Her eyes dip to my cock and back up again.

She knows what she does to me.

It's the first word I've said during this whole encounter. "Yes."

"Great." She smiles. "See you later."

And just like that, *poof*, she's gone again.

I need a shower to jerk off because my dick seems to have his intentions set now and it's all about her.

Only her.

43

VIOLET

Arms spread wide, shoulders hunched, I clasp the bathroom vanity in the staff restrooms.

Looking at myself in the mirror, I exhale a long breath. "Right, Violet. You've got this."

I'm trying to keep it all together; however, it's a bittersweet situation I find myself in now that I am here in Scotland.

Flying thousands of miles to be with him seems like it was a completely stupid idea. I'm so happy I took the leap and the job is incredible, but Lincoln looks so broken and tired. He looks lost. When I caught him checking me out earlier in the corridor, I could almost see his brain misfiring. He wants to be with me— I know he does deep down—but he's struggling with the decision he made when he left Santa Monica, knowing he hurt both of us, and he can't quite believe I am here. He's having a hard time accepting I would do that for him and he's at war with himself to take the leap in my direction again.

Maybe Knox's plans are not going to pay off after all.

And even after Lincoln kissed my neck this morning, he's

still keeping his distance. He's avoided me all day. If he's not, it sure seems like he is.

I pull out my phone and text Hannah and Ruby.

ME

Please tell me I did the right thing.

HANNAH

You did. You are going after what you want.

RUBY

Why? What's up, baby girl?

ME

I have my doubts. I might be home sooner than planned.

HANNAH

There is no way that is happening.

RUBY

Give him time to adjust.

HANNAH

Call us later and we can cheer you up.

ME

It will be the middle of the night.

HANNAH

We don't care.

RUBY

You know me, I'm always up!

HANNAH

It will work out.

RUBY

And remember we love you and so does Lincoln.

I hope that's still true.

44

VIOLET

It's been four long days of learning, Lincoln avoiding me, car hunting, and I'm still yet to figure out what these Scottish people are saying half the time. They talk so fast sometimes, and I've had to ask a few of my staff members to slow down.

I've met several of the girls from America; they are here on a hotel exchange program the hotel has a partnership with, so that's been wonderful, and I've also met a couple of local girls who are around my age too who said they would love to take me for a night out. Apparently, there is only one nightclub in town, The Vault, and next weekend is ladies' night. Sounds like fun.

Laying on my side, I stare out into the night sky.

He didn't come to bed with me again tonight. His bed.

Instead, he's currently sleeping in the room across the hall. Again.

This might all have been a big mistake.

Moving to Scotland was an easy but huge decision for me. Knox and I sat down for several hours, and then he made me an offer I couldn't refuse. It made sense.

Now I'm not so sure.

Lincoln doesn't exactly seem all that happy to see me either.

I'm guessing if someone moved into my house uninvited, I would feel the same. A smirk pulls my lips, remembering his look of horror as I entered his hallway with Pom-pom.

Best. Moment. Ever.

I love him.

Now I am here, and all I've wanted is for him to wrap his loving arms around me and tell me he loves me too.

But he's shut down.

His barbed-wire fence is high and, trust me, I got the message. *Please keep out.*

It was kind of fun when Eva, Eden, and Ella all helped me move in. I was nervous and had serious doubts whether our plan would work out but championed through it, even when my nerves kept shimmying, trying to stop me.

Hunter and Fraser assembled a new dresser for me too. I'd like to say it feels like home, but it's not.

Although Lincoln's place is very homey compared to my beach house, I still feel alone.

My favorite part of the house is the coal fire in the living room. I can see myself sitting around the oversized white marble fireplace all winter. That's if I am still here.

The photographs Lincoln showed me all those weeks ago during our first date didn't do Castleview Cove justice.

The town is stunning, but I have yet to visit the castle or the ice cream shop, and I'm desperate to walk the sweeping beach and the pier with Pom-pom because I was in hiding from Lincoln for a few days, then I jumped straight into work. I'm making that my priority at the weekend.

But what I have seen of Castleview is beautiful and green.

Everything is very, *very* vibrant green and the air is pure and clean. It's wonderful.

Lincoln lives within his father's walled estate that appears to go on for miles. Knox even has a custom-built ten-car garage full of supercars off to the side of his Victorian nine-bedroom mansion.

The street I now live on is called Cherry Gardens Lane. It couldn't sound quainter if it tried.

Knox also has a pond full of koi carp, which Pom-pom has become fascinated with. He sat on the edge of the grass for twenty minutes yesterday, tipping his head back and forth; it was very cute, and luckily there is thick safety netting to prevent anything going in or out. Perfect for keeping small Pomeranians and children out.

The vast green garden is littered with multicolored plants, secret pathways, and seating areas, and there's a huge treehouse at the bottom of the garden that Archie and Hamish spend a lot of time in. You can hear their shenanigans and laughter for miles as it echoes around the estate.

Pom-pom is still yet to get used to Coal and Jet, Knox and Eva's two black Labradors. Pom-pom looks like a mouse in comparison to them both and they can't decide whether to play with him or eat him. Every time Pom-pom barks, which is more like a yelp, they both jump and run away. End to end, the whole of the Blacks' walled estate is picture-postcard perfect.

Although it's supposed to be the end of summer, it's anything but summer. It feels like winter already and I'm dreading the coming cold. However, I have only ever seen snow a handful of times, but in Castleview Cove they get it every year, like clockwork, so that makes me excited. I've never built a snowman before. That's if Lincoln wants me to stay.

When I appeared in the ballroom the other day, it looked like he'd been slapped across the face, and then Knox and I ran off and hid through one of the secret entrances. Knox has had way too much fun planning Operation Violet, which is what he's been calling it, and I've seen a side of Knox that showed his sense of humor too.

It's been fun playing with Lincoln, but now I'm alone in bed again, and I don't know how I feel. Maybe he truly doesn't want me. Maybe he doesn't love me like he said he did.

I can feel the confidence I had coming here slipping a little and it terrifies me.

I live in a perfect new home, within a perfect walled garden estate, have a perfect job with a perfect new family, but it doesn't *feel* perfect.

A small tear escapes and I let out an unintentional whimper.

"Can you not sleep?" Lincoln's deep voice that I so love asks me in the dark.

I quickly wipe my face to hide my emotions. "No."

"I'll make us a hot chocolate. Come down to the living room when you're ready."

"Okay," I whisper.

After a few minutes, I make my way down the white wooden stairs. I love Lincoln's house. It's warm and modern all at the same time. It has deep charcoal carpeted flooring covering the top floor, with a matching-colored wooden floor on the bottom floor. It's much smaller than mine, but he has white wood throughout and a white Shaker-style kitchen, making it look bigger than it is.

Lincoln is finishing lighting the fire just as I enter the living room. He's placed a couple of cushions on the floor for us to sit on.

"It's colder at night in the house. That's the problem with stone houses. Come and sit down by the fire." He passes me a super-soft gray blanket and I make myself comfortable beside him. It's the closest we've been since he zipped my dress up for me, and his familiar aftershave assaults my nose.

I've missed that.

The warm orange glow from the fire illuminates the entire room.

It lights up Lincoln's handsome face but highlights the deep bags under his eyes. He looks tired.

He passes me a hot mug of chocolatey liquid. "Are you okay?" His voice is full of concern. "Have you been crying?"

"I'm still jet-lagged. I'm no good without sleep. Makes me emotional," I lie, then I blow the top of my hot chocolate before I take a sip. Oh, that is nice.

"Me too."

According to his dad, he hasn't slept for weeks.

He clears his throat. "So you're here?" He stares into the crackling, dancing flames.

"Yeah," I whisper.

"You left your father's business?"

"It was time to move on. I get job offers all the time. I needed a change."

"And my dad made you a good offer?"

"Yes." I can't wait to manage the suspended restaurant. "Your dad asked my dad if he could steal me."

Lincoln shakes his head back and forth in astonishment. "He always does the honorable thing."

"You're just like him."

"I'm not. He's a much better man than I am. He wouldn't have left you." He wraps his hands around his mug. "When did you arrive?"

"Two days before the ballroom meeting."

"Where were you staying?"

"Ella and Fraser's house."

"With Pom-pom?"

"Yes."

"And how did you get Pom-pom here? Did he not have to quarantine?"

"No. He is microchipped, has a pet passport, and he has all of his vaccinations."

"And your belongings?"

"Shipped them express the first week. They've been at Ella and Fraser's house."

"That simple?"

"Yes."

"You worked everything out."

Yes, for you, you dumbass.

"What about your house?" He stares deep into the hypnotic flames of the now-roaring fire.

"You mean my dad's house? He sold it. Not his style."

"To your sister?"

"Hell, no."

He's thinking, and he's yet to look at me.

"I'm sorry," he whispers.

I don't want to cry. I'm too tired and emotional for this conversation. It's been four weeks of no contact with so many unspoken words between us, but all I can say is, "It's okay."

He lets out a big sigh. "It's not. I'm a fucking disaster."

When his *yaya* dropped by the first day I moved in, she told me he was crying the other night in her arms and my heart broke for him all over again. She asked me if I could fix her broken boy. I hope I can.

Placing my hot chocolate on the white marble hearth, I kneel in front of him.

He's so handsome, and his tan is still deep considering he's been home for over a month; maybe it's the white tee shirt that makes him look darker or the low warm glow of the fire. Although I'm guessing his Greek heritage will help prolong his tan too. Whatever it is, he's still my dark and mysterious man.

He has no choice but to look deep into my eyes as I cradle his face with my hands.

"You are not a disaster." I thumb his cheek. "Your heart may feel broken right now, but you are not a disaster. You have people in your life who love you. I saw that with your family in Santa Monica, Linc. The people in your life are the people who matter the most." His eyes become glassy with emotion. "You need to focus on what you have and not what you don't. Maybe one day your mom will want to get in touch with you; maybe she will realize what she lost, and I know you said she was dead to you, but I know you. You will give her a chance if she ever does come looking because you are exactly like your father in every way. Never doubt that." I give him a reassuring smile. "I think you are way more handsome than he is, though. Just don't tell him I said that." His gentle laugh ripples through the air. "It's going to be okay. The fate of us meeting, and the way we did, it showed you what you were destined to always find out anyway. Just remember you are surrounded by people who love you, Lincoln."

"She didn't want me." He blinks and one lonely fat tear slides down his cheek. "It hurts so bad."

I give him a caring nod. "It will get better."

"I'm so tired."

I don't kiss him. Instead, I gently coax him to lie down with me. I create a makeshift bed for us and lie on my side facing the fire, instructing him to spoon me.

He snuggles into me and says an almost inaudible thank you.

With his warm body pressed against mine, in his giant bear arms, we fall asleep together in minutes to the sounds of the crackling wood. And it's the best night's sleep we've both had in weeks.

45

LINCOLN

I woke up this morning with Violet wrapped around me. Her soft hand lay over my chest as she gently snored away. I didn't want to move. I stared at the ceiling for half an hour before I had to get up for work.

It's the first straight eight hours of sleep I've had in weeks and I feel like a new man.

I don't deserve her. I've been a bastard to her, leaving her without a goodbye.

But she came for me.

She's too good and kind.

Why would she move her life to be here?

Moving into my house the way she has is fucking wild and I still can't understand what the hell she was thinking.

I'm daydreaming about her when she steps into my office, a vision in her fitted dress. Never have I ever thought our staff uniforms were sexy, but she makes everything look sensational.

"We are meeting Jacob, Owen, and Skye at Wee Oscars for dinner at seven tonight. So be home in time to change. See you then." Her small figure turns and leaves.

I fly off my seat from behind my desk, chasing after her.

"What do you mean, Jacob, Owen, and Skye?"

Her footsteps come to an abrupt halt. "Exactly what I just said. We are meeting your friends for dinner. Don't be late."

Then she wiggles her way down the corridor and I take a moment to appreciate the gentle sway of her hips. With a springy bounce, she turns the next corner and is gone.

"It's a nice view." My dad's voice startles me.

"What?" I discreetly try to adjust my hard cock. It's been hard since I woke up this morning.

"The sun is shining across the bay." He looks out the window at the end of the corridor Violet just walked down.

Then he winks at me and disappears.

46

LINCOLN

Following our meal with my friends tonight, I'm desperate to throw my arms around Violet and tell her what a fool I've been. I feel so fucking stupid and yet I still can't.

We had a lovely evening where Violet held my hand and didn't for one moment let me push her away.

I don't know why I do that.

Am I protecting her from me?

Why the hell am I like this?

"Good night, Petal." I stand against the doorjamb of the spare bedroom and give Violet a wave across the hall. Because we're still sleeping in separate rooms, which is madness.

"Night." She smiles as she gently clicks my bedroom door shut.

I jump into bed and grab my phone.

ME

Were you just checking my abs out?

VIOLET

Maybe. *winking face*

ME

I may have been checking you out too.

VIOLET

I noticed. I find your abs very distracting.

ME

I find everything about you distracting.

VIOLET

Me too and I like everything about you.

ME

I like your ass. You have a great ass.

VIOLET

Ever the romantic.

ME

And your smile.

ME

And your waist. That's my favorite part.

ME

And your kindness.

ME

And the fact that you gave up your life. Your friends. Family.

VIOLET

Sunshine.

ME

Just to be with me.

VIOLET

For starters I needed a change. I leveled up.
Your hotel is one of the top-rated hotels IN THE
WORLD. And the suspended restaurant is going
to be an incredible project to be part of.
Something to be proud of.

ME

But what happens when the project ends in
three years?

VIOLET

Your dad has other plans. I don't know what
they are yet.

ME

One step at a time.

VIOLET

Yeah. My dad understands I needed something
new. He has his own life, and my mom and
sister don't play any part in my life anymore.
And regarding my friends, Hannah has taken an
editorial job in New York and Ruby will continue
to be Ruby. She will party hard with all of her
other socialite friends and her father is so rich,
she can visit me anytime using his private jet. I
went out with them once or twice a month. I
hardly had a huge social life.

ME

That makes me feel better.

VIOLET

On a serious note... and we haven't spoken
about this, but are you okay with me being
here?

ME

I didn't really have a choice.

VIOLET

I'm sorry.

ME

For?

VIOLET

Forcing myself on you but we didn't think you would talk to me otherwise or buy into your father's idea and vision to bring me on as a Sanctuary team member.

ME

He was right. He's always right.

VIOLET

You are very stubborn.

ME

And you are very persistent.

VIOLET

There is another reason for me being here.

ME

Oh yeah, what's that?

My bedroom door swings open.

"Because I love you, Lincoln, and I've missed you." She's crying.

I immediately throw back the bedcovers and go to her.

"I don't want to be apart from you ever again. I don't like that feeling." She clutches her chest.

I've never seen her like this before.

"I've come all this way. Just me and my dog with a few of my belongings. To a strange, unfamiliar country where you all talk funny. It's rained five times this week already. I'm so cold. And I don't think I can do the job. I do not know what I am doing." Her voice cracks.

"Petal," I whisper. I'm lost for words. *Tell her you love her, for Christ's sake, man.*

"I'm too scared to ask you directly if you want me here because I see what's going on behind your eyes; half of you wants me to stay, I think, but the other half is questioning everything about me, us, and begging me to leave." Her shoulders bounce up and down as she pours out her thoughts she's been keeping in.

"I'm sleeping through there and you are here, and I've been trying to keep it all together and be strong, but I need to know if I did the right thing moving here, Linc."

"Oh, Violet." I loop my arms around her and press her tight against me. "Shh, shh, shh." I rock her.

I've been selfishly thinking about myself with no thought of Violet living in a foreign country with no friends and no family.

She cries out, "It was supposed to be fun, a way to get you to snap out of your funk, surprising you and moving in, but when you saw me in your house it didn't feel like fun. Knowing you didn't want me here."

That's not true. I *do* want her here.

She struggles to get her next words out. "I'm here because here is where you are. I would go wherever you are in the world to be with you because you make me feel special and like I finally belong somewhere. You made me feel like I am perfect just as I am back in Santa Monica, but over the last few days, I somehow feel like I'm not enough for you anymore and I don't want to stay here if I'm not what you want." She pauses, trying to catch her breath.

"You're using your mom as an excuse not to let love in, while she is out there living her new life without a care in the world.

She doesn't care if you are upset or hurting, Lincoln. But I do. That's why I am here. You hit the stop button on us, but I never got a say in it, and pressing stop was never what I wanted."

As if someone has flicked the switch in my brain, everything appears clearer.

She's right. I've been a fool.

I rub my hand up and down her back to soothe her.

"Your father moved heaven and earth to bring you the girl who loves you, to prove to you that she means business." She stutters as she tries to get her words out. "I am serious about us, but you need to meet me halfway. You need to open your heart to me and trust me. Trust that I will never break it. Trust me to piece whatever your mom broke back together. Because you broke mine when you left Santa Monica, and I'm not sure my heart could take it again if you turn around in a few weeks' time and tell me to go back to America. I would rather go now." She gasps for breath.

I thread my fingers into her hair and smoosh her into my chest. She must feel my heart beating faster than a prestissimo beat.

"I miss you, Linc. I miss your touch." She pushes herself closer. "I miss *us*." Her tears soak my skin.

"I miss everything," I whisper.

I broke my girl.

She's been so strong on the outside, keeping it all together for me, but she's breaking, and I was too self-absorbed to see it.

"I don't want you to leave, Violet. I want you to stay with me."

She almost collapses in my arms and I momentarily have to hold her up.

The thought of her leaving now runs a rusty nail along the pit of my gut.

In complete contrast to my selfish thoughts, she thought I needed her, but what *she* needs is *me*.

I move us to the edge of the bed and pull her sideways onto my lap.

Her red-rimmed eyes stare back at me when I cup her face.

"I've been such a fool," I confess. "I'm sorry."

She closes her eyes and lets out a long exhale, wafting her fresh pear scent around me.

Her face is covered in raised blotchy patches, and knowing I'm the one who caused her sadness does not sit right with me. This is not who I am. Not with her.

"I've been a big baby."

She shakes her head. "You're hurting."

"So are you." I didn't notice.

"It doesn't hurt so bad when you hold me." She leans her forehead against mine. "Or when you kiss me." This woman is my everything. She loves me and is there for me even after everything I've put her through.

I kiss her softly at first, then dip my tongue into her mouth as all of my resistance to the messed-up thoughts I've been having fade away. I should have done this the minute she turned back up in my life. I should have shown her what she means to me. I should have rushed out and bought her a car, taken her shopping, introduced her to my friends, made love to her every day. I should have done it all.

I reposition her and straddle her legs around my waist. It feels as if it's our first kiss again, where we were reckless with each other and wild with desire.

"I need you, Linc," she gasps.

She grinds herself against me and I quickly rise to my feet, cupping her ass with my hands, and stalk along the hall into my bedroom. This is where we should be, together, in my bed, *our* bed.

Our lips never leave each other as we fall onto the mattress, and I know this is it. This is the moment that changes us forever.

47

VIOLET

I'm on top of Lincoln, his back against the mattress.

We said all the things that needed to be said.

We've been holding back. Me included.

Holding it all together was becoming too much of a burden, and I couldn't take it anymore.

My heart just grew butterfly wings, and it's gently fluttering in my chest because he said the words I've been desperate for him to say. He said he wants me to stay.

I want that too.

I couldn't think of anywhere else I would rather be because my love will never change for him.

Lincoln pulls my oversized sleep shirt up over my head to remove it. As soon as it passes my lips, I crash them back against his again. I don't want to stop kissing him.

In a moment of desperation, I free his hard cock from his boxers and lower myself onto him.

He groans loudly and mumbles against my lips. "I've missed you so fucking much."

I slide up and down his cock, breathing heavily with every stroke.

Holding my hips firmly, he pushes up into me with punishing thrusts.

"Always so wet for me, Petal," he moans.

This isn't lovemaking; it's pure carnal fucking and what we both need to solidify us.

Lincoln wraps one arm around my waist as he keeps on fucking me hard and with his other hand, he grabs my ass.

"Fuck me, Linc. Make me yours."

I push against the headboard to fuck him back.

He fills me to the hilt with his punishing hips as he slides himself in and out of my body over and over relentlessly. His thick crown finds my sensitive spot; at the same time, I grind my clit against his pelvic bone.

"Come for me. Call my name, tell me who you belong to." His dirty words set off a blazing shock of pleasure that burns, radiating into my thighs and through my wet core. With a few more furious thrusts, we come together.

"Linc," I moan.

Unapologetically loud, not giving a damn that we just gave our hearts to one another in our moment of frantic fucking, our orgasms intertwine, molding into one. He's breathing hard and fast as he jerks himself into me while my inner walls pulse around him.

Our breathing slowly subsides as Lincoln slides himself leisurely in and out of my body, lovingly escorting us back down from our ecstasy. His hips continue to move back and forth as if he doesn't want to stop.

Slowly now, we kiss. Lincoln clasps my face with his enormous hands and slants his mouth against mine. "I love you," he whispers.

"I want to look at this face for the rest of my life." I smile at him.

"Is that a proposal?" He tucks a strand of hair behind my ear.

"No." I blush.

"Are you sure? It sure sounded like one."

"Do you want it to be?" I ask nervously.

"Is that not my job?"

"Is anything we ever do conventional?"

"Nope. I realized that on the first—sorry, Lucy, second—day we met, when you fell over, and flashed me your hoo-ha." He winks. "Or maybe it was the epic, *I'm sleeping with your husband, Mrs. Black*, that I realized, or when you gave me a chili dick and knocked me out." He points to his forehead scar that's healed rather nicely but will leave a small mark. "Or what about moving into my house without me knowing?" A confetti of giggles leaves my throat. "You are going to send me to an early grave with all your shenanigans. Or a trip to the emergency room again if you continue to fuck my dick until it's raw, like you did back in Santa Monica. You are a horndog, Ms. West." He tickles my ribs.

"I feel so much better already." It's the truth and I feel warmer than I have in days.

Lincoln rolls us onto our sides. "I'm sorry I've been such an asshole."

"Yeah, but you're my asshole."

"I can't believe you gave up your career and life and moved five thousand miles to be with me. I'm astounded that you didn't hop on the next flight back when all I've been is a self-centered prick. Are you okay? Are you happy here?"

"Yeah. I like it more now." I glance down at his cock.

"Oh, I'm sure you do." His eyes narrow. "Are you, though?

You're my responsibility now, Violet. My job is to make sure you're happy and I've missed my happy Violet."

"Just promise me you will never push me away again."

"I promise." He holds out his pinky for me to take, in exactly the same way he did when he threw us off the leap of faith.

I link my pinky with his. "And promise me you will explain what the hell a bahookie is."

Lincoln chuckles. "It means 'ass.' Why?"

"Michael, in reception, told me yesterday I had a nice bahookie. Don't be mad."

He grins wide. "Oh, I have nothing to be mad about because Michael has a boyfriend."

"Oh."

"He's not wrong, though. It's fucking amazing." He squeezes my *bahookie*. "But you haven't been eating properly. Let's shower, and then you can destroy my dick."

I throw my head back, laughing.

"Then tomorrow I am taking you to my *yaya*'s. She is going to love feeding you, and then we are going grocery shopping together. I've always liked watching couples shopping. I want to do that with you and take walks on the beach hand in hand, bringing Pom-pom with us. We are doing all the shit. I want it all. I'm going to take you to the stationery store and you can buy washi tape. What the fuck is that anyway?" He doesn't let me answer. "We also need to get you a car. I want to sign us up for a place on the next dance retreat at the hotel. I want to dance with you properly and Eva will teach you better than I can." He's so excited. "Oh, and we need to buy loads of shit for the house—flowers, cushions, ornaments, and especially more candles. They make the house smell nice. Anything you want to make it feel like it's yours."

"Like ours," I counter.

"Yeah, like *ours*." He sighs blissfully.

48

LINCOLN

Violet is currently kissing me in such a tender way, it's as if she is hand-stitching my heart back together, piece by torn piece.

"I love you." She ghosts my lips with hers. "I will spend my life showing you how much I love you, Lincoln. I will always be here. For you and with you."

There is nowhere else I want her to be. This is where she belongs.

She moves south, laying a gentle path of kisses everywhere as she moves with grace down my body. It feels even better than sex because this is us connecting on a deeper level than we have ever before, as we fully commit to one another.

"This is mine." Her lips press against the skin over my heart and my newly stitched-back-together heart melts in my chest. It feels full of unconditional love for her.

She's been patient and caring and put me first, and it's the most extraordinary feeling to know that she would literally do anything for me.

Her lips find mine. My hands trace and caress her hourglass curves that I am completely obsessed with.

Wrapping my arms around her, I roll over, her back now against the mattress, and reacquaint myself with every one of her freckles, her soft skin, her warmth, and her curves.

Goosebumps dance across her skin in waves when I kiss her stomach, navel, cleavage, up to her neck.

Sweeping her hair to the side, I kiss the sweet spot behind her ear and whisper against the shell of her ear, "I love you."

She lets out a soft gasp as if she's on the verge of climax.

Her legs open wide for me and I slowly ease myself into her wet pussy. She lets out another soft gasp and if I didn't know any better, she might purr like a kitten with how turned on she is.

I run my nose down hers, then kiss her with everything I am. Because I'm not the guy who runs; that's not who I am and I will apologize to her every day for the momentary brain glitch I had. Choosing to leave without a backward glance was a terrible decision, and one I will never make again. Not in this lifetime.

I've learned my lesson.

Violet needs me just like I need her.

She whimpers when I slowly move in and out of her body, gently gyrating and moving my hips in slow waves as I lose myself in her addictive sounds and curves.

I kiss her with the lightest of touches and our tongues tap each other briefly as I push the seam of her mouth open.

I feel her heart beating in rhythm with mine.

I move a little faster when I sense her impending orgasm.

Leaning back slightly, she looks up at me and blinks, before her jaw hangs open and I know this is it. *She* is it for me and I'm never letting her go.

Picking up the pace, I thrust into her, cupping her ass to push myself deeper.

Our heavy breathing and faint sighs are the only sounds to be heard.

Her little mewls are my undoing and my muscles pull from my stomach and my thighs into my balls and I can't hold back any longer as Violet shatters all around my cock, clenching and pulsating her inner wall and taking me with her in our euphoric moment.

It's what we needed to connect us again and erase the last month as if it never happened.

Slowly coming down together, I kiss her lips and she smiles sleepily when I lean back.

"That was beautiful."

"You are beautiful." She is.

Inside and out.

49

LINCOLN

Four days later

I yawn.

"Are you still not sleeping?" My dad's concerned face tells me he's worried about me.

"Oh no, I am *trying* to get to sleep and *can* sleep, but somebody *won't* let me." I look over at Violet, the woman who has recently reinstated Mission: Ruin Lincoln's Dick.

I shouldn't complain; it's fucking epic. Every single minute of everything we do together is epic. Hand-holding, walking the dog, beach walks, even shopping.

She's currently playing on the kitchen floor with Thea and Pom-pom. Thea thinks Pom-pom is a cuddly toy and is a little overzealous with him, so she has to be watched like a hawk. She keeps trying to put him in her mouth.

A silent laugh makes my dad's chest shake. "Everything good?"

"Everything is epic." Contentment rests easily in my bones. It's an odd warm feeling I'm not fully used to yet.

When I was in Santa Monica with Violet, my departure was ever present and loomed over us like a creaking three-hundred-year-old tree, but now I'm here and so is she and we aren't going anywhere.

"You're not mad at me anymore, then?"

"Hell, no." I have the girl of my dreams living under my roof. She makes everything shine brighter and smell better.

When Violet showed up in the doorway of my spare bedroom four nights ago, we stayed up all night talking. We shared our fears, our hopes, our goals, and more importantly, we fixed us, and I'm doing everything in my power to make all my wrongdoings right again.

The truth is, accepting my mother for all that she is and how I can't change her, or the past, has been my biggest revelation over the past four days.

I was preventing acceptance.

"So I did a good thing bringing her here?"

I nod my head and laugh. He's always right. "Yeah." I pick up an apple out of the fruit bowl and take a bite of the glossy red fruit.

Noise from the hall alerts me that someone is entering the house. Although it's not just someone, it's a crowd. The motley crew, no doubt.

"We're having a barbecue," my dad informs me.

"Are we?" I frown.

"Yeah, to welcome Violet." My dad gives me a curt nod.

I eye him suspiciously. "Am I being ambushed again?"

He winks. "Maybe."

As he says that, Hunter and Eden with their triplet boys toddle in. Then Ella with Fraser, who has Mason in his arms. Along with Jacob and Owen.

I place my half-eaten apple on the work surface and I'm on

my feet in an instant to welcome my grandparents, who appear next.

My *yaya* smacks a kiss on my forehead, then ruffles my hair. "Love always finds a way. See? Your grandmother is always right. Now I need to cook." And she's off.

My grandfather goes straight over to Thea. "C'mon, you wee rascal." He lifts Thea into his arms, and she squeals with happiness; she's such a happy baby. "And you too, you wee bit of fluff." He lifts Pom-pom up next. "Maybe we should use you to clean out Thea's ears." That would work; he does look like a cotton swab.

Violet pushes herself to her feet and greets everyone in her usual cheerful voice, hugging everyone and charming them all with her questions about their lives. She remembers everything about everyone and always manages to make people feel special.

I'll never get tired of that or her.

Jacob and Owen wave.

"We're on drinks." Jacob points to the champagne bottles that have appeared from nowhere. They make themselves at home and pour drinks for everyone. They both spent hours here growing up and they know this house like it's their own.

"You good, Linc?" Fraser tilts his head in Violet's direction.

"Never better." I grin. "Thanks for helping with the ambush, by the way. Although you and Hunter are shit at assembling furniture. I've had to realign all the screws and readjust the squint drawers you haphazardly put together."

He snorts. "We only had a few hours to move Violet in; give us a break."

I laugh but hold out my hand for him to shake. "Cheers, man. For everything."

Jacob and Owen hand everyone drinks.

Archie and Hamish burst through the back door.

"Linc," Archie yells, laughing. "Zac and Caz are doing *The Sex* on the grass."

Oh, dear fuck.

Archie and I do have a laugh and giggle when our garden tortoises get a bit frisky. It's only recently Archie had his sex education class at school, but he doesn't discuss it with his mom and my dad. He discusses it with his big brother: me.

I shake my head and widen my eyes, trying to secretly tell him *not now*, but he keeps on giggling. "Zac fell over." I think he's gonna wet himself. "He landed on his back and his legs were all wiggling about." He makes small T-Rex arms and flaps his hands.

"Why is it so funny? They looked like they were playing together. I helped Zac," Hamish says in his sweet voice. Archie's explosion of contagious giggles makes everyone else laugh along.

"Okay." Eva appears in the kitchen looking every bit the ethereal goddess in her floaty cream summer dress. "Enough silly talk. Rubber boots off, then clean your hands."

"They were *doing it*, Linc." Archie can't stop giggling.

"Enough now, Archie." Eva raises her voice.

I press my pointer finger to my lips, urging him to be quiet and mouth *later* to him.

"Okay," he shouts back. Subtle, Archie, subtle.

"We are all having dinner together," Eva informs the boys.

"A barbecue?" Hamish's eyes light up.

Eva nods.

"Yes." Hamish and Archie punch the air.

"I need a poo first." Hamish toes his boots off and runs out of the kitchen.

Eva pinches her nose. "Remember to wash your hands." She lets out an exasperated sigh. "I need another vacation. Knox..." She spins around on the balls of her feet. "No more babies."

"Whatever you say, sunshine." He winks at her.

I think my dad has other plans.

Violet appears by my side and we both hop onto the white leather chairs around the kitchen island. I drag her seat closer to me, making the metal legs squeal along the marble floor as I do.

She shivers. "That noise is like nails running down a chalkboard."

I lean in and kiss her cheek. "You're not shivering because you're still cold, then?"

"Nope. I put three layers on today. How Eva can wear a short-sleeved dress on a day like today is beyond me." She lays her hand on my thigh.

"It's supposed to be the hottest day of the year today." Hunter chuckles.

"What?" Violet exclaims. "That's insane. I might join Zac and Caz when they go into hibernation for the winter."

"Or we can hibernate together in front of our coal fire all winter." I wiggle my eyebrows.

"Sounds like heaven," she says dreamily.

Movement around the kitchen island makes me turn my head.

All the adults are now standing around the kitchen island, and we all have a glass of champagne bubbling and fizzing away.

"What are we celebrating?" I sweep my gaze over my family and friends.

My dad says, "Family." He picks up his glass. "We are celebrating having each other. For always having each other's backs. For taking care of one another come rain or shine. Today we are celebrating the fact that family is not defined by the blood that runs through our veins. Family is made up of the people standing here today around this kitchen island. Family are the people who stand by you, lift you up, and support you through whatever life throws at you. And that includes the time your American girlfriend flew over five thousand miles to be with you and moved herself into your house without you knowing. Family are there for you for times like that."

Everyone chuckles.

My dad raises his glass higher. "Family."

I struggle to swallow the bubbly liquid as emotion catches my throat.

The people I needed most in the world and who accept me as I am were in front of me all along.

Violet lays her soft hand on my forearm. "Are you okay?"

"Yeah, yeah, I'm fine." I throw my head back and eye the ceiling to stop any tears from forming. I can feel everyone looking at me.

I haven't cried since I was a little boy, but I've been so emotional lately, breaking down a few times in less than a month.

"Can I make a toast?" Violet asks.

"Go for it," my dad says confidently.

I relax my shoulders and exhale. Picking up my glass, I take a huge gulp. "I'm fine," I say to no one in particular. Jacob slaps my back.

Violet raises her glass up. "I would like to make a toast to my father, who kindly dumped Olivia, because if he hadn't and if they ended up getting married, then Lincoln and I would have been..."

"Brother and sister," I shout too loudly. Oh my fucking God, that never even crossed my mind.

And the kitchen erupts with laughter, chinks of glasses, and lots of *oh my Gods*.

As I look around the kitchen at my blended family, I feel loved, just like my grandmother said I was. *I am loved beyond measure.*

And I have everything in my life I need.

Right here.

50

LINCOLN

Four months later

"Jonathan, remove yourself from this ballroom and get back to work," Violet calls out from across the room. "According to Michael, you were supposed to be in reception twenty minutes ago."

"Oh shit, you had better go," I say through the side of my mouth. "She looks pissed."

I turn around and Violet is standing at the back of the room with one hand on her hip and in the other she is holding on to a sparkly bright-pink planner.

Jonathan runs, fucking runs, through the room. "Sorry, we were talking about cars," he blabs.

"Well, you should have been talking about work, not cars." Violet narrows her eyes. "Go."

Jonathan flings the wooden doors open wide and disappears.

"And you. Come with me." She beckons me with her pointer finger and goes out the same door Jonathan did.

Oh shit, I'm in trouble.

I run toward the exit. Christ, what am I doing running? I know exactly why I am running. She has me by the balls.

Violet is standing and waiting for me.

"How did you know I was in there?" I thumb over my shoulder.

"CCTV."

"What were you doing in security?"

"Looking for you."

"Why?"

"Because there is a problem down here."

She walks down the hall. My eyes fall to her hips as she wiggles herself swiftly down the black-and-white marble corridor and I have to skip a few times to keep up with her.

Everything happens at once. She stops walking, unlocks the laundry closet, pulls me by my tie into the small room, slams the door behind me, and locks it, then shoves me up against the shelving unit that houses dozens of white towels and smashes her lips painfully against mine. I'm pretty sure she just drew blood.

"I thought you said we had a problem," I say between her frantic kisses.

"We do. I haven't seen you since this morning." She unzips my dress pants.

I don't think she knows she doesn't have any shares in the hotel yet, so she won't get a penny from the hotel when she kills me; she's going to fuck me to death.

I pull her dress up to her waist and move us around as she unbuckles my leather belt.

With her back now against the shelves, we're all fast hands and clumsy maneuvers as we desperately try to undress each other.

I grab the back of her thighs and she knows what to do as she loops and locks her legs around me.

I slip her lace panties to the side and drive myself into her. There are no airs and graces about what we are doing. It's fucking at its finest. The need to be together because we can't keep our hands off each other. Making up for our lost month, we don't care how and when we fuck; we do it all the time, and I'm not complaining.

She lets out a moan and clutches on to the back of my neck as I fuck her hard against the shelving unit behind her.

As I drill her hard, she bites my neck and moans into my ear. Her whimpers drive my dick crazy.

Her pussy soaks my hard cock and I fuck her even harder, pushing myself into her with grueling thrusts. Her body begins to shudder, and it tells me everything I need to know; she's on the precipice, about to fall off as the walls of her pussy contract around my cock and she lets out a loud moan.

Her breathing becomes heavy. She throws her head back and her mouth hangs open in the shape of an O.

Her whimpers tell me she's right there and she takes me with her, coating my dick in her orgasm.

We work in harmony with each other on every level, from sex to business.

We just work.

Soft pants are the only noise to be heard as she lays her forehead against my shoulder.

"Problem solved." I chuckle and lower her to the ground.

Still breathless, she fluffs out her long hair with her hands. "I feel better. I'll be able to concentrate this afternoon," she says, wiggling her dress down over her hips.

Until tonight.

I buckle my belt and straighten my tie.

"Do I look like I've just had sex in the laundry closet?" She runs her hands across her dress, trying to smooth out the creases.

"You look freshly fucked every day. You don't look any different." I cup her face and softly kiss her lips.

"We have to go. I need to visit the ladies' room to clean up first. I will meet you in your dad's office for our meeting."

"See you up there. Love you."

She throws me a cheeky smile, unlocks the door, and then she's gone.

My life couldn't be more perfect.

51

LINCOLN

Violet and I are sitting in my father's office for the meeting he summoned us to.

"Say that again," I say in complete shock.

My dad repeats himself. "You and Violet are going to run the hotel for the next two years together. You, my boy, will take my position, and Violet will step into yours. In six months' time, I am taking the next two years off as a sabbatical."

"Why?"

"Because Eva is having another baby."

Violet claps her hands together excitedly. "That is wonderful news, Knox."

"But I have never done your job before." I start panicking.

"I'm not disappearing off the face of the planet, Linc. I will be around, just not every day. I'm going to be a stay-at-home dad." He grins like a Cheshire cat. "While you two"—he wiggles his pointer finger back and forth between us—"run this place. We have six months to train you, Linc, and you have the same time to train Violet, and you will both attend every board meeting from now on."

"You're going to be a brother again, Linc." Violet lays her hand on my thigh.

"I'm going to be the main director," I whisper. I can't believe my father is giving me the control to run this vast enterprise we own.

"With Violet." He sits back in a black leather chair and drums his fingers against the armrest.

"I'm so excited," Violet cheerfully coos.

And I'm in fucking shock. Violet detects how I am feeling; she always knows.

She grabs my chin and forces me to look at her. "We've got this."

The sight of her face calms me. I lay my hand over hers.

"I will sail this giant ship with you, Linc. I won't let it sink."

My heart batters in my chest. "I love you, Violet."

"Will you marry me, Linc?"

My eyes bug out at her unexpected words.

"Oh, Jesus Christ, I shouldn't be here," my dad mutters.

"Stay, Knox." Violet smiles, her eyes never leaving mine. "You brought us back together." Her smile grows wider. "Will you?"

My heart just took a step into the unknown. "Yes." It's a solid yes. "But only on one condition."

"What's that?" She looks concerned.

"You'll let me buy the ring."

Her shoulders sag with relief.

"We're getting married?" She goes all girly.

"Yes, we are, Petal."

"I have a condition too."

I frown.

"Can Pom-pom be the ring bearer?"

"He can be anything you want him to be. Just promise me you won't ever fire me again?"

"When did she fire you?" My dad chuckles.

"When I lived in Santa Monica." I hold her gaze. She's put me under her spell with her golden eyes.

"He worked for me for all of one day."

"Then she fired me."

"You were working when you were supposed to be having time off to travel and explore?" my dad says, aghast. "You are unbelievable. I give up."

If I hadn't, I never would have met Violet.

"I love you, Lincoln, *your-dad-has-a-crap-surname-and-I'm-going-to-sound-like-a-color-palette-when-we-get-married*, Black."

"I love you Violet, *your-mom-should-have-called-you-Susan*, West."

Never in a million years did I think traveling to America would lead me to this phenomenal woman in front of me.

She's my life buoy. She calms me and makes me a better person. She makes everything better.

I'm addicted to her and her lips, her hips, and this life we are building together.

I smile and kiss her, knowing that she's the best leap of faith I've ever taken.

EPILOGUE
LINCOLN

Three years later

"Oh, thank goodness I found you," Violet wheezes, out of breath.

My black patent dress shoes squeak against the marble floor as I swivel around.

"You shouldn't be here. It's bad luck; you have to go." I point back at the open door.

She casually waves her hand in the air. "Hocus pocus. I needed to see you." She rests her hands on her hips and tilts her head back to catch her breath. "I should work out more. I'm so out of shape."

She's not. She works out three times a week like clockwork, and the more squats she does, the better in my opinion. Her ass is looking mighty peachy these days, even more than usual.

"If my *yaya* catches you within a twenty-foot radius, she won't share any more of her recipes with you." And we need them. I need that famous moussaka recipe of hers; she makes the best, but she's yet to share it with Violet.

Every Saturday morning, Violet visits my grandparents'

house, where my *yaya* teaches her how to make traditional Greek desserts and dishes. I live for Saturdays; dinner times are the best.

In contrast to the rest of the week, Sundays are our non-negotiable day off together. We completely switch off and it's a relaxing day where we don't do anything other than eat, rest, walk the beach with Pom-pom, who has become a bit of a star in Castleview Cove, and of course my favorite, playtime in the bedroom.

Ella encouraged Violet to set up a social media account for Pom-pom and he now has over a million followers on that stupid video platform that everyone is nuts about. He's a star in his own right and I'm certain he knows how special he is.

"Okay, I'm good." She fans her face with her hand. "I needed to let you know something because I am freaking out."

"Okaaaayyyy."

"There is no easy way to say this." She clears her throat. "My mom is here. With. My. Sister." She looks worried when she bares her teeth.

Her sister came? "Wow."

"Right. Wow. I think I'm going to be sick." She grabs her neck with her hand. "My sister is going to complain about everything."

"She won't." She might.

"She will moan about the weather." Yep, she probably will.

"We can't control that." I chuckle.

"She will blame me for it raining today." I know she is genuinely worried, but her freaking out is the cutest thing I've seen. I'm trying to be serious and console her while holding back my own laughter.

"Our whole day is inside. It doesn't matter. And it's February, so it's colder now."

"She will hate the venue; she suffers from vertigo." She suffers from being a royal pain in the ass; that's what she suffers from.

"I'm sorry our thirty-million-pound *suspended-over-the-cliffs* venue isn't good enough for her," I reply with a hint of sarcasm, throwing my hands on my hips, tantrum-style, as if I'm so offended she won't like our venue.

I couldn't give a shit if her sister doesn't like the venue. However, there is no chance of that because it's been featured in every architectural, structural, and engineering magazine. We didn't just build a venue. We built a magnificent piece of art, and today is its maiden voyage.

Today, our wedding day, marks its official opening.

And we made it more than just a restaurant; we made it an events venue too.

The Cliffs is split into two sections. Both sides can be opened up for larger parties, but the entire front part of the structure features floor-to-ceiling windows over one hundred feet wide. For miles, all you can see is the wild inky blue North Sea. It's breathtaking.

The only thing close to it I have ever seen was the restaurant Violet and I dined in at the top of the gondola in Queenstown.

We took a vacation to New Zealand last year and spent a well-deserved month off from work. The Cliffs was almost completed, and we needed the time to relax, away from everything. It was the best month, and I even persuaded Violet to take another leap of faith with me and bungee jump. She screamed the entire time, but she did it and I was so proud. She's much braver than she thinks she is.

"My mom will absolutely hate the fact that Francesca is not a bridesmaid." She bites her lip.

"But Hannah and Ruby are and they love you."

"My mother, Francesca, and Richard aren't on the seating plan. I've had to get Nicola to shuffle everyone around." Violet spins her pointer fingers in the air. "So stressful."

"I hope you placed her as far away from my *yaya* as possible." Or she may attack her with her wooden spoon, which I would pay money to see. I chuckle at that thought. My grandmother is livid that Violet's mother didn't want to come or take part in any of the wedding preparations.

Instead, Eva, Ella, and Eden have helped organize everything for our wedding with Violet. They've become like sisters to her, more than her real sister has ever been.

"I broke a nail already." She flips me the bird.

"Well, that's not very nice," I say with a smirk as I move closer to her to calm her down.

"Oh God, sorry." She lowers her raised finger and wraps her other hand over it to hide it.

She screws her face up. "What if she doesn't like my dress?"

"You look absolutely beautiful."

She looks down and puffs out her long ivory satin dress. "Do you like it?"

"It's perfect."

I pull her into a hug.

Her dress is covered in dozens of tiny crystals all along the neckline. They scatter down her delicate lace-covered arms, and every time the light hits them, they change to an iridescent northern lights purple.

"I love it too." Her megawatt smile is so wide it might very well blind me. "I better go." She lifts her shoulders in excitement as she slips out of my grasp, her face beaming with happiness. "We're getting married."

"I know."

Her eyes blow wide. "Oh my God, I do have to go. It's bad luck for me to be here."

"I did say th—" She stops my words with a kiss, then dashes out the door and I hear the clacking of heels disappear down the corridor, but they start to get closer again.

Her face appears around the doorjamb, her long hair falling like a waterfall off to the side. "I forgot to tell you something else."

I raise my eyebrows.

"You look really handsome. You had better not be wearing anything under that kilt; there is a closet along the hall waiting to be christened." Before I can even respond, she blows me a kiss, and she's gone, clip-clopping down the corridor.

She will be keeping me on my toes for years to come.

I close my eyes and take in a deep breath. I want today to be perfect for her. I hope her mother doesn't ruin it.

"Are you ready?"

I open my eyes, and standing in the doorway is my dad.

"More than ready."

All in black, he strides toward me.

He dominates the room in his pitch-black kilt with matching black leather brogues and flashes, sporran, shirt, waistcoat, and two-button jacket—black everything to match our family name.

He proceeds to straighten my purple cravat. Our cravats are the only flash of color.

That's our theme—purple. Figures.

"Was Violet in here?"

"Her mom showed up." I stretch my neck to give him better access to my cravat.

"I saw. My job is to keep her as far away as possible from Violet today. I have assembled a 'keep Violet's family busy' team. We will not let anything spoil your day."

He makes me laugh. "Thank you."

"Anything for you. Now, let's get this show on the road." He lays his hands on my shoulders.

"I hope you haven't embarrassed me in your speech."

"It'll be exactly like your stag was."

I groan. "I hope not."

"As the best man, it's my job to embarrass you." He laughs.

Oh, great.

My dad brushes the fabric on my shoulders. "Ready?"

I have been for the last three years. "Absolutely. Let's do this."

* * *

Everything went without a hitch today and Violet and I have had the most incredible day surrounded by our family and friends, some of whom have traveled thousands of miles to celebrate our wedding day. Some from California, some from Greece, and we are very grateful they came. Our day has been filled with fun, laughter, and one hundred percent happiness.

Violet has been smiling all day, but I have yet to catch her speaking to her mother or sister. Or even her brother-in-law for that matter.

My father's plan worked.

"Hey, you." She pinches my backside.

"Hello, Mrs. Black."

She lets out a little squeak at her newly married name.

"Come over to the window." I hold out my hand for her to take. She lifts the front of her long dress to stop her from tripping over the delicate fabric, which is highly likely for Violet. We mosey over to the furthest point of the gigantic space, and I pull her into my arms, her back against my chest. We haven't had a minute of peace and all I want is one small moment with her.

Then she can go back to doing what she does best—chatting, mingling, and using her snake-charming skills on anyone she talks to.

I hold her as we stand and enjoy the ferocious waves, gray skies, and cliffs of Castleview Cove.

After some time, I turn her around in my arms.

"Did you like the wedding gift I bought you?" She begins giggling.

"It's getting hung above the mantelpiece." Violet had a body cast of her backside made for me and made into a bronze sculpture. She remembered what I said all those years ago. She even had it coated in vibrant violet paint.

"It was a nice surprise to have delivered this morning. The best wedding gift." I kiss her neck. "Have you had a nice day?"

"Ocht, I suppose it's been okay." She tries hard to hide her smirk and her Scottish accent is appalling.

"Yeah, I was thinking your dress could have been nicer and the venue is pure shite." We both burst into a fit of the giggles.

I lift her hand up and brush my thumb over her black brushed titanium wedding ring. It matches her engagement ring perfectly. It too is black brushed titanium, and set inside six prongs is a rare purple diamond, also known as an orchid diamond, and it couldn't be more perfect. It's truly a reflection of me and her—black and violet.

"Did you have a look at what I had engraved inside your wedding band yet?" I look into her eyes.

"No. We agreed we would do it together. Let's do it now. You first." She gets excited.

I pull off my matching black titanium band with one tiny purple diamond inset into the metal.

I tilt the band back and forth and move it between my

fingers. "*I am your missing piece.*" I read the heartfelt words I said to her on the first night we spent together.

I reach up and cup her face. "You are. You are everything to me, Violet."

"You are going to make me cry again, Linc. That's all I have done all day. Especially when *Yaya* handed me her coveted moussaka recipe."

"It could be a ruse; she may have left an ingredient out. Don't get too emotional. She's sneaky like that."

Violet giggles. "My turn."

She slides her engagement ring off first, then her wedding ring, and tilts it to read my hidden message, meant just for her.

She reads it silently and her eyes turn glassy. "*You complete me.*" She repeats the engraved sentiment.

"You do."

"We are a pair of oversentimental twits."

"We are."

But I wouldn't have it any other way.

Injecting humor, she asks, "Fancy a shag?" Violet bites her lip and scrunches her nose up.

"Sounds so romantic."

"Just kiss me." She grabs my cravat and smooshes her lips to mine.

This is how it's always going to be.

Her bossing me about, joking, laughing, having fun, but most of all, she's always going to make me feel like a million dollars because I hit the jackpot when I found Violet.

She's my orchid diamond.

Rare, unique, and all mine.

* * *

Violet

Two years later

I stand in the doorway, admiring my naked-from-the-waist-up husband with our tiny nine-month-old daughter scrunched into a pastel-pink ball on his chest.

Pom-pom is snoring away at the foot of the bed. At eight years old, his snoring is getting worse as he gets older.

Lincoln is rocking our daughter back and forth on the black wooden rocking chair his *yaya* gave us. It's the one she used when Knox and Lincoln were babies; it's a true family treasure. It's now being used for our Melina. The little girl whose Greek name means "honey." It's perfect for her—sweet.

I take a mental picture as my ovaries explode.

The care and love Lincoln has for his daughter warms my heart more every day.

He's utterly smitten with Melina and very protective. There isn't a moment she isn't in Lincoln's arms. Melina may never need legs, but I am sure it's because he never wants to miss moments of her day.

He loves teaching her new things, making her giggle, and chasing her around the coffee table. She learned to crawl only a few weeks ago, and Lincoln has taken it upon himself to babyproof the house. It will take some time getting used to those stupid but necessary kitchen cabinet safety locks and I've broken several nails being overzealous opening them.

Tiptoeing across the plush, thick carpeted floor, being careful not to wake the baby, I brush Lincoln's cheek. "Hey," I whisper.

Lincoln pops one eye open.

"She's sleeping. Come back to bed." Lincoln looks down at his cute-as-a-button dark-haired baby girl.

"Are you sure she's sleeping?" He looks down at her through tired eyes.

He doesn't want to put her down.

"Yes." I grin.

He lets out an *if I must* sigh.

The rocking chair stops moving when Lincoln places his feet flat on the carpet, then gently leans forward. His whole hand is almost the same size as Melina's little back.

He cups the back of her head, slowly rises to his feet, and makes his way to Melina's crib.

As he gently lays her down, she raises her hands in the air and does a big stretch, then sucks the air for a few moments before she pops her thumb in her mouth.

"She's so cute." Lincoln looks down at our sleeping daughter.

I clasp the side of the wooden crib. "She is but we have a big day tomorrow and we need to sleep."

"Do we?"

"I am making moussaka for your grandparents tomorrow."

"Oh, yikes. Yeah, you need to rest and limber up for that tomorrow." He grins and wraps his arm around my waist, a simple gesture that sends tingles through my body every time.

Lincoln plants a kiss on my temple before I drop my head to his shoulder.

"I don't think I was your missing piece."

"No?"

I draw my head back and look up at him. "No, I think she was."

We both look down at our sleeping cherub.

"She completes *us*," he whispers.

She does.

But for Lincoln, she's taught him the true meaning of unconditional love. Melina loves him without question, without conditions.

I do too and he loves us even harder back.

I am truly loved beyond measure by him, and it's the best feeling in the world.

My life is perfectly complete.

* * *

MORE FROM VH NICOLSON

Another book from VH Nicolson, *Jacob*, is available to order now here:

https://mybook.to/JacobBackAd

ACKNOWLEDGMENTS

Ah—Lincoln's story—it was just begging to be told. He wouldn't shut up after I finished writing *Unexpected Eva*, and as usual he got his own way and he finally got his happy ever after. He deserved it after all, and he needed someone a little fierce and fun—Violet was the one for him.

This book would not be possible without the support network I am surrounded by.

To my incredible husband, Paul, who continues to feed me never-ending words of encouragement, thank you. I couldn't do this without you, babes.

I want to give a massive shout-out to my super-talented author friend Esme Taylor. Esme, I am so grateful for your read-throughs. You are one in a million.

To Carolann... my enthusiastic beta reader... thank you for taking the time out of your busy days and nights to read for me. You have been an enormous part of my author journey and your continued excitable energy for my books keeps me going.

To Lizzy—wow—my beautiful alpha reader from across the pond—I feel like I was meant to find you. Fate played a massive part in us meeting, I just know it. From your development suggestions to your intricate edits, I was blown away by your passion for Lincoln's story. I cannot thank you enough for being in my world. Love you, lady.

To all of the book bloggers, Bookstagrammers and Book-Tokers—a huge thank you for all of your support and the beautiful graphics and videos you create; every day you blow me away.

And to you, the spicy book reader, thank you for taking a leap of faith on a new author; you have no idea how much that means to me—I am eternally grateful. THANK YOU! Mwah x

ABOUT THE AUTHOR

VH Nicolson is a Scottish author of spicy romance fiction. She was born and raised along the breathtaking coastline in North East Fife. For more than two decades she's worked throughout the UK and abroad within the creative marketing and design industry. Married to her soulmate, they have one son.

Violet is up to her capers again... sign up to VH Nicolson's mailing list to find out what she does to Lincoln in an extended epilogue, and download the recipe for Yaya's secret moussaka recipe...

Visit VH Nicolson's website: www.vhnicolsonauthor.com

Follow VH Nicolson on social media here:

- facebook.com/authorvhnicolson
- instagram.com/vhnicolsonauthor
- tiktok.com/@vhnicolsonauthor
- bookbub.com/authors/vh-nicolson
- pinterest.com/vhnicolsonauthor

ALSO BY VH NICOLSON

Lincoln

Jacob

Owen

Boldwood
EVER AFTER
xoxo

JOIN BOLDWOOD'S
**ROMANCE
COMMUNITY**
FOR SWEET AND
SPICY BOOK RECS
WITH ALL YOUR
FAVOURITE
TROPES!

SIGN UP TO OUR
NEWSLETTER

HTTPS://BIT.LY/BOLDWOODEVERAFTER

Boldw**oo**d

Boldwood Books is an award-winning fiction publishing company seeking out the best stories from around the world.

Find out more at www.boldwoodbooks.com

Join our reader community for brilliant books, competitions and offers!

Follow us
@BoldwoodBooks
@TheBoldBookClub

Sign up to our weekly deals newsletter

https://bit.ly/BoldwoodBNewsletter